Dread upon the Waters
Joe Gaspe and the Portable Nukes

Richard A. Minich

Copyright 2010 by Richard A. Minich. All rights reserved.
No part of this document may be reproduced by any means,
Mechanical, electronic, digital, or otherwise, without
The expressed written permission of the author

ISBN: 978-09758728-5-7

Library of Congress Control Number: 2007904242

All Esox Publications
P.O. Box 493
East Aurora, NY 14052
www.AllEsoxPublications.com

Theresa Meegan – Cover
Patricia A. Lanigan Eberle – portraiture
Theresa Meegan – pen and ink drawings and oyarons
Book Design by Janice Phelps Williams

*To the members of the US Army, Air Force,
Coast Guard, Navy, and Marines
past and present.
Thanks for your
Service to our country.*

Acknowledgments

The help that Janice Phelps Williams gave me in the design and the copyediting of this book was of incalculable value to me. In addition, she often nudges me in a direction that is less self-indulgent than the one I would have taken. The artists of the portraits, Pat Eberle, and the cover, oyarons, and pen and ink drawings, Theresa Meegan, did their usual great job with little to go on.

Thanks to Doug Minich, my big brother, for touring, researching, and climbing around West Point with me. I know he had fun but, thanks anyway.

My two critical readers on this book were Rick Jackson and Margaret Rose. Rick had several helpful suggestions and Margaret was encouraging and thorough and had fun, too. Chris Zeth again did some work on technical aspects of the story. Thanks.

The enhanced stories from his checkered past always lead to fun adventures, thanks to Jim Reynolds.

I appreciate the folks at General Welding in East Aurora, NY for letting me be photographed in their cool fish chair.

Thanks to my wife, Joan, and children, Jackson and Holly, for their help and encouragement.

Cast thy bread upon the waters:
For thou shalt find it after many days.
Give a portion to seven, and also to eight;
For thou knowest not what evil shall be upon the earth.
Ecclesiastes II: 1–2

Preface

Pantherville

Thomas Andre didn't know what he'd be getting into when he hired Joe Gaspe for his Special Projects Group. It was his nimbleness of mind, ability to adjust on the fly, and willingness to allow his teammates to work independently, that made Thomas Andre, Assistant Special Agent in Charge of the FBI office in Pantherville, the perfect choice for leading the covert team.

Musky fisherman Joe Gaspe had proved himself when he formed a network of operatives to watch the northern coastline of the US border and led the charge in preventing an attack on the Friendship Bridge connecting Canada to the US. Then Andre stepped back and allowed Joe to unofficially take on the Russian gangsters involved in human trafficking, only stepping in at the climax to keep the results as clean and sanitized as possible. The fact that Joe's operation in Ohio had exposed a problem within his office cemented Agent Andre's faith in Joe.

When Andre contracted with Joe, he also took on Joe's network of associates across the region. Foremost among them were sundry members of the Mohawk Nation spread across that porous border between Canada and New York.

Joe and his cousin Moses Snow have now come to Andre with a threat that will require him to quietly spread his irregular FBI assets in a thin line across the area. They will have to be unobtrusive and

Dread upon the Waters

stealthy. A meticulously planned and far-ranging attack will prove to be the most difficult and dangerous yet encountered on the north coast.

Introduction

Muskedaigua: August 15

Little Kendra stepped down from the sliding door of the van and headed directly to the back door of her house. Though she was the second youngest, in the family she was the only child of the four awake. Her father got out of the driver's side and walked to the back of the van. He was going to unload the picnic gear, the extra clothes, the baby's kit bag, and the cooler. The car needed to be empty for tomorrow's day of work. Kendra's mom carried the baby toward the back door. She planned to return and wake up the two boys when she had the girls inside.

Kelvin heard four car doors slam behind him one by one. This neighborhood was always very quiet at the end of the weekend. His family was getting home late from the amusement park because he'd had to fix a flat tire on the road.

"Hello Joe." Kelvin turned to see who was there. Arrayed like the four horsemen of the Apocalypse were burly men in black suits and ties. All were big, all were white, and all were overdressed for a Sunday night. Kelvin thought about his wife and two daughters, inside, and his two sons sawing logs just on the other side of the back seat. One man had a gun in his hand. The others had their hands inside their jackets. They stared at Kelvin who looked through the near darkness from one to the other under the light from a nearby streetlamp.

Dread upon the Waters

"Schwarze! We are not looking for a black man," said the man with the gun.

"Where's Joe? Are you his servant?" said the first voice. Though in obvious danger, Kelvin was processing information as he'd been trained to do. He was ticked off at being called anyone's servant. Though he'd bought this house from a man named Joe. He knew that accent from his time as a Marine guard at the US embassy in Moscow. These were Russians. That, and the bad suits and the lousy haircuts, gave them away.

"I am no one's servant," he stated firmly.

Two sets of high-beam headlights from cars across the street came on illuminating the scene. Yard lights and porch lights all around the neighborhood lit up; then there were noises and voices.

Ka-ching, the slide of a pump shotgun loaded up.

"You okay, Kelvin?" another shotgun was heard being armed. "Anything I can do to help?" These came from theright and left of the Russians who began looking around with worry.

From behind them a voice asked, "These guys bothering you, Kelvin?" Dogs were growling held back by leashes. "Need anything neighbor?" said another man and another pump gun chambered a shell.

Gus, Kelvin's next-door neighbor and the only one of these men he knew as more than a nodding acquaintance, said, "I've got your back." He chambered a round in his nine-millimeter, then he continued, "We don't want any trouble in this neighborhood, so we have been watching these guys and planned a little welcoming party."

Looking less sure of himself, the lead man said, "Wrong person. We go." The four turned and walked back to the Volvo station wagon, got in, and drove away. No one fired a shot. No dogs were unleashed.

Kelvin looked after them, shaking his head. Kiesha walked up beside him and said, "Those kluxers leave?"

She carried a child's baseball bat and the fury in her eyes shined like flashes of lightning.

Kelvin felt the tension drain from his neck and shoulders. He began to laugh. "Girl! Were you gonna fight guns with a kiddy bat?"

"I'll protect my babies with whatever I have!" She was angry but started to laugh as well.

Joe Gaspe and the Portable Nukes

Gus said, "I called the cops. Those guys have been sitting out there awhile, and I got their license plate number when I walked Buster an hour ago. I'm glad you got home. I was falling asleep."

"Do you know them? Are they local?" Kiesha challenged. Kelvin and Gus had planted a birch tree together on Saturday and they were pretty well acquainted. Kiesha hadn't warmed up to Gus yet.

Shaking his head, Gus responded, "New Jersey plates, not local. I worried about racists too, for a while, but they seemed so out of place. Several of your neighbors kept an eye on them." Kelvin noticed porch and yard lights winking out as the neighbors retreated to their homes. Gus waved and the headlights across the street went out. In a few moments a squad car showed up.

Chapter 1

Tuscarora Falls: August 16

Assistant Special Agent in Charge Thomas Andre was usually frank with his burly white driver. The slight, black man straightened a crease in his trouser leg and said to the back of the driver's bull neck, "Talking with the Mohawks will be slow and tedious it will require gifts to be given—you brought those Havanas didn't you?"

"The cigars are right here." The driver held up the wooden box.

"I mention this because you may be standing at the door for a while."

The driver shrugged his shoulders.

They arrived at the Tuscarora Falls Inn. Andre was unsure what to expect from Joe Gaspe's cousin Moses X Snow. Having been advised that Mo was very concerned about his message and that the issue was serious, "very serious," Andre had taken time to scan a pair of reference books. Because of the importance of speechmaking to Mohawks, he acquainted himself with the etiquette that he needed to observe in the situation. Thomas Andre, while an important man, was down-to-earth enough to realize that since Joe had given him suggestions on how to behave, he should heed them. Andre had to prove to the Mohawks that he was a "big man," in influence. The FBI agent projected confidence that belied his slight frame and dressed in such

Dread upon the Waters

an impeccable manner that no one would think him frivolous. He was five foot seven, barely one hundred fifty pounds, and intimidated no one physically. His carriage and intelligence, however, were impressive. Andre's reputation had preceded him with Mo Snow and he had made it clear to his honored companion and tribal leader that this man had juice.

Mo and Joe were sitting at a table overlooking the falls for which the Inn had been named. Though there wasn't much water in the creek in August, the scene contained a wild beauty that was both invigorating and relaxing. With the coming autumn rains the creek would be brim full, but those rains didn't usually come until well into November. There was a stranger sitting with Mo, another Indian, older, robust, dressed in a Western-style shirt and hat, wearing straight leg jeans and cowboy boots.

Andre's driver was left on guard at the door outside the separate room, Joe, his appearance rumpled in contrast to Andre, stood as the agent approached. He reached out and shook Agent Andre's hand, Then introduced everyone. Joe was very respectful, and finished up by saying, "This is Brant Johnson Tribal Chief at Akwesasne. He is here to listen and to demonstrate the understanding and agreement of the tribe in what Mo is going to say."

Joe's head bowed as he sat down. Andre's grip had been firm all around. He sat at the table across from Mo. A panoramic view of the falls was behind the Mohawks. Mo spread his arms, dropped them to the table and pushed a small package, wrapped in soft leather and tied with a string, toward Andre who grasped the table edge, then released it, turning his hands palm up. Andre nodded to acknowledge the gift, but did not touch it. Mo's eyes shone with fire when he looked at Andre. Joe thought he heard a quiet grunt of satisfaction from Chief Johnson.

"Go ahead, cousin, tell him what you know and also what you have deduced," Joe said.

Mo paused for a few minutes. His hair, no bigger than a playing card at the top of his forehead, was black sprinkled with gray and freshly cut at one-eighth inch in length. The neatly shaved sides of his head and his "better" clothes indicated the seriousness of this council of war. Andre noted all of this.

Joe Gaspe and the Portable Nukes

"For many years we have been suffering from bad advice in our nation," Mo began. "These ideas have come from everywhere. From Canada, from America, from government teachers you have sent to us, from your magazines, and TV, and movies. Our young people are divided against themselves. They live a confused life, and we have not been able to contain them or restrain them. They call themselves 'warriors' yet most do not even hunt or fish. They have no connection to the founding beliefs of their ancestors, what you would call our myths. They drink too much and take drugs, street drugs, and when they lose their money they huff chemicals that cause them to drop their minds more quickly. The sachems and elders of our tribe have exhausted themselves trying to boost the sagging spirits of these youths who have lost all reverence for their mothers and grandmothers.

"I speak here as a pine-tree chief, allowed to participate in councils but not one of those who decides. The youth of our tribe and all the tribes of the longhouse are consumed by desire for the advantages of the world of your civilization but they despise and reject all that is whiteness. They hate you and they consider us," he moved his arm deferentially, palm up toward the chief, "ridiculous. They are overtaken by America but accept only its ugliness. They have become half one thing and half another. Only the vigor of youth keeps this from tearing them up. When they age—those that are not actually killed by this nothingness will be destroyed from within."

Mo raised his palm toward Agent Andre. "To calm your guilt, both sides of the border have provided teachers for our schools. Yet they teach us your ways, not the ways of the Mohawks. We see the many things you have to teach us. Those practical things, technical things, skills and understandings, are needed. But you provide us with many teachers who send the minds of our young men and women on a wandering journey to nowhere. Under the title of history your teachers show us that they hate themselves. If the victors hate themselves what are those who have been defeated supposed to think? It is easy for our young men to hate your culture…" Here Mo raised his arm and took in the main room of the inn, tacitly excusing Agent Andre from the statement. "But that hatred does them no practical good and greatly harms their spirit."

Dread upon the Waters

Mo took a breath, sipped his clear tea and closed his eyes for a three count. Thomas Andre was a polite man who knew enough about Iroquois culture to understand that a pause did not mean Mo was done. He would signal the end of his speech. Joe had warned Andre that this speech was being made for the chief as much as it was for him.

"A Mohawk traditionally respects the one who wins the conflict and feels no pity for those who are defeated. Your self-hatred when victorious has been a tumultuous thing for our people. Since the time when the French and English fought over our land we have been on both the winning side and the losing side of many wars. It wasn't until the wars of this century that we have all, those Catholics at Kahnesetake educated by the black robes, and those Protestants at Akwesasne educated by the English, been on the winning side.

"Now there is a teacher of great learning and charisma who teaches at the community colleges in both Quebec and New York. He bends the minds of our young men with grievances from the distant past. He has words that are so flowing and enticing that many young men believe that he has been sent, like Island Woman once was, to bring us to glory again.

"This man has developed two study groups of young people, only men are instructed by him, who plot against the State of New York. Chief Johnson and I do not know all of what they speak and plan but each of us has cousins and nephews in these groups, and we have overheard things. These are bad things, sir, very bad things. The young men who think that we..." Mo gestured to take in himself and the elder at the table, "have lost our ability to lead the people. They have grown to disrespect our women of power—those who choose our chiefs and sachems—they have been convinced to participate in a plan to take back our ancient lands for the people of the longhouse. This teacher, an Arabian man, has convinced them that they can bring about the surrender of New York to our people through a series of raids. Do not scoff until you hear the details of which we are aware.

"There are going to be three or four or five raids, all planned to come off at the same time. These raids are designed to take out New York. They target the city and state. West Point because the Army's brain is there; Niagara because the electrical power is there; and New

Joe Gaspe and the Portable Nukes

York City because that's where the Jews are. They have other targets in mind that I do not know exactly.

"While many of our young people do not have faith in the dreaming anymore, some of them do have a limited power to dream. A few of the old ones can enter those dreams and see what the young men are planning. This is what I have to tell you." Mo, who had been standing, sat down. He finished the tea in his cup and poured more from the pot.

The waitress came in and asked, snapping her chewing gum, "Are you guys all set or do you want sumpin' ?"

Andre said, "Coffee please, miss."

"I'll have a Yuengling," Joe said. "Chief, how 'bout you?"

"Nothing." Brant Johnson was stoic in aspect and attitude.

The waitress left and Andre wrote a few notes on a pad. He said nothing for several minutes. There was an open window near them and the sound of the waterfall soothed the four troubled minds.

Andre placed a small box of cigars in front of each man. Mo's and the chief's were left untouched. Joe took one smoke out, admired its fresh green leaf wrapper and ran it under his nose, moaning in satisfaction. Finally, Andre said, "I have a few questions."

Mo nodded. Joe grinned like a man who knew what was coming. Chief Brant Johnson was as impassive as the Great Stone Face. Andre spoke.

"I understand the power of dreaming to your people, and I have become semi-convinced since I've met Joe. But, selling ideas reached through dreaming, ideas about events that are yet to occur, will be impossible with regard to the government of New York or the federal government." All three listeners nodded. Andre lifted an eyebrow to Mo, inviting comment.

Mo said, "We know this. That is why we came to you, because you have agents like Joe and because there are things we can do to help. We expect nothing from the government except what is too little and too late."

Andre didn't respond directly. He said, "Nevertheless, I need details. How, what, where, and when. I don't care about why very much and I don't expect to know all the information on who until this is over. Tell me how they plan on doing this, if you will."

Dread upon the Waters

Joe spoke up, "Suitcase nukes, which have nothing to do with suitcases, as you know. These devices are already in Ontario, perhaps even on the Rez. They are going to use a waterborne assault—actually several of them. They are coming through two foreign countries, Canada and Vermont," Joe chuckled at that. Mo frowned at him and Andre raised an eyebrow.

"So Lake Champlain is one of the routes? Am I right?" Andre said. He again looked at Mo.

"We think so." Mo dropped his open palm on the table for emphasis. "They will purchase boats, lake boats, and four-wheelers in bulk for cash. They are also shopping for two ocean-going boats to approach the city."

"There isn't that kind of money on the Rez, is there?"

Mo shook his head. "The purchases are being handled by someone else with money, oil money I'd guess."

Joe stared right into Andre's eyes.

"These nukes, where'd they come from?" Andre asked.

"Russia would be my guess. There are two components to each nuke that are being kept separate until the targets are reached. Then a clamping device of some sort would connect one with the other, activate them, and ... There are at least eight of these two-part devices."

"Jesus!" Andre said. "Go on."

"They have been after New York City for a while, and they are not done with it yet. They think that taking out West Point will decapitate the army's ability to wage war in Afghanistan and such. They plan to take out the power grid at Niagara to darken the entire northeast, at least. There are other targets but I don't know specifics."

"This isn't enough?" said Andre.

Joe shrugged, "They are going to double up on each attack to reduce or eliminate the chance of failure."

"Taking out the power station at Niagara will devastate Canada as well. If this were to succeed, large areas of the State of New York would be uninhabitable for many years. This would be a catastrophe." Andre said as he continued to take notes. "I guess I do want to know the who. Who is behind this?"

"The same Taliban bastards who attacked us before!" Joe brought down his fist on the table.

Joe Gaspe and the Portable Nukes

"What do your young men have to do with this?" Andre looked at Chief Johnson.

Mo framed the response to this question. "They are going to be guides because they have unique access to the areas of which we speak. They can handle boats and they blend in better. Political correctness, an area of weakness for you, means that they can travel unmolested through these waters."

"If this happens, they will all die."

Brant Johnson said, "Yo hay," and made a chopping motion with his right hand.

"Your ancestral homeland will not come back to you. It will be a moonscape, no one will be living there."

Johnson said, "Yo hay," again.

Then Mr. Johnson spoke briefly, "We have always lived in this country. Since time began we have been happy with the difficult conditions we have faced. We have laughed, accepted our life calmly, and taken joy in being bound to the land of our ancestors. Our people have struggled for some time with boys who cannot hunt, will not learn their language, consider all our beliefs to be old school, don't want to learn. But this coming thing is worse. Much worse. You whites have books to keep your history. We have only stories, in a language no one speaks, kept by old ones who get fewer in number every year. Now even the land—our land that is in your possession is going to be lost." The chief nudged a dream catcher across the table toward where Agent Andre sat. When Andre accepted the gift a bargain would be struck. This was offered as a contract by a Mohawk just as a mortgage was a contract to a homeowner.

Andre went over some details again. He ended the meeting by promising to put some things in motion to combat this plot as much as he could. Mo and Joe confidently promised to work on a plan of their own.

At the end of the meeting each man accepted his offering. The Mohawks shook hands with Andre. Brant Johnson, who towered over the FBI agent grasped his right hand, took Andre's elbow in his left and looked long and deep into the agent's eye. After thirty seconds the chief nodded once.

Dread upon the Waters

Joe was sitting at a blackjack table with Uncle Mike, the Seneca sachem, and the dealer. Uncle Mike had four cards in front of him. The dealer waited for him to indicate his preference. There were no other players in the Sachem's Sweat Lodge, a private gaming room upstairs in the Seneca's casino in Niagara Falls, New York. Uncle Mike was of an indeterminate old age, wrinkled and brown like an orange left on the porch over the winter. His stature, never huge, had become shrunken with age. This evening as a guest of honor at the casino, he wore his best clothes, pressed chinos over cowboy boots; a string tie closed the neck of his rhinestone-buttoned Western shirt. The clasp of the tie was a silver stylized wolf's head given to him by the clan mother years before. He wore an incongruous snappy blue blazer with the crest of an extinct British Army Regiment on the left breast.

Joe and Uncle Mike were smoking, a perk provided only to Indians in the casino. Joe dragged on his cigarette while Uncle Mike puffed a pipe just enough to keep the embers alive. Joe wasn't entirely comfortable, he felt under-dressed and disheveled, because he was. His presence had been requested by Uncle Mike and, as senior sachem of the entire Seneca Nation, Uncle Mike, whose name was actually Joseph Buck Brant, got what he wanted.

The Sachem took a card from the dealer and turned over his hand to show a winner at five and under. The dealer paid off.

"I'm done. Lost all I can afford at one time," Joe said.

The Sachem pushed a short stack of chips over to Joe's position and said, "Stay. Play some more, then we'll talk." The dealer dealt another hand. Joe didn't think this dealer looked like an Iroquois, but who could tell? It wasn't logical to have an Anglo dealing in here. Many non-Indians worked at the casino, but here, where only the elite could gather, all the workers were of The People.

"Our people love to gamble, as you know, Joe. The funny thing is, many of us don't care one way or another about winning. Until these casinos came along, there weren't many Seneca capitalists. All assets were shared with the clan. A tough position in the white man's world but, maybe better in a way." They both went bust on the next deal and tossed in their cards. Joe sipped a Yuengling while Uncle Mike drank tea from a cup on his right.

"One more deal and we'll chat over there," Mike cocked his head towards a round table covered by a clean white tablecloth.

"Do we have secrets?" Joe asked this of the Sachem while looking at the dealer whose right eyebrow moved a millimeter up and down.

Mike laughed until he began to cough. He recovered himself and said, "No secrets. Just a subject important to the entire survival of our people." The Sachem smiled so that the wrinkles in his face doubled in number and his one tooth glinted in the light from the chandelier.

Twenty minutes later, they were at the table. Joe had lost the chips given him by the Sachem and Uncle Mike asked the house to hold his stack for later. Joe ordered a cheeseburger platter from a comely black-haired waitress. Uncle Mike asked for more tea, "English Breakfast if you please."

"We need to talk about your daughter. Amelia is a special women of power sent to our people, and she needs to learn more about her dreaming." Uncle Mike held up his hand silencing Joe before he spoke. Ignoring Joe's continued attempts to interrupt he continued, "I know she has been having very disturbing dreams, each more affecting than the last. The power grows within her and she drops back into the same dream with shocking regularity. She is in touch with our ancestors in that Real World and since there are so few of us who can dream true, many many ancestors come to her in those dreams.

"She has awoken from difficult dreams and shaking, fearful, and exhausted, gone right back into them, unable to resist the craving to learn more. She has told you she hates this knowledge, wishes that she was just a normal girl worried about her appearance." Mike paused and Joe nodded several times.

"Now she must take the next step. She must learn to dream in a way that we, as a nation, can benefit from. She must be trained to dream with all the power of all the people of the longhouse.

"There is a man, in the Adirondacks, who has been sent to us to re-teach us how to dream true. He is, like Island Woman, from a different culture sent here to help us to reclaim our place in the Real World and the Shadow World. He made a lot of money, purchased a

Dread upon the Waters

huge old estate, and created a dream ways school for the Iroquois. This Irishman, the son of a son of a son of a son of Warrighiyagey, Sir William Johnson, will be able to instruct Amelia and other power dreamers of the people—mostly women but a few men—in the methods and techniques she will need to learn.

"It has always been the Mohawks who led the dreaming of the Six Nations though the Onondagas have been jealous of this. Island Woman came to the Mohawks and this man whose tribal heritage goes back a thousand years, this Ruland Rush, must teach our people their way forward. The Mohawk woman who will lead is your daughter, Amelia Gaspe. It cannot be changed. It is so."

Uncle Mike lit his pipe and Joe smelled the sweet essence of Kinnikinnick mixed with his harsh Kentucky Burley in his smoking mixture. Joe remembered his manners and waited in case the Sachem wished to continue.

After five minutes, Mike had said nothing. Puffing his pipe he finally nodded to Joe. Joe said, "Amy has learned how to go in and out of her dreams. We sometimes dream together. But she has moved far beyond my ability to lead her. So, I guess you're right. When does this all happen?"

"Tomorrow."

"But she is going to be in school, studying to be a dental technician. She starts next week."

"She must take a leave. Call it independent study. She will go to the camp of the Irishman, Ruland, and study until the double moon of January. Then she can resume her schoolwork. Our people will need her as a dental health provider. Perhaps some of us still have our teeth." He laughed loudly, smiled, and tapped his one tooth with the stem of his pipe.

"She's not gonna like this, and her mother will like it even less."

"You underestimate them both, Joseph. Kate knows that this daughter is different than the others, and she will be energized in raising the younger ones without the distractions Amelia causes. Amelia will not be alone, a distant cousin of hers, the eldest sister of Moses Snow will also represent the wolf clan, the part of the clan in Canada, with the Irishman this fall."

Joe Gaspe and the Portable Nukes

"Okay, I guess." Joe looked at his cheeseburger, unbitten these twenty minutes. He remedied that situation.

"Raiding," Mohammed Ahmed Ibn Al-Sayid Abdullah said. "That's what it will take to recover your ancestral lands. A constant stream of minor battles won because you are able to strike and disappear." The Mahdi, an honorific by which he allowed himself to be addressed by his core group of Muslim followers, was talking to sixteen recruits for his big operation. They were all Native Americans; mostly Iroquois—Mohawks, Onondagas, and Senecas, but also Aquinah and Narragansetts.

The Mahdi was a highly intelligent man, scion of a family awash in oil money. He had subjected himself to severe and austere religious training. He found himself more intelligent than his teachers and more devout as well. He had agreed to his father's requirement that he obtain a university degree in the west. First at Oxford and then in the United States, he found himself increasingly disgusted by the obsequious groveling professors who thought that by denying the West's victories and apologizing and bemoaning their culture, they would win over those whom they saw as oppressed. Instead they inspired only his bitter and absolute contempt for their weakness.

In some ways he was naïve. He believed, often in spite of an obvious logical disconnect from reality, all the anti-western scholarship run rampant through academia. He swallowed the line with enthusiasm. While contemptuous of the weak sisters of the left, he believed their arguments implicitly.

When given the chance to recruit, his message changed with his audience. It was one of inspiration and fanatical devotion for the Islamic warriors of the jihad, and one of resentment and lingering, bubbling grievance for the Native Americans. The Mahdi had nothing but contempt for the intelligence of both groups, a contempt he nurtured as justification for his own existence. Historicism, the belief that his own life was the culmination of history, that all of mankind's progress and regress up to now led inevitably to him, was his reason

Dread upon the Waters

for living. The Mahdi had been mentored by a self-hating teacher in England and at Harvard College, where he followed him, a man who would sacrifice his own people, including his children, just to be thought of as progressive by the elites in the university systems. That man had shown him how to triangulate Americans. So interested in finding the best in everyone and in having themselves considered tolerant and broad minded, they were eager to believe anything negative about their country. Perhaps it was the self-knowledge they had about how venal they really were that made them so easy to dupe.

Native Americans were another case. They were more than willing, eager even, to nurse a colossal sense of grievance for the wrongs previously done to their ancestors. Their unfilled need for a physicality in existence, no longer satisfied by war and hunting, left them brimful of energy to be expended. The logic of an argument need not be rigorous for them as long as the promise of violent action was held out there.

With his Islamic devotees he could combine all this: a lingering sense of resentment, even older and less relevant that that of the Native Americans, a thousand year-old grudge, a guilty conscience—all his "students" were wealthy sons of wealthy scholars, engineers, and the royalty of Arab society. They were like the Americans in their guilt and like the Indians in their desire for combat. As if they were American middle-class dropouts, they had done nothing in their lives except aim for the big noise that they hoped to make on the upcoming mission.

The Indians had practical skills with boats and motors with trucks and ATVs that his ideologically pure and physically inexperienced co-religionists lacked. They also contributed access to the hated State of New York through their ability to move seamlessly from Canada to the US and back through the 30,000-acre reservation on the border. This huge area, spanning two provinces and the State of New York had a water border that could be crossed unmolested by anyone, as it was never patrolled. A constant stream of smuggled untaxed tobacco products invited any and all other contraband to move across the border as well.

Joe Gaspe and the Portable Nukes

Addressing his followers, the Mahdi encouraged, as much as possible, their natural tendency to despise all unbelievers and especially those he told them were their oppressors. Nurturing hatred carefully, one could move the followers on to fighting with a mere logical progression. It would have been easier to build the desire for jihad if the oppressors had been guilty of better-documented brutality. Evil and brutality went together so well. But repeating easy-to-understand messages from the Koran to people eager and grateful to hear it, instilled in them the belief that kindness was weakness. There could be no gratitude to a Christian from a Muslim. It was anathema to them. Dispatching infidels, when it caused one's own demise, was a cherished path to paradise.

"When you have gotten past the sentries at the border you can look for an opportunity to eliminate these primitives. Some of you will need them longer than others. We will decide this in our detail sessions," the Mahdi explained.

He was in the office at the boatyard near Montreal that had been purchased in order to get possession of the two ocean-going salvage tugs that would be used when the critical shipment was ready. None of his adherents would ever know the total mission. Each would know only the part he was to complete. Planning sessions, all aimed toward that same Saturday morning, would nail down the details.

"We are going to destroy the State of New York. The enemy's country will be ripped in half with the least patriotic, most easy to subvert part, the Northeast, ripped from the rest. The invaders of the Tenth Mountain Division will be removed. The officer corps of the crusader's army will be dealt a fatal blow. The power grid of the eastern half of the continent will be devastated for years to come. The center of the cabalistic Zionist financial fixers will be destroyed. And finally, the worldwide Jewish conspiracy will be beheaded by eliminating New York.

"Your Indian guides are to think that they are on a raid to regain their homeland so that they will be taken seriously by the occupiers. If and when they begin to suspect that they are merely tools to achieve our goals and not theirs, you will dispatch them to their happy

Dread upon the Waters

hunting ground." An evil smile crossed the dark face of the Mahdi. His flashing eyes, as always, assessed his audience.

The four groups of jihadis received different orientations. To one group of four he taught: "Lake Champlain and the Hudson River are an historic invasion route for the Indians. These Iroquois, who think of themselves as the wisest of Indians, will find the irony delicious in your use of the water route to eliminate the infidel's war college at West Point."

A different foursome of jihadis was told: "The looseness of the reservation's boundaries and the fear at being seen as politically incorrect, will enable you to use the Indian guides to cross into New York without difficulty. You will need your guides to drive your ATVs all the way to Fort Drum."

A third group of four heard: "The Senecas, who consider themselves to have highly developed political techniques, are like the Mohawks in considering Canada to be an extension of Iroquiana. Theys can be exchanged for the divers you'll need at the Niagara Bar."

To the group that would be guided by the Aquinah brothers, he dropped the Iroquois mythology all together: "Your guides must take you all the way in to the center of Zionism, even if at the point of a gun. As dry land people you are not ready for the piloting of ocean-going tugboats. Keep them alive and driving. You will have additional helpers. You must succeed."

Mo's fishing camp at the Lake of Two Mountains was primitive, absolutely primitive. His wife, Olivia, had gotten used to the outhouse, the lack of running water, the wood-fire cooking. She had a lot of trouble with the lack of noise. No electrical hum, no ticking clocks, no computer buzzing in the background, no furnace fan, no water pipes hammering. She had spent the last four days and nights here but most of the time she'd been in the boat with Mo. In the cabin, alone after dark, she was aware of the millions of animal and wind noises and at the same time oppressed by the lack of house noises. These sounds by which she'd slept at night were gone.

Joe Gaspe and the Portable Nukes

Night noises on the Ottawa were all suffused with the sound of moving water. Liv had come to accept those sounds by cataloging them before she drifted off, understanding the ones that were expected and being aware of any unnatural change or stoppage. This trick of sorting out the regular sounds made drifting off to sleep an easier task. In New Orleans, Liv had been an insomniac—here in camp or on the Rez she tranced herself into dreamland.

Olivia had been living a different life within her imagination since coming to the Rez. Now she was semi-divorced from modern life and convenience, and had come to accept an existence where she contemplated the conditions and sanctity of the inner life in her mind as the true reality. She smelled the difference in her life and it smelled like sanctuary.

At the beginning of September, Cornflower, her young helper, had asked her how she liked living at the north, after the easiest, but not the prettiest season.

"Very different from home weather-wise, but, like home, lots and lots of water and many good folks to keep me company. Are snowstorms worse than hurricanes? I don't think so."

Granted she had not gone through a winter yet, something that would be a long hard challenge for a southerner. But she accepted her primitive conditions, understood them, and was more aware of nature. She overcame the nervous worry that she had stumbled into a prison or was in a perilous situation. Her understanding of Mo and the women of his clan had led to the realization that the sure road, where one knows everything that will happen in life, is a living death. A life spiced with uncertainty and even peril is the true life. Living life where nothing ever happened except drinking and partying, she'd be as good as dead.

Mo's main residence was at Akwesasne in a house next to his business, but he kept this fish camp in Quebec and a hunting camp at Kanesatake in Ontario. Liv had been staying with him at the New York Rez, in her own cottage, since late March. The living conditions were quaint. She lived in a heated, snug cottage and kept her own garden and a few farm animals. One of Mo's nieces, Cornflower, was a salaried helper. When Mo visited, he asked permission, which was always granted, to stay the night. Mo traveled regularly for work and for sport. He'd stayed at his Ottawa River Camp twice before he took Olivia along.

Last fall, Liv had returned to New Orleans after helping to rehabilitate Randi Deschutes. Her parents weren't too surprised when she announced that she would be returning north in March. They were used to her peripatetic ways, suspecting a man to be the lure but, feeling guilty about their own marital failures, they were unwilling to inquire.

In March, Mo had picked her up at the airport in Albany, brought her home and, after a rapturous night, left for deliveries of bait before the season opener on April First. For two hours Liv wondered what she'd gotten herself into. Then, while she was exploring her back yard, she heard a pick-up truck pull up in the drive, the doors slam, and the truck pull away. Olivia came round the side yard near the driveway and saw two women standing there: a slim girl holding a cardboard box and a heavier older woman with a mesh carry bag.

Without preamble the older woman said, "I am Jane, cousin to Moses Snow: this is my niece Cornflower. We're here to tune you up." She laughed a happy laugh at her own jest. Liv didn't understand the reference, a problem she would have many times in the coming days.

Jane began instructing her in many of the ways that a Mohawk woman lived. She explained that Mo was a pine-tree chief among the members of the tribe. He was important and listened to in council but had neither hereditary nor appointed status and did not vote in council. She explained that Cornflower, who spoke Mohawk and French but little English, was there to assist her in her household and farm duties and would be around all the time until fall and then occasionally through the winter. Coming from New Orleans, Liv knew some Creole French and she and Cornflower developed a pidgin of their own that combined French, Mohawk and English in a unique way. Liv learned that this house and garden were hers. Mo was the owner but must seek her favor to visit or stay overnight.

Jane had explained the requirement that Liv do two things to signal to the entire tribal community her status. She must provide a symbolic meal to her man's mother, or if she had passed away, his oldest living female relative, an aunt in this case. Bread was suggested as the offering and Liv had stunned the community with the quality and aroma of the rosemary-flavored loaf she walked across the road and left on Auntie's doorstep. When the woman ate the offered food, the suitability of the marriage was confirmed to all Mohawks.

The second thing Liv needed to do was grow her hair long enough that she should wear it in a single braid. This would take time. The single braid meant that she was no longer unattached. Two braids were worn by any unattached Mohawk woman.

The most important thing that Jane told Liv was that a Mohawk warrior really appreciates a warm sleeping robe. For this she unpacked a smooth oval soapstone and instructed Liv to heat up the stone on the stove and place it in her bed before each night spent with her man,. She laughed at this and Cornflower, overhearing, tittered a bit. It was made clear to Liv that the faster she produced Mo's children the happier the entire community would be.

Jane and Cornflower were the female relatives who Liv saw most often but there were many more who came around on occasion. Liv, used to people from the southern United States who came in an infinite variety of odd looks with a generous sprinkling of the ugly and the obese, got used to the appearance of Mohawk women. Most were handsome and graceful in youth, distinguished in age. All but a few had black hair worn long. There were none that were striking beauties and none at all that were ugly or misshapen. It was not uncommon for them to be stout but they were too underfed to be sloppily obese.

Liv had found that sleeping rock to be useful well into June and here, in August, it had been brought out again. It sure did work to keep her man attentive.

Liv had been confused for a while by the interchangeable nature of the terms; aunt, cousin, and niece, for example. Rather than representing a strict biological or marriage relationship, the terms seemed to indicate the relationship at the time of the interaction. Thus Liv could be a cousin with an equal, a niece with a superior, and an aunt with a younger person. In separate circumstances, one could have those different relationships with the same person.

Dread upon the Waters

Now, though she was settled in her house and living the Mohawk way, there was still much which she did not understand. Her acceptance by the women of the clan and community had become more thorough when she had begun baking bread and biscuits with her special southern recipes. This she did most Mondays. Mo's nieces and others, so many that some had to sit on the floor, would watch the entire operation, but only Cornflower would help.

Gesturing toward the assembled women and girls, Cornflower said, "They are not here to learn your process or techniques but to build their anticipation and most of all to eat the bread." This was said in the pidgin that Cornflower and Liv had invented.

Mo had towed his boat to the Lake of Two Mountains—actually just a wide spot in the Ottawa River—and brought his new wife to show her the lure of musky fishing in a place where there was a good chance to catch a trophy fish. A trophy in musky fishing is defined as a fifty-inch or longer fish (Canada may use the metric system in commerce but they still seek big fish that are measured in pounds and inches) and is harder to catch than the ten-pound largemouth bass of the southern United States. Mo and Liv had been on the Ottawa for a few days and had caught several muskies in the mid-forty-inch range but no trophies.

Mo trolled downstream for most of the fish he caught. Dragging lures on short lines along high weed edges was a preferred pattern on the Ottawa. But he had also taken a page from his friends at Red October Baits and begun casting monster tubes to likely spots where the depth changed rapidly. He did this while slowly inching back upstream against the current, controlling the boat while his partner, Liv in this case, made casts to likely spots. A short cast, against a drop-off with the bait in free fall, had elicited several monstrous strikes and lost fish over the days. Liv just dropped her tube with a spinner blade ahead of the plastic off the front of the boat. She could see the weed edge and had no need to cast it very far. Mo short-lined a different lure behind the boat but kept his attention on positioning the boat. Liv could just flip the bait and let the lure fall as the weeds gave way to a twenty-foot deep pool. It was on the free fall that she noticed something.

Joe Gaspe and the Portable Nukes

"Hey, my line is moving against the current. What's up with that?"

"That's a fish! Strike him!" Liv looked at Mo but didn't react. "Rip his head off! Now!"

Liv pulled back with all her might and the line spun out against her thumb.

"I've got a submarine or something!" She held on as her rod tip pulsed. Head-shakes alternated with steady pulls against her efforts to stop the fish. Mo put down his rod and moved up next to Liv and used the bow-mounted electric motor to keep the fish out of the weeds.

"I can't stop him. What do I do now?" Liv asked

"Hang on for the sleigh ride. She'll get tired." Mo smiled as he watched her experience the kind of fight a trophy musky will etch into one's memory. He had turned the boat broadside to the fish and edged out into the current.

A troller passing by yelled over, asking, "What have you got Mo? A big 'un?"

Mo knew the charter captain and yelled back, "Might be." Then more quietly to Liv, he said, "She's coming up. Try to keep your rod low and give her no slack…" Before he could complete his sentence a five-foot long olive green missile launched itself completely out of the water and propelled the white-colored monster tube twenty feet up into the air. "If you can," Mo finished his sentence.

"It's gone isn't is? Is it gone? Is it? …I can't believe it's over." Liv stared at her rod tip.

"That's why a near miss is so exciting to a musky fishermen. I hate that sound."

"What sound?"

"Didn't you hear it go ptui when it spit the lure?" Mo laughed out loud.

"I didn't hear that." Liv had an agonized look on her face as she'd never had an encounter like this before.

"You'll be reliving this one for the rest of your life." Mo put his arm around her shoulders. She turned into his front and was consoled with a full body hug. He beamed over her shoulder, knowing that now she would understand.

Dread upon the Waters

Transcending from her city life into the Mohawk way, Mo wanted Liv to be a good hunter and fisherwoman who would often, but not always, travel with him. He also wanted her to help run his bait operation, keep his nephews in line, and trade fairly but firmly with his customers, Indian and non-Indian alike. He was very content with the way she was adapting to the life.

Chapter 2

Tuscarora Falls: August 28

Joe had to work at it to listen to the boss when his mind was somewhere else. He'd noticed that women in conversation could talk and listen at the same time, while he, thinking he was typical of men, could not even think about anything while listening. Never a multi-tasker, Joe tried to get his mind to concentrate.

Joe was thinking about Agent Andre's intelligence forces. He admired how this man could overcome the bureaucrats with their quid pro quo needs to closely hold anything they knew and only give up something if they got something in return. Somehow, Andre had executed an end run around the "stove piping" of information that made Homeland Security another denser, more monstrous, layer of bureaucracy—more nitpicking, obstructive, and jealous than all the others—and succeeded in foiling numerous attempts to attack the US. He also knew that these failed attacks would be secret for years because telling what had been stopped might reveal how the plots had been discovered. Better for the public to think that there had been no attacks than for the enemies, the terrorists who had declared war on the US, to gain any information on how the attacks had been prevented.

On the subject of killing terrorists, Joe recalled Andre saying to him, "If you're ever confronted by the accusation that you have done these things and you can no longer deny it, don't apologize. That would give our enemies the idea that you might not do it again and that would embolden them. Make it clear to them, unashamedly, one way or another, that you will keep up your defense of our country." This was why Joe loved working for Andre. Joe could understand and endorse that.

Today, Andre was conducting a briefing at a truck plaza. He was speaking to Moses Snow and Joe Gaspe about things they needed to know on their upcoming "kinetic operations." Andre's sources of intelligence were legion. No one knew who all of his operatives were, and he never confused any of them with details about where other information came from. He had assigned each person a theater of operations. He spoke first to Mo.

"In the east it will be a big time for the leaf peepers. Boats will be out to see the displays on the hills on both the Vermont and New York sides. That isn't such a big deal in the north where you will be, Joe. Since the trout season will be over on Champlain the only charter captains out in any numbers will be the perch fishermen. The enemy hopes to blend in with the tourists and transit the entire lake without drawing any attention. However, I've got a roster of cooperative captains who have been advised that you," he nodded to Mo, "will be in contact with them. They expect your call." He handed a sheet of paper to Mo and turned toward Joe.

"The musky fishermen on the St. Lawrence will be still plying the waters so they may be even more helpful since they are going to be more active. You are in the same situation, in that I have a list of cooperative, and eager-to-help, captains. You two, rather than the Coast Guard or county sheriffs, are doing this for two reasons. Plausible deniability for the government and overlapping jurisdictions with foreign countries." Andre paused as he pushed the lists of cooperators to Joe.

"Vermont as a foreign country! That's a joke huh? Andre, you're too much some times." Joe smiled.

"All foreigners to me," said Mo.

Joe Gaspe and the Portable Nukes

"You both know why we do things this way. Enough said about that." Andre motioned to the door of the banquet room, if that is what a private dining room at a truck stop can be called. Andre's aide opened it to admit a tall man with a light complexion who would have had blond hair if he hadn't shaved his head to ward off the appearance of impending male pattern baldness—as if, by preempting nature, baldness would be contraindicated. Andre motioned him to sit at the table and made his introductions.

"Chief Warrant Officer Rhinelander is an operative in the United States Coast Guard's Intelligence Service. He works for the Special Agent in Charge out of the Cleveland Office, coordinating with the Field Intelligence Support Teams and on the Ports, Waterways, and Coastal Security mission. This is an investigative task." Andre completed the formal introductions.

Then he said, "Through some helpful acquaintances and international agreements, CWO Rhinelander will be on a training mission with the Canadian Coast Guard in the Lake Ontario and St. Lawrence venue for the next few weeks. He will have this cell phone, with a recognizable number. If you get a call from this number it will be important. Joe, you take this one. You and Rhinelander will have a walkie-talkie feature exclusive to you two. Any amount of time that you meander into Canadian waters should be limited. Let the CWO be your eyes and ears."

Andre sipped his coffee. Joe gave CWO Rhinelander a slip of paper. "Here's my partner's cell number just in case." He looked at Andre, shrugged, and said, "Electronic stuff breaks when I have it. The devil in the machine makes a cell phone in my pocket stop working."

Andre considered that explanation and said, "These are high-grade items, the latest technological equipment. I doubt that you'll have a problem."

Joe nodded, tapped the slip of paper and motioned for Rhinelander to put it in his breast pocket. The CWO did.

Dread upon the Waters

"Are you going to climb down into every one of these boats? Geez they're all the same," Mel Dumke asked this of a man who was upside down scanning the bilge of a Lund with a penlight. Ian Drakulitch's head and one shoulder were all that could fit down the hatch, but that was enough to press the sticky-back Velcro loop to the aluminum hull. Then he placed a little item with a sticky-back Velcro hook against it. The RF transmitter would now passively wait for a detector to come looking for it.

"I guess you're not gonna answer that." Mel mumbled.

Ian's head appeared above the gunwale of the boat. "I'm sorry, what did you say?"

"Nothin' just get on with it, will ya?"

"That one's okay. Four to go." Ian had a contract to inspect and approve twelve seventeen-foot Lunds for an unidentified purchaser for whom Dumke was the agent. Drakulitch had asked for one hundred dollars per boat and was being paid one hundred fifty dollars at the insistence of the customer. This whole project was suspect in the extreme, but Ian was happy to take a Saturday off from attending his son's moto-cross races in order to earn eighteen hundred dollars.

The boats sat on four gang trailers for transport by semi-truck and would be shipped as soon as Ian approved them. They were new, had low-horsepower, high-quality Honda outboards, and were bulk priced at twenty thousand dollars Canadian each, plus GST. Mel and Ian had driven to Peterborough, Ontario for the purchase because they had found a dealer who was happy to take cash, no questions asked. Mel stood with a huge backpack hanging from his wrist while Ian climbed down and moved to the third trailer.

"Look, let's make the deal and go home. All these boats are the same." Dumke was nervous.

"It's been awhile since you worked in a factory hasn't it, Mel? A thousand and one things can go wrong. And they do." Ian signed a check sheet and moved it to the bottom of the pile on his clipboard. He filled in the heading on his next sheet. He looked up at Mel who was fidgeting and sweating in the August sun. He despised Mel Dumke but a big payday was a big payday and he was going to get another twelve hundred dollars from the Department of Homeland Security for placing the RF transmitters in each boat.

Joe Gaspe and the Portable Nukes

Ian Drakulitch was an original member of Joe Gaspe's network of people who kept an eye on the north coast of the United States. Ian's expertise in boats, their qualities, capabilities, and peculiarities had already been helpful. It was a natural for Agent Andre and Joe to use him to find a way to track these Lunds on their journeys.

John Talor and his brother James were talking, over coffee, in a small restaurant. James, the younger brother, was trying to relieve John of his doubts. They had been hired at wages well above that to which they were accustomed to pilot two ocean-going tugboats to New York where the boats would be sold. One, the larger and older boat, had been laid up for several years and needed considerable refurbishment. The other had been in service until recently and had been reasonably well-maintained considering the owning company's financial difficulties.

"Hey, it's good money they're offering. Excellent money. Who else offers that kind of cash to a couple of half-Aquinah half-Portagee tugboat pilots? We can't even get a look at the union hall,.." James said.

"But they don't seem to wanna listen to anything. They are re-welding some of the plates on the *Madison* [renamed the *Eastern Sun*] but they wanna take out all the electronics, except one cheap depth finder. We're going out on the ocean with no radio, no fax machine, no radar—nothing. And the *Lillian* (renamed the *Eastern Star*), that needs a terrible lot of work. The plates are rusted nearly through. I was surprised to hear the engine even worked on that museum piece. I'm not sure whether a vessel in that condition can endure the North Atlantic in October." John said.

"Hey, weather in October can be outstanding, you know that. Al said all that stuff was inoperable, anyway and he didn't want to buy new for a one-trip ride. I guess I understand."

"Do you? And what about this limited crew stuff. He wants you and me 'cause we're sailors and two other guys each to provide relief with the piloting, but we're not to meet the others, the engine-room guys, the deckhands, the cook. Both crews will be dangerously short-handed, unless I miss my guess."

Dread upon the Waters

"Hey, ten grand to go out the Larry for a few hundred miles 'round the Gaspe and down through the Strait of Canso. Then another ten large when we bring her in to New York. Easy money I say," James hoped this would end the discussion.

And it did, it was obvious that they were going to do the job. They sat in silence and drank more coffee. East of Quebec City, they had nothing to do but go to their hotel room and wait or sit here and wait. The refit of the two ocean-going tugs in a nearby shipyard would take a few days. There were things to do but these brothers had both taken the pledge to shy away from alcohol and when they were together they could keep their word. Separated, they were more easily tempted.

James looked very different from John. Sometimes when two people of different races and skin tones have children the offspring are an amalgam of the two shades. Other times one child looks like mom and the other looks like dad. These men were the offspring of a Native American man, specifically an Aquinah from Martha's Vineyard, and a Portuguese mother. John was tall with a long torso and broad shoulders. He had the coppery skin and black hair of an Aquinah with only the curl in his hair to give the lie to his look. James, short, broad-shouldered, and olive skinned, looked like his mother except he had the straight coarse hair of an Aquinah. One needed to look long and hard at them to see any resemblance. There was a way that their eyes crinkled when they smiled or were concentrating that was identical, but their differences were more obvious at first glance.

They waited. It was an uneasy time for them. Coffee didn't calm them but it was something to do.

Finally John spoke to put the matter to rest. "Let's look at this as our main chance to get ahead on our own. Our persistence finally paying off, you might say."

James didn't think John really believed that.

The truckers didn't know what they were carrying when headed to Kanesatake in the Quebec side of the Mohawk Nation. They were used to asking no questions. There were four flat-bed trucks, two of which

Joe Gaspe and the Portable Nukes

were of the lowboy design, carrying portable generators of various sizes in wooden crates strapped to their beds. The crates would have to be unloaded by cranes. The lowboys had two large crates each and were slated to pass through the nation and move on to the container port at Levis across the St. Lawrence River from Quebec City. Then the trucks would return to the Wolf Clan Marina on the Rez.

The last two trucks, carrying six smaller crates each, were to stop at the marina in Kanesatake. The crates were to be off-loaded near a tiny cove that was separate from the main commercial area of the boatyard. The non-union truckers would be paid in cash, loaded into a short bus returning from Levis, and be taken back to Ontario where they were instructed to know nothing. Having no knowledge was easy when one was paid five times the going rate for a gypsy trucker. Who would know that anything was wrong over the next few weeks if each of these drivers met with an unfortunate and random fatal accident?

Chapter 3

Muskedaigua: Labor Day Weekend

Neither Joe Gaspe nor Moses Snow was embarrassed when Joe's daughter Amy suggested that they dream together before she went off to her three month's of study on the other side of the state. Both men accepted the power of dreaming and they accepted the leadership that came from a woman of power even when that woman was hardly more than a girl. In truth, Amy had a harder time accepting her leadership role than either of the older men did. She was not completely over her teenage resentment of her father and his checkered history, a history she only knew a tiny bit about. The three sat on the deck outside Joe's house. It was a new house he had only been in for a few weeks. Three Adirondack chairs were in a semi-circle when Amy began tapping rhythmically on the wooden armrest of hers.

Birds began to take off and land randomly: herons, hawks, ravens, snipes, egrets, woodcocks, grouse, and pheasants, heading in all directions. A woodcock went east, followed by a heron and an egret. A snipe met them in flight and turned east with them. A great horned owl swooped through these birds dispersing them. Hawks went north and west then turned farther north and farther west. Single ravens accompanied all of them and more ravens seemed to appear, recede into the background, and reappear.

Dread upon the Waters

A woodcock flew through a flock of ravens that parted for its passing and reformed. Each time a bird headed in any direction a raven followed it. Behind the first raven came several more.

The door to the deck slid open. Joe's wife looked out, shook her head, and said, "Joe, get in here."

The dream ended with no one saying anything. Joe got up and went through the sliding door. Mo Snow looked at Amy and said, "Ravens mean mischief or danger. An owl means death."

Amy's eyes shone luminous and piercing, "We're all going to be in it now." Moses Snow nodded his head.

A few days later Joe sat in the bait shop in Pantherville talking to Rudyard Loonch. Rudi swamped out the barroom at Jackie B's Draft Beer and Live Bait while simultaneously doing independent research on one esoteric subject or another. Joe was at the shop to collect a few dollars from the sale of one of his custom fishing rods. He never questioned why an educated man like Loonch occupied himself with a lowly job such as he had at Jackie B's. Joe was aware that Loonch was part of Andre's intelligence collection system and deduced that overhearing things was the real purpose of his being a fixture at the round table in the corner. Joe sat down with a schooner of beer and greeted Rudi.

Without preamble he started in, "Amy's gone off on her internship. Her mother drove her out there. I'll miss her but, in a way, we'll be better off at home without her influence on the younger ones. I swear she's turned my youngest into a protest radical. We'll be at dinner and that little one will start banging on the table chanting, 'More ketchup! More ketchup!' then they'll all start. It's like being at an anti-war rally. I'm sure it was Amy that put her up to it." Joe stopped. He looked at Rudi, who had one eyebrow raised, then said, "That's not what I wanted to talk to you about, though.

"I'm kinda wondering what I've gotten myself into with Agent Andre. Are you aware of the mission he's got planned for Mo and me?"

"I know some things."

Joe Gaspe and the Portable Nukes

"In the river I could understand me being the guy, especially with the whole attack being cross border from Canada and such. But now he wants more…"

"He needs more, Joe. We all do," Rudi said. "Our way of life is at stake, as you know." Joe nodded.

Rudyard marked his place in a loose-leaf binder and closed it. Joe noticed the title, "*Operation Sidewinder.*" Joe knew that he was asking for a lecture from an erudite man. He got one.

"In 1979 when Iran declared war on the United States we were too busy to notice. We have always had three ways we could defend ourselves. Unfortunately, for many years we've not defended ourselves at all. Iran and her proxies, in all the different terror groups they funded, had free rein to attack us. Until the second attack on the World Trade Center Towers we were too oblivious to even take proper notice of the incidents, though they were much more than pinpricks in our hide.

"Most of the time, political correctness prevented us from doing anything more than taking a law-enforcement type of approach. That, of course, means that the attack has to have already occurred before we act, like the first one on the trade towers. Since the early fifties, our public discourse has been overtaken in politics, newspapers, and education by people who have never ventured into that half-world out there; a half hidden world that you or I can step into and out of but which these leaders, who have done nothing but criticize the doers all their lives, don't even acknowledge as existing." Joe nodded his head in agreement.

Rudyard continued, "You know people on the fringes who move about below the radar, cross borders, provide and use forged papers and exist in a world of half light, sometimes for their whole lives. Drug dealers are only the most obvious of these people. Our scribblers never see these people unless they are romanticized by Hollywood. You and I know that they are anything but romantic.

"Right after 9/11 we pulled together as a nation and seemed to understand the nature of our enemy. But now we are several years along and those enemies have done a lot of work putting us back to sleep in our comfortable lives. They are still intent on making bad things happen to us. Meanwhile we have taken to telling ourselves lies. Ironically we get more complacent each month because we have been able to prevent any major attack since then. These adversaries of ours take the long view. They are meticulous planners. They understand the vulnerability of our ports and seacoasts, our pipelines, our over-the-road trucks filled with chemicals that are toxic, caustic, flammable, and explosive. Our elites talk like a piecemeal approach to protecting all this will work forever when it most certainly will not."

"Jeez Rudi, you are depressing me," Joe smiled, looked at Rudyard's stern expression, stopped smiling, and said, "Go on."

"We live in denial though we know that these people are patient, tenacious, creative, and technically savvy as they probe for weakness. If they weren't so committed to the spectacular they would have already pulled off some vicious attacks. Two examples of what is wrong. We westerners do not consider attacking children to be in our interests because of bad publicity and international outrage. They think of such an attack as a strategic bonanza. If they were to kill a large number of children and incite our anger against all Muslims they could redefine the conflict as a religious rather than ideological war and bring the entire Muslim world in on their side against the weak western democracies.

"The other thing we do as a society is that we lie to ourselves. We say, for instance, that we will protect our ports by aggressive patrolling outside our borders by a newly tasked and robust Coast Guard. Then we don't change the Defense Department procurement priorities to upgrade the ships and boats that this overworked agency needs. The average boat in service is twenty-seven years old and the replacement time frame is on the order of thirty years. In 2038 we'll be patrolling with fifty-year-old ships!"

"You're not making this up are you?" Joe looked in Rudi's eyes. "No, you're not."

"The odds against catching these guys if we follow business as usual, which is what we are doing now, are worse than the odds of hitting the lottery. It is only their arrogance that trips them up, and they will not always be so overconfident. The millennium bomber who was caught bringing explosives into Washington state on a ferry

Joe Gaspe and the Portable Nukes

boat was only stopped because; a) he'd gotten malaria in Afghanistan and he was suspicious because his state of illness was obvious, b) his was the last vehicle off the ferry so there was no hurry to inspect his car and send him through, c) he was unfamiliar with English and handed over a discount card instead of proper ID, and after he was asked to open the trunk he tried to run away. That trunk contained enough bomb-making materials to equal four explosions the size of the one that destroyed the Murrah building in Oklahoma City.

"Still the border inspectors thought that they were looking at drugs being smuggled. At that port of entry, they had no way to test for explosives. The US Attorney, who was consulted, expressed the opinion that there was no cause to hold him. INS delayed long enough for the one bomb-testing team to show up. As you can see, there was a lot that could have gone wrong here."

Rudyard Loonch waited for this to sink in. He rearranged some books and picked up a highlighter, then put it down. He looked Joe in the eye and said, "There's more."

"The bureaucracy that is tasked with controlling all this is uniquely unprepared to accomplish it. It is an iron-clad rule of government work that an agency request all the money it got last year, in order to do the exact same things it did last year. There is no incentive to innovate, no reward for having done so, and no money available for anything unproven. No official sticks his neck out without resources already in the budget pipeline.

"So how can we defend ourselves without giving up all our freedom? Well we have four levels of defense: preemptive defense, forward defense, defense in depth, and reactive defense. There are problems with all four, and we will need all four in the years ahead.

"I'll start with reactive defense first. First responders: police, fire, emergency medical, and hazard response teams, need all the equipment and training that we can give them and most important of all they need to be nimble replacing outdated equipment with newer, better technical innovations. This has to be done more quickly than the way it is presently done. Ask the postal clerk to look up a zip code for you and it takes ten to twelve minutes. Google the address on your home computer and you'll get the answer in one second. It takes an

Dread upon the Waters

Act of Congress, literally, to get new software in the government. In the private sector it happens every few months. But the big problem with reactive defense is that the disaster has already happened. Remember Katrina? Of course you do. Private companies and faith-based charities were able to provide relief supplies faster and in greater quantity then the federal government for many reasons. American people and companies are more than ready to step up to the plate if the government will not impede them. Budweiser was shipping bottled water to New Orleans within a few days of the crisis. After all, they have the bottling plants. There are many examples of this. But reactive defense is, by its nature, after the fact.

"Defense in depth is where you come in, Joe. This is Agent Andre's area of expertise and it is a tricky one. Here we must defeat the attackers as they cross into our homeland and at the same time refrain from destroying the village we are seeking to protect. The US military is too proficient and too thorough at destroying things for this task. They are able to take out enemies but they cannot be tasked with this without taking out many friendlies as well. A combination of high-tech and low-impact weapons wielded by unknown and unpublicized assets is the only way to keep this a viable alternative.

"Forward defense is what our outstanding military is able to do. They are the best and most deadly in the world. They are able to change their tactics on the run. They are good at blowing things up. And they are busy. Every fighter they kill is one fewer that we will have to suffer from over here. They are active in many places about which the public knows nothing. Unfortunately, the enemy is numerous and has a large cohort of volunteers to die for jihad. It is a symbiosis. They come to die for jihad and our troops go there to kill them for the same reason. But the military's efforts are outside our borders.

"Preemptive defense is one that the political situation makes difficult to pull off but it does have resonance in the minds of the terrorist sponsors. For example, with Iran at war with us since 1979 and killing Americans through proxies everywhere they can, we could take them down readily if we were willing to, and had the political courage, to do it. The one oil refinery in Iran that makes gasoline could be removed. Their ports to import gasoline could be readily closed by our naval forces. Their forces would be much slower to arrive in Iraq if they were walking to the battlefield. The greater dangers that we face from China and Russia will be more difficult to deal with and the political will to do that is lacking today and may be lacking forever.

"This is why you are doing what you are doing. Andre's teams, consisting of nameless assets, are a vital part of our surreptitious defense in depth. What is to be done must be done by unknown and unlikely people such as you and your cousin Mo.

"The long-term need for our government to stop treating the American people like children, stop them from believing convenient lies, and enlist all of us in our own defense, is a big problem that I am not sanguine about."

"Sanguine? What's that mean?"

"Optimistic and confidant the way I'm using it but it also means bloody." Rudyard laid down his marker. He had finished.

"Bloody, huh? Well I don't know whether I feel better or worse, but I guess I know why I'm helping out Andre."

As a member of Andre's far-flung intelligence force, Rudyard Loonch knew some things about Joe Gaspe that Joe had never admitted even to himself. Joe was not brilliant and not even all that insightful but he was determined and he had stamina. His best quality was that he would be unfazed by setbacks and most difficulties he encountered would go unnoticed. He would bull ahead until he reached his goal, and while alive, he would never stop until he got where he was going.

Joe had perfected the habit of not feeling guilty. It wasn't as if he could rationalize or justify his bad behavior. It was just a technique he had worked out where he compartmentalized his life so that he thought about what was in front of him not what someone else, his wife for instance, wanted him to think about. In front of him was the forty-acre shoal in the Thousand Islands area of the St. Lawrence River. At home Kate and the four younger daughters were trying to get settled into a new home. His wife had her sisters and brothers to help her and they were legion. Here, Joe had musky fishing to take care of.

Joe's regular fishing partner, Marv, wanted to stop and cast at every likely looking spot: Seven Pines Island, Black Ant Shoal, Black Duck

Dread upon the Waters

Island, everywhere. Joe thought that this expanse of water in front of Gananoque, Ontario was an area where a trolling bite was more likely to get results. Traditionally, Joe was correct. As a change of pace, Marv had a point. Lighter in weight and more nimble than Joe, the blonde-headed Marv fished the front of the boat with his ball cap on backwards and his manic energy keeping up a slight rocking motion on the bow.

"Let's offer 'em sumpin' they haven't seen a million times." Marv was clipping his favorite black and white spoon onto his casting rod. "I'll let you throw towards shore while I hit the Canadian side." Marv meant the deep water where the conventional wisdom stated that the thrown lure would never go deep enough to reach the fish. That traditional wisdom had been proved wrong many times lately. Notable musky guides, like Mike Hulbert of Indiana, had shown that the deep, or Canadian, side often held suspended fish that would come up for a lure cast their way.

Joe shrugged, clipped on a Red October Monster Tube, and flung it toward Black Duck Island. He would bounce and rip that tube back to the boat. The tube could be fished with success as a slow bottom bouncing jig, or it could be retrieved by reeling quickly and ripping in to cause the pulsating plastic skirt's vibrations to draw in active muskellunge. The wind had set up nicely for this drift and they skimmed down the shoal with Joe pounding the break line and Marv tossing his heavy spoon into the void. Joe wasn't confident that casting was the best technique. Lack of confidence is a fatal flaw in musky fishing, but at least Marv would stop ragging on him for a while.

For the next two hours they were able to drift down the shoal edge alternately farther from or closer to the line of islands, and motor back for another drift. They were blown along steadily but not too quickly for effective work with their baits. During that time, Joe had three fish on and had lost them all. They destroyed the tube each time. The first two strikes on the lure went unnoticed by Joe. He was trying to eat a submarine sandwich about two feet in length, and he'd let the tube drop while he took a bite. Then, when he saw the line heading the wrong direction, he struck and ripped the tube right out of the fish's mouth. The third strike, after he'd finished eating, had resulted in a brief hard fight with the fish coming right to boat side, opening its mouth, and letting the tube fly into the air over Joe's head. He did some cussing at that point.

Marv caught a slim forty-two-inch male musky on his spoon, released it, and kept on fishing the deep side. He was throwing that big spoon for all he was worth, counting it down to a ten-one-thousand count and bringing it back on a straight fast retrieve. Marv was eating his favorite mini-doughnuts, which, being one-bite noshes, didn't tie up his hands as Joe's sandwich did. On the third drift over the spot where he'd landed the forty-two, his lure stopped dead in the water. His rod doubled over and he said, "I've got bottom. A log or somethin'."

"It's eighty-feet deep over there. You've got a fish. Strike him! Rip it in!" Joe was fired up. Marv pulled for all he was worth and fought what felt like a monster for a few minutes. Then it was gone. He reeled in his spoon to find the treble hook having one point straightened out.

"Look at this Joe! He must've been a monster!"

Joe looked and said, "Reminds me of Musky Bill's saying. 'Whatever you've got, there's a musky that can defeat it.'"

By the time Marv put a new hook on the spoon, the weather had brewed up, threatening a storm, and the wind kept them from drifting any more that day. They trolled into the evening without another strike. On the way in to camp Joe said, "All that action came as the weather was getting ready to change didn't it?"

Marv was heartsick. He didn't respond.

Amelia Gaspe, five foot six, pretty but not beautiful, looked like her mother, not her half-Mohawk father with whom she had spent the last six years in low-intensity conflict. She didn't want to be a Mohawk power dreamer but she was one. She could no longer deny it. The dreams came to her unbidden and at least the Mohawk thing was an explanation. She no longer thought that she was going crazy. God had

Dread upon the Waters

Amy Gaspe

Joe Gaspe and the Portable Nukes

given her these dreams and now she must learn to deal with them. Driving across the state with her mother, she looked forward to her course of study and she dreaded it as well. Her fate was to be a dreamer. Now she must become adept at dealing with it.

Amy was tired of being misunderstood and having nobody to talk to about the visions that came to her. Any attempts she had made to explain herself had led to embarrassment and difficulty. Amy loved her mother but Kate couldn't understand because she had no ability to dream. Since Amy had accepted her power dreaming, her relationship with her father had improved but only on the dream level. In everyday things he was still just a big pain in the neck to her. She thought about all this as she watched the autumn landscape stream by. It was incredibly beautiful but it presaged a long, cold, nasty winter that never seemed to loosen its grip on the state.

Amy was coming to the realization that fully half of her inner life up to this time had been inaccessible to her until she became conscious of why she had such strong and vivid dreams. She'd never been one to pine for an existence in the natural world. Hiking, fishing, hunting, and camping had never been fun for her. She'd tried camping with her dad a few times, just as a way to mend fences, but it always led to frustration and difficulty. This dream world, in and out of which she moved seamlessly, was a primitive world with campfires and caves and swimming in rivers. This was the world of her ancestors for which she had never had any use at all. The ruggedness and difficulties of the natural world were something that she saw as having been replaced by comfort and modern conveniences. In her dreams the tests and trials of nature were the school where she would teach herself how to live.

Often she found herself in a cave with other women many of whom seemed dried out, drunk, and shriveled and always there was "The Old One" who looked, with his silly wolf-skin cloak, to be a semi-pathetic figure. But her grandmother was always there also. Aksotha, shining and beautiful, would tell her that she did not create these women in her dreams anymore than she created the animals in the zoo. They were there to show her what was happening to those

Dread upon the Waters

people who had lost the dreaming and succumbed to the ways of the wicked world. "And The Old One, he is there for you. He is your teacher and your helper. Without him to go out in the dreams of those you influence, they will not believe what you will be telling them. When the old one tells them the people will believe. Show him what you want to say and he will see that they hear it.

"When you move with him into the depths of your mind I will be with you as well. You will never be alone as you plunge into the world of the unknown. Your knowledge, strength, and power will increase and lead us all. The challenges are great but you will know that you are doing right."

Amy's thoughts were interrupted by her mother's voice. "Check the Mapquest printout, I think we have to make a turn soon."

Later, after her mother had dropped her off, Amy met her dream teammate, Moses Snow's older sister Molly. They sat together while they listened to an orientation lecture by Ruland Rush. He was a stout, ruddy Irishman, graying now but a natural reddish blond. He paced as he talked and had an unlit pipe he waved around.

When Rush stopped pacing and looked over the group, his eyes bored in on Amy. She wondered if everyone had the same feeling. "You will learn to accept the dream state as a feeling that is more consuming than your imagination. You will see today, yesterday, and tomorrow all at once. Things that have not begun will take place at the same time as things that have ended and things that are happening right now. You must abandon your need to see this as an intellectual situation. You must just accept it as it is. You don't need to know why it is like this. You just need to accept the things that are offered to you. Take note of it. Honor it.

"When you dream about something that later comes to pass, you will have had foreknowledge that did not originate with you. It is not something that you have deduced. It cannot be, because until the events take place at a later time, you did not even know that it was foreknowledge. This is an inspiration. An inspiration, by its very nature, is a gift. This is a revelation that you have been chosen to receive."

He waited for what he said to sink in, then started again. " You are going to be dreaming, meditating, and relaxing here. That's all. We are going to make your mind more labile than it has ever been before. Lability is the ready capacity to change or adapt. Your mind in dreaming can move from idea to image and back or onward. It is more open to influence. For one thing, no one is watching, so how others react to an idea or image is not a concern. You will be more receptive to change from its accustomed patterns. These images will often seem random and chaotic without the conscious mind imposing order on them.

"After you have become used to this, your spirit guide, your oyaron, will appear to you. This will be a bird or animal. Because this vision is so real, it may seem like the devil to you, but ride with it. If it is a ferocious animal the thing it tells you about will be dangerous or evil, though not necessarily for you. If it is a harmless animal it is foretelling something beneficial. When they warn you, you will not always be able to understand because it is seldom clear enough to be obvious. Do not be alarmed if you misinterpret. That is usually caused by you reading into it more than is there."

Ruland Rush abruptly stopped his talk. He stood before them quietly. An assistant stepped to the front and instructed the dream workers when they would be fed and what the evening's activities would be. There was no hum of conversation as the people moved off. Molly and Amy were assigned a bedroom in the mansion, spare as a cell, where they were to practice their individual and team dreaming when not being taught or led by Rush or his assistants. They were quiet with a lot to think about.

Far to the south and eastward across the Atlantic Ocean, the Cape Verde weather machine had begun its work. At 20-west longitude and 20-north latitude a wave became organized that would become a named storm in a few days. Squeezed by a ridge of high pressure to its north, this storm wave started to track to the westward.

If this wave became better organized by atmospheric conditions, a depression bordering on a hurricane would advance into the Caribbean. Moving at forty miles per hour to the west, the storm was predicted to organize and follow a track to the west because the huge

Dread upon the Waters

continental high to its west and north constrained it. Should that continental high weaken, the storm could push rapidly north in the western ocean and create a large nor'easter in the western Atlantic.

Chapter 4

St. Lawrence River: September 30th

Joe Gaspe sat at the picnic table drinking coffee. It was late morning, the sky was a shimmering blue, the air no longer crisp. Mist rose from the inlet where the Boston Whaler was moored. Marv was on the dock casting a bucktail. His throws quartered the stream and created a fan pattern of ripples on the still water. Joe was using a flat file, a round file, and a hook hone to put razor sharp edges on the treble hooks of the lures they had used the previous day. They didn't plan on fishing from the boat today. Last night they had trolled several of Marcus's runs. This was the mighty St. Lawrence River and they had bounced their lures: deep divers, mid-depth and shallow runners off of rocks, logs, and through weeds. Because even weeds made them dull, hooks had to be examined. Joe worked contentedly, happy not to have to listen to Marvin's chatter. Marv cast his lure repeatedly, happy to work out the kinks from a night on a lumpy mattress. They didn't speak to each other.

Best friends and longtime fishing buddies, Marv and Joe were content with silence. The hangovers would dissipate, the coffee would take hold, and they would start their banter soon enough. Today was going to be a busy day spent entirely in camp. An abandoned campground and resort turned into a private playground was their setting for two important meetings. Joe glanced at Marv's cell phone sitting

Dread upon the Waters

on the table, wondering again whether his brother Frank and Johann Hatchett had this number. He knew they did, but his mind looped into worry when he didn't keep his hands busy. He had five lures laid in a row, their three treble hooks had been touched-up by the round file. He picked up the flat file for a go at them.

"There ain't no muskies in this crick, maybe a northern but no skis." Joe said this to aggravate Marv, not looking at him but concentrating on his work.

"Fish can swim, right? There's water in through here, right? Why wouldn't Mr. Toothy be in here?" Marv said over his shoulder, his body turned away from Joe as he kept casting.

"It's your turn to cook breakfast. I built some good coals here and the potatoes are peeled and sliced. Coffee's hot. I make the coffee and fire. You make the eggs, spuds, bacon, toast." Joe said.

Joe looked back at his work but his eyes shifted, once more, to the phone. Sitting there, glowing green, it didn't ring, vibrate, or flash. He could hear Marv walking up to the fire pit as he examined a non-existent nick on one of the hooks.

"Did you wash your hands? I don't like musky slime on my toast, Joe said."

"Yes, I washed," Marv answered. "We haven't caught a fish for two days. Where would I get slime anyway?"

"There is that." Joe cracked a small smile.

Though on their most serious mission yet for Assistant Special Agent in Charge Thomas Andre, Joe and Marv still had time to pursue their passion for musky fishing. For the last week it had been a day of fishing, a day or two of pursuing bad guys. Life was good. Boys never grow up if they can help it. Outdoor play and dangerous adventures, what could be better?

They were in Wesley Walden's compound, an isolated seven-acre campground with abandoned RV hookups scattered about. Being an old friend from Muskedaigua, "Whiskey Nose Wes" had let Joe and Marv use the main cabin, which was just a log shack big enough for a wood stove for heat, two beds, and a tiny bathroom. There was a gate at the road with a Tennessee latch (a loop of wire over the end of the gate that fitted over the first fence post) and a huge sign above the gate

Joe Gaspe and the Portable Nukes

that said, Posted, No Trespassing; Violators Will Be Shot. The inlet that the camp had used to moor boats had a similar sign. That waterway was blocked by a plastic snow fence strung from a chain and sagging right down to water level. This top hinged gate could be raised for entry with a convenient notched pole so that boats could go up and down the creek. Neither of these security gates was any way to prevent forced entry but Whiskey Nose Wes's reputation as a crank, that discouraged the locals, and the closed gates and threatening signs were enough to discourage tourists who didn't go anyplace that one had to get out of the car to reach. Wes had decamped for Florida after Labor Day and allowed Joe to use his property.

He'd had been Joe's brother Frank's best friend and a thoroughly delinquent person as a boy and young man. Than his rich uncle left him this campground and piles of money and he had moved north for the summer and south for the winter. As the years passed, Wes closed the camp except for a few weeks per year and spent most of his time down south. Joe and Marv had used the camp for fall musky fishing the last several years and closed up the property at the end of their stay. Today they had a strategic rendezvous planned; later they would skedaddle with the Whaler.

Marv fried the whole pound of bacon, poured off half the grease, and then added the sliced potatoes and onions. He started the eggs in a second skillet, recharged the coffee pot and sat on his haunches with his head cocked to one side trying to keep the smoke from his dangling cigarette from getting in his eyes.

The pan sizzled and popped as the smell of cooked bacon—probably the best smell in the universe—drifted off to the west. Almost immediately, a dog showed up. He was a mixed breed, looking to be part Lab and part German shepherd. A man, whistling tunelessly, trailed along behind the dog. Joe looked to the westerly woods, paper-company land as far as he knew, and watched the man, who looked to be in his sixties, amble down toward him with a double-barreled shotgun in his the crook of his arm.

"Smelled your bacon and I knew Rammer would head this way. Just came to gather my dog." The man wore a red and black checked hunting shirt and a bright orange cap. His shotgun was open at the

Dread upon the Waters

breach as it cradled in his arm. Perceiving no threat, Joe didn't go for any of the weapons that, though concealed, were readily at hand.

"What you huntin'?" he asked

"Rammer and I are just killing time. Stay out of the house when the she-one has it occupied. She heads to the outlet mall downstate in a little while, then I'll go home and putter around."

"Want some breakfast? We've got plenty."

"Breakfast? I ate that five hours ago. But I'll share a cup of coffee if you don't mind." He stood at the end of the table taking everything in as Joe poured coffee into an enameled tin cup. "I take it you know Wes and are familiar with his security arrangements."

"Old family friend. Marv and I have been shutting this camp down for the last four years. How 'bout you? Are you a friend?"

"Friend and neighbor. I used to own the gas station when they were called service stations, back in the day." A wistful look crossed his face as he raised the cup to his lips. He blew across the hot liquid and took a tiny sip.

"Yeah," said Joe. "Now you can't even get someone to fix a flat."

"Tires don't get flat anymore—roads and tires are better today." Marv seemed to want an argument.

The hunter looked at Marv, smiled, and said, "There's roads around rough enough for any tire, but I take your point. I'm Floyd Zepf by the way." He offered his hand. Joe wiped bacon grease onto his pant leg and shook hands.

"Joe Gaspe. This is my partner Marv Ankara. We're up here for a few more days. You live nearby?"

"Other side of that mountain, about a mile and a half over there." He waved his hand to the northeast.

"I hope we won't disturb you this afternoon. There may be some loud reports. My brother is bringing up some guns, primitive weapons, we'll be doing some shooting." Joe was searching the old man's face for signs of worry, alarm, whatever.

"I'm your closest neighbor and I won't pay any attention. This is hunting season. Nobody out here cares about gunshots."

Joe tucked into his country breakfast while Marv set the fry pan down for the dog. Rammer scarfed the few remaining potatoes then

Joe Gaspe and the Portable Nukes

began worrying the greasy pan with his tongue, pushing it up against the picnic table leg. He wagged his tail and worked hard over the delicious grease.

"That dog's not going to lick away the iron is he?" Marv asked.

"Rammer! Come here!" The dog immediately walked over and nuzzled his master behind his right knee. "A dog can lick meat off a bone. He thinks he can lick through anything."

Joe washed out the pans after Rammer was done, burned his paper plates and all three men were having more coffee and talking fishing when Frank's ancient bush car, a Ford Bronco, came up the driveway. Joe noticed that Frank had a passenger. That was a change of plans. The car stopped at the gravel patch thirty yards away. Frank walked up to the table and was introduced to Floyd the hunter, who then took his leave, following Rammer down toward the shoreline road.

Joe turned to Frank with a questioning look and raised his eyebrows.

"Yes, I've got everything and plenty of it. DeXFactor, slow matches, pyro papers, fuse cord. Enough for fifty snappers or thirty-five long snappers." Frank looked at Joe again. Joe raised his eyebrows, cocked his head toward the truck and raised both hands in a "What's up with that?" gesture.

"Oh her? That's a long story." Frank waved for the woman in the car to come out.

Marv and Joe both took a double take as a slim woman with a stunning face and raven black hair strode up to the table. She was dressed in an oversized hoodie, jeans, and running shoes. She looked awfully familiar to Joe. He couldn't remember where he'd seen her.

"Sherry, this is Joe and Marv, his partner. Sherry is looking for you, Joe."

Joe's brows shot up again. He said, "Me?"

"You don't remember me do you? You gave me your card once in Pittsburgh. At a club. I looked for you in Muskedaigua but you'd moved. Luckily I found Frank." She tapped Frank on the sleeve.

"Er, I remember you. You didn't have so much clothing on though. Heh, heh, heh."

Dread upon the Waters

Frank spoke next, "Sherry found me at my shop and didn't hook up with Kate or the girls. So, you're safe there brother."

Sherry faced Joe. She was four feet in front of him.

"Word about what you guys did, at Sweet Cherries in Cincy, got around over the last year. I remembered you, and I know some girls who ended up in those dives working for the effin' Russkies. All the girls I know want to meet you guys and thank you for taking on those bastards. Too many girls got messed up dealing with them. I had your card, I made my bogey and nothing held me back from coming to look for you guys."

Joe was edgy. "'Er, I'm married, more or less happily."

Marv cleared his throat. Loudly. Everyone looked at him. Sherry spoke again, "I'm a free agent, and I've got a three hundred dollar bottle of single malt Scotch. I just want somebody cool to drink it with."

"Frank's going home this afternoon. We are on the boat there until we get back to Cape Vincent where our truck is." Marv cleared his throat again. "I mean Marv's truck. We have some things to accomplish. Important things. I don't think we want a lady along. Could be dangerous, uncomfortable, cold. We can't be looking after no little lady."

"So, a girl's okay when she's stripping and dancing but other than that you don't want her around." Her eyes lashed Joe, and Marv thought he saw a bolt of lightning pass between her and Joe.

"Well…yeah. Pretty much." Joe knew he should shut up.

Frank had walked back to the Bronco and was unloading boxes, cans, and gear. Marv piped up. "I think you'd be great to have along. You can help with our project, and I'm not married."

"I like you," Sherry said. Turning back to glare at Joe, she pointed out, "Men are a dime a dozen, you know, nothing special about most of them. I thought when you pulled off that raid you had something going for yourself, but…"

"That was Marv's deal. He had the plan…"

Sherry interrupted, "OK, you can stop now." Taking several trips to the truck, Frank had set gear on the table. Joe didn't notice as he slid two pink backpacks under the edge of the picnic table.

Joe Gaspe and the Portable Nukes

An hour later the team had built twenty snappers and twelve long snappers and carefully placed them in compartmentalized plastic boxes. It turned out that after some instruction Sherry was adept at building snappers and could do it better and faster than any of the men. Frank was a pyrotechnic—a fireworks expert—who had invented the snapper for fun and giggles. A sheet of pyro paper, slow burning, stiff paper, was laid on the table. A tablespoon of DeXfactor, improved black powder, was poured into the center. Then a three-corner double-fold was executed to create a triangular item about two inches on a side. A fuse piece an inch- and-one-half long was folded in so that it stuck out of one corner. When the fuse was lit, one had fifteen seconds before the snapper exploded.

"A snapper is the equal to a quarter stick of dynamite. A long snapper, which we'll make next, is equal to a half stick. These will sink the Lunds that we are trying to stop. I hope." Joe said this for Sherry's benefit.

Joe walked over to an old grill on the property and lit the fuse on a snapper, tossed it in the grill, put on the cover, and scooted quickly backwards. "Fire in the hole! Cover your ears and open your mouth."

With a snapping sound as loud as a tree being broken in half, there was an explosion in the grill and the cover went ten feet straight into the air.

"Whoo hoo!" yelled Marv as the grill cover came back to earth and the smell of burnt powder headed downwind.

Frank had seen this before. He said nothing. Joe looked at Sherry wondering what she'd do.

"Cool..." She wasn't fazed. Yet.

Later, after Frank left, they built some long snappers. Long snappers, with two heaping tablespoons of DeXfactor and a longer fuse, were a more difficult folding job, requiring two sheets of pyro paper. The long snapper that was tested blew the grill cover into bits that flew twenty feet into the air in all directions. Sherry said, "Maybe you should tell me what you are up to." Joe did.

After his explanation, Joe was relaxing with a coffee cup full of fancy Scotch when he saw a great blue heron step into view in the shallows of the inlet. The bird turned and looked at him. Joe got a feeling at the edge of his mind that there was something about to happen.

Johann Hatchett showed up mid-afternoon in a red refrigerated pick-up truck with the Mo's Bait company logo on the doors. He was alone. Sherry noted that Joe seemed to be expecting him. She looked Johann over: blond hair, almost translucent skin, slight build, chin a little weak, he was dressed for the mountains with camo paratrooper pants, webbed jungle-style combat boots, and a black tee shirt that said; "I like my leather" on the front.

He and Sherry eyed each other up and down. Joe asked, "You two know each other?"

"You look familiar. Did we ever work together?" Sherry asked, betraying nervousness about some of her past experiences.

"No, I don't think so. Ever work in Columbus?"

"No."

"How about Pantherville? Weren't you a cashier at Rick's hardware?"

"I'm a professional—I don't do hardware," said Sherry. Joe marveled that a stripper could look haughty and too good for any job. He knew that Johann had a past that required dissimulation, times in Massachusetts and Virginia that were best left hidden from prying eyes.

"You look like a co-worker of mine who worked part-time a few years back. Just a coincidence, I guess. No offense intended." Hatchett turned to Joe, nodded, then turned to Marv and said, "How's it going?"

"Hey Yo, you here for your pick-up?" Marv asked.

"Yeah, I've got something for you to try and a video clip on my iPod from Mr. Snow."

"We already have a dozen snappers and six long snappers for you to take. What more do you need?"

"Mr. Snow sent along some special papers you might want to use for this mission."

Johann placed a plain black briefcase on the table. He opened it and reached for a stack of stiff white papers. "Everyone has to extinguish smoking materials before I can show you this."

Joe Gaspe and the Portable Nukes

Sherry and Marv stubbed out their cigarettes. Johann picked up the coffee pot and poured some cold dregs on the butts. Marv and Joe looked at each other with raised eyebrows.

"Hey, were you ever in Virginia?" Sherry seemed to be getting a flash on Johann.

"These are special papers," he said, ignoring Sherry's question, "Infused with white phosphorus. Watch this." He stuck a scrap of paper the size of a file card into the opening of an empty beer can. He walked over to a bare spot on the ground ten feet away placed the can on the ground and lit the edge of the paper. A brilliant white flame roared to life spewing thick smoke and, with a loud hiss, melting the aluminum can into a blob in seconds.

"A man named Rhinelander got them for Mo. Those Lunds we're going to be hunting have aluminum hulls. Just in case we don't blow the bottoms out, these will burn holes in them as they sink. Even burns underwater. Combined with DexFactor we'll take them down." The grin on Johann Hatchett's face was pure evil, delighting in anticipated violence.

The thick smoke was gone and the beer can was a black blob as small as a nickel. Joe looked at Sherry, then at Marv. He eyed the camp fire embers, turned to Johann and said, "Let's take our equipment over there," he pointed at a picnic table forty feet away, "We'll build some special snappers and some special long snappers. Marv, stay over here and build up some coals," he pointed at the campfire. "We'll probably have an appetite after this."

They packed the special snappers in tissues inside the boxes used to transport them. Not unreasonably, they worried about friction and heat as possible tinder to start the explosives going early. After they were done, having packed all their DexFactor into snappers, they had twenty regular and twenty special snappers and ten of each type of long snappers. Half would go with Johann and half would stay with Joe.

The four had an early dinner, finished the bottle of Scotch and Johann prepared to leave. "I almost forgot, Mr. Snow wants you to see this Joe."

They crowded around the one and half inch square screen on the iPod.

Dread upon the Waters

Mo's face came into view and he said, "Hello, Joseph. Here is the latest news. You will find it as worrisome as I. CWO Rhinelander has confirmed the following facts. Mel Dumke has purchased twelve Lunds, seventeen-foot Pro-Angler models. They have gone by trailer to Akwesasne. He has also bought eight John Deere Quad Runners delivered in New York and Vermont. Previously, Mr. Dumke had been in the Quebec area where he was the agent for the purchase of a bankrupt boatyard and two down-at-the-heels ocean-going tugs. They are being refitted and they wait for instructions to sail on the St. Lawrence. Dumke is using OPM, other people's money, and the purchases are being made in Ontario for the purpose of disappearing into the Mohawk nation. Our enemies are coordinating this as a four-phase simultaneous attack on the State of New York. The timing is going to be hard to pin down but the targets are clear. Down through Vermont, Lake Champlain, and the Hudson River—they plan to attack West Point. Down the St. Lawrence and overland they plan to take out Fort Drum. Down the Larry and across Lake Ontario, they are going to blow up the power plants at Niagara. Around through the Ocean and down through Long Island Sound, they are going to nuke the Throgg's Neck Bridge. They want these four to be as close as possible to simultaneous in order to make New York a wasteland for a hundred years.

"These are obviously strategic targets in the state. They have a plan to hit everywhere at once. We are needed to stop them or to disrupt their timing at the least. This is our ancestral homeland that is going to be laid waste. We won't let that happen, will we cousin?" Mo's image blinked out.

Radleigh Loonch, tall, slim, and professional, a fine-looking career woman, was letting her hair down at Olivia's Aunt Sally's place in the hills of rural Cornwall, Connecticut. Rad was still having a time of it, getting used to the idea of Olivia being married to Moses X Snow. He was twelve years older than Liv, from a completely different culture, and she had known him only for one summer. Rad asked, "Doesn't the cold bother you? Weather up there is worse than at Saltillo University, way worse."

"I don't love the cold climate but he does, and he's my man. Mo's big and brown and mine, and he growls softly like a huggy bear," She said smiling. Both women laughed. "The harder thing for me to grab ahold of is the early rising. He starts his day at five, unless he gets up early, in which case, it starts at four." Liv stared big-eyed at Rad, emphasizing her sacrifice.

"No more party girl for Ollie. Did you say that your parents don't know that you're hitched?"

"They're coming along this weekend to talk me out of doing it. I guess they'll find out then. The fur will be flying. Marrying what they'll call a yankee, going to live in the north, an older man, an Injun to boot. It's not like they are experts at picking mates, although they have gotten some practice."

Radleigh Loonch and Olivia Shanio, college roommates and lifetime friends, were sitting in the kitchen of Sally's farm, where her raptor rescue operation consumed almost all available resources and space. Rad had driven up from New Haven in her new Jeep on a two-day break from her sojourn at the Port of New Haven. She was on assignment for her job with the Customs and Border Patrol (CBP) Agency. Liv had dropped down from Cornwall, Ontario near the Mohawk Rez to Cornwall, Connecticut to visit her crazy aunt.

"Your mother will support you, I don't know about your dad. I never could read him. Tell me about your man. Are you happy?" Rad asked.

"I wanted something different, didn't I? I wanted somebody who didn't see getting drunk every day as the end of a perfect day. Well, Mo stays away from booze, doesn't usually even drink beer. It's been different. When we got up there to his house on Akwesasne, that's what used to be called the St. Regis Reservation, he settled me in a small house, a cottage really, and went to check on his business. So I was in this house relaxing, when two women showed up. Everyone around there is called a cousin so I don't know the real relationships, but these two couldn't have been more different. His cousin Jane wore a business suit, had half glasses dangling around her neck and spoke

Dread upon the Waters

English like a British subject. Turns out she is the tribal accountant and also does the books for Mo in his bait business. She made it clear that I was welcome, though some jealous people would be unenthusiastic, and that she was pleased for Mo. Probably pleased that he had any woman, not specifically me. She made me feel good.

"The other woman, a girl really, who stayed after Jane went off on business, was a cousin named Cornflower also called Maria. She speaks Mohawk and French and only had a few words of English. But, she is a dear, and we communicate in a combination of my high school French, hand signs, New Orleans Creole French, English, and the Mohawk words I've learned. They have, taken the time to teach me their culture, and a wife's role in it. It sounds odd, but they were gentle and I wanted to learn these things.

Mo and I were separated then while I was preparing for my wedding. The traditional clan mothers schooled me, with Maria smoothing the way. I didn't see Mo for three days. Then, we were married by a black robe, their name for a Catholic priest, and a tribal sachem simultaneously. It was so cool—I said 'I do' in Mohawk."

Liv made a sound that Rad couldn't begin to understand or spell, but which she assumed was, "I do."

"So, you were married three days after you got there. Did you know that was what would happen?"

"Not exactly. But it's all good. I have my own house, one of four owned by Mosie. He has a hunting camp in Ontario, a fishing camp at the Lake of Two Mountains, that's in Quebec. His main house and mine are on the Akwesasne Rez. These are cottages really, not big or fancy but my place is about seventy-five yards from his, he asks for permission to visit me—which I never deny – but, as a woman of The People, I could do so. I have room for my own garden and livestock. One of his girl cousins or the other comes by every day to help me around the place. We chat. Plan next year's crops and garden. They tell me how to behave like a member of the Flint People.

"It's so cold up there that we were sleeping under comforters in August. They've shown me how to warm up a smooth round river stone on the stove and slip it under the covers to warm his feet. That rev's him up, I can tell you." Liv got a telling look on her face that Rad interpreted to be rapturous. She smiled.

Joe Gaspe and the Portable Nukes

"You're really happy aren't you?" Rad knew the answer to that.

"When it was clear to everyone that I was his choice in a mate, they all took me into their hearts. It's wonderful up there. In spite of the cold, a lot of time is spent outside; fishing, camping, just living. We move around to the other cabins too, into Canada and out with no one asking questions. As long as the border agents profile you as a Mohawk, they ask no questions."

Rad squirmed a bit at the mention of border security.

"Did you have midget jugglers at your wedding?" Rad asked this because of wild and crazy conversations from their college days.

"No, there wasn't time. There was no one riding a unicycle either. But you remember that blond boy who claimed to be a Shawnee—Johann, the one who was sweet on you? He was there and he's a magician now and a juggler. He entertained the kids—Mo has a million nieces, nephews, and cousins."

"Johann Hatchett? He was at your wedding? He was hot." Rad replied.

"Yeah, but he's got some issues now. Mo says he's at Akwesasne because he's hiding out from the cops. Trouble in Massachusetts. I'm not sure what, but it's serious. He's gotten weird with the magic thing though. He's let his hair grow long, and he wears a top hat like he's an undertaker or something. He also has a falcon that he's made into a pet. But, you won't believe the things he can do with his hands. He's quite the magician."

Olivia gave Rad a searching look, saw her apparent interest in the story of Johann and said, "He'll be along with Mo later. He's in danger of arrest crossing Massachusetts and can't go to Virginia, but he's safe in Connecticut and New York, I guess."

"He's coming here today?"

"Yes he is."

"Ollie, are you happy with your big Indian?"

"He is a big man on the Rez. They look up to him and revered him. He is forgiving, patient, and pleasant. I thought he would be good, but I never knew a man could be *this* good. I'm *very* happy." Olivia beamed and she and Rad hugged again.

Dread upon the Waters

Olivia was direct. "If you like Johann, you've got to let him know."

Rad waffled. "Well, I don't know. I thought he was all that when I watched that basketball game in Ohio, but he hardly spoke to me afterward, and the more I hear—"

"He's a man, He's not gonna say what he wants, might not even know until you make it clear to him. You've got to take charge here. Use your work personality. Assertive, isn't it?"

"I'm not going to chase him. He's got to make the first move."

"Don't be waiting too long, girl." Olivia left it at that.

Rad thought about a move she might make, and then reconsidered. She sighed and shrugged her shoulders.

Olivia Shanio had gotten sick of arguing with her four parents: Mom and her latest husband and Dad and his latest wife. So she was as happy as could be when her husband and his friend Johann showed up in the bait business's reefer truck. Mosie was here to take her home to Akwesasne and, she hoped, defuse a tense situation. The two parental couples, normally tense rivals, had joined forces in a grilling at the kitchen table in Aunt Sally's house to berate Liv over her choice of a man. They were batting her peccadilloes back and forth like a tennis ball as both Dad and Mom had been dismayed to hear that she'd; a.) been married, b.) married a Yankee and would be living up north, and married an older man. They were beyond reacting when they learned that the older northern husband was a full-blooded Mohawk Indian businessman. Each parent had a bobble-head partner to reinforce the points they were making and support them anytime they wavered in their objections to the matter.

Liv had been prepared for this. When she asked her aunt and Rad to go take care of the animals, she had been alone in the kitchen, resolved and resolute. She was neutral toward her mom's latest husband and negative toward her dad's bossy new wife, but she was prepared to be stoic and stay strong during their assault. She knew it would be all about them, as it always had been, and that they would get over it by being wrapped up in themselves again. She would not yell. She would not defend herself. She would just say three things: It's done. I love him. I'm happy.

Joe Gaspe and the Portable Nukes

It hadn't been easy to control her desire to get nasty, especially when looking at her dad's wife. But she had. They were all going over the situation a third time, though she noticed that her mom's husband had shown some body language that indicated reluctant acceptance. She was standing at the window when she saw Mo's truck pull up the winding driveway. Johann got out of the passenger's door and Mo exited the driver's side. He lifted out a grocery bag and greeted Rad who'd come from the barn. He spoke to her and headed to the house. Rad and Johann engaged in a conversation that appeared to be stilted and distant. The last Liv saw of them they headed down a woodland path at Rad's direction.

Moses Snow was in his better clothes, was freshly groomed, and stood before the back door. He neither knocked nor spoke, but waited for those in the house to bid him to enter. They were being given time to prepare for a visitor. Liv walked to the door, opened it, and gave him a light kiss on the cheek as he entered. An unmistakable lilt came into her voice as she said, "Mo, I want you to meet my parents." After introductions all around, during which the older generation were subdued and meek, Moses Snow placed his grocery bag on the kitchen table, extracted two wrapped packages and extended them toward the two women present.

"I commend you for the skill and wisdom of raising this daughter who brings light, beauty, and grace into my life and to the life of a people oppressed and in need of such a woman. I have wandered for years in a darkness that oppressed me. I went forward against the storm, alone, and resigned to a gloomy life. A life no Mohawk should live. We are a happy people who should laugh and enjoy this best of all worlds that we can live in. But, I was alone and consumed by surface things, unable to see those things in the background that make my life so good.

"Then Olivia came to me in my dreams, and because I honored those dreams, my cousin's friend Radleigh introduced my own snowy egret," he gestured toward Liv, "to me. Your daughter makes me happier than I have ever been. She lifted the clouds of sixteen years. She has helped me push back the gloom that has been flowing with

Dread upon the Waters

me, into the past as if it had never been lived. During these months when my time has been spent with Olivia, I have been able to protect that little light in my mind and keep it from being snuffed like a candle in the wind, Together we can go forward in lightness, laughing at the storm. She is honored by my family, my clan, and my tribe."

He reached into his bag and pulled out two three-cigar cases, each clearly labeled Havana. He placed these on the table toward each of the men. He began again.

"Clearly, you are great men to have brought such a beautiful and capable person from a girl to a woman with your skill. I know how hard it is in the white society, with many dangers and false paths out there, to lead such a beauty, no matter how wise and all-seeing she may be, to become self-reliant, stable, and capable. So many take wrong turns, become arrogant, or self-defeating, or small in their ways. It is through your efforts that she has become the wonderful woman who is now going to spend her life as my wife and bear me sons and daughters."

Mo stopped talking. He looked into Olivia's eyes and she beamed back in admiration. Liv was vibrating to an emotional rhythm. "Admiration, loyalty, and appreciation—that is what I have for my husband." She said this looking at his face; stoic, noble and savage as it was.

To her parents, she said, "Take your gifts and accept the bargain."

None of them spoke but all pulled their small tokens in toward themselves. Overcome by the masculine and spiritual aspect of Mo's broad shoulders, massive chest, and distinguished face, Liv's mother looked at her gift, a dream catcher, and said, "Well, all right."

Radleigh Loonch walked down the path, a trail that looped through the woods. Accepting a sense of dread, she was aware that any magic she had felt with Johann Hatchett back in Ohio was gone. Her emotions said, "It's nothing, give him a chance to explain." But there was an annoying rational side to Rad and this side said, "Well, that's a disqualification. He's a non-starter."

Joe Gaspe and the Portable Nukes

He'd gotten weird, too weird. He almost looked like a Goth with his black top hat and long coat—a duster like an Australian would wear to cross the Nullabar Plain. Beyond his appearance, there was an unspoken thought between them that he had come here because he had things to do with Moses Snow and not because he wanted to see Radleigh Loonch. They talked of banalities as they slowly covered the loop going around the base of a small hillock. Rad was listening to the debate in her mind and not seriously thinking about what Johann was saying.

"I killed two men in Massachusetts. It wasn't a fight exactly, but I was protecting myself. They were going to humiliate me. I wasn't having any of that. I had to face it. They needed killing. That's when I went to Ohio. But eventually they came looking for me in Ohio. They had found my relatives, don'tcha know. So I ended up in Canada with cousin Mo. At Akwesasne you can go back and forth, except in the dead of winter, by boat, and nobody from the US or Canada knows a thing about it."

Rad rubbed her earlobe. She'd only been partially listening. Not sure she'd heard correctly, she tried to force herself to concentrate.

"Even though the authorities haven't caught me, and probably won't, I have to live with my conscience and that's harder than jail time. I've done some time and it is nowhere near as hard as the punishment I have visited on myself. I'm hoping that I can work with Mr. Snow and balance the scales of justice a little bit. I know it won't make a difference with the law, but it might change things in my mind, where I'm under punishment all the time."

Rad stopped and Johann turned back to glance at her. Her face was dappled by the sunlight filtering through the yellow leaves of a maple tree. "I'm an officer of the law. I didn't hear what you just now told me. My mind was elsewhere. Don't say anything more and don't tell me again. If I know these things I am required to take action." Rad had a hard look in her eyes.

Johann nodded. "I've been learning juggling with an expert. Juggling and magic tricks, slight of hand. You'd be surprised by how much you can improve hand-eye coordination with a little—well

Dread upon the Waters

actually a lot of—practice." Johann was moving an old silver dollar across the back of his hands, rolling it between his fingers back and forth as he spoke. They resumed their walk in the woods.

An hour earlier, when Liv knew that Mo was bringing Johann she had told Rad, "If you want him: if you are sure he's the one, go after him. Don't wait for him to ask you. You can catch him if he's the one. Just set your mind to it and go. I've seen you get what you've wanted too many times for you to act all demure and shy now. If you're sure he's right, then go ahead." Trouble was, Rad wasn't sure he was right anymore. The feeling was too strong that he wasn't the right guy.

Nevertheless, when she came back to earth and started listening to Johann she understood that the mission she was on, at Agent Andre's command, was going to bring her and Johann and Mo and Liv into very close proximity and some little danger, for the next few days. That nagging little voice in her head said, "Well, maybe things will change." She suspected, though, that they wouldn't.

Marv hadn't lived with his mother for years, but since he moved from apartment to apartment, looking for love or having been rejected, he still used her apartment as his legal address. It was a place to pick up mail and avoid changing things like driver's licenses all the time. As such, someone looking for Marv had discovered that he was hard to find. That's what convinced Marv that it had been he the thugs were looking for, when there was an incident at his mother's apartment. He had gotten a call on his cell phone, while on the St. Lawrence, from a cop saying that he should report to the police station in Coleman and talk to them about an incident. He dropped his kit bag at his own apartment, a rundown second floor walk-up in a semi-industrial area, and washed his face and changed his shirt before heading to the station. The cops had told him not to go to his mother's apartment.

Nothing about this sounded good. Marv knew a fair percentage of the older cops in Coleman, either from growing up with them or from various run-ins of a minor nature in which he had been involved. It was eleven-thirty PM when he walked up the front steps of the

Joe Gaspe and the Portable Nukes

Victorian building housing the police station. He identified himself to the desk sergeant, a man he had gone to high school with but had barely known. He was directed to a hard wooden bench to wait for the appropriate officer. The building was musty and dark. The feeling coming over him was ominous. Marv fidgeted and thought about walking back out—he never had been comfortable around the cops. Few people were moving in the building. The night shift was already out on patrol and the evening group that quit at eleven had left the station. Down the stairs and headed for him, came his younger brother's boyhood nemesis, John Brinkman. Marv groaned.

Brinkman walked up to Marv and said, "Hello, Mr. Ankara, come with me." He abruptly turned on his heel and waved his arm in a follow-me gesture.

"What's going on? Why am I here?" Marv asked these questions to Brinkman's back as he followed a man he really didn't like up a set of stairs that doglegged to the right. Officer Brinkman led him past a door that said, "Major Crimes," and turned down a hallway. The cop opened a door and stepped back saying, "In there."

Marv entered. There was a table and several chairs, a few file cabinets, and a barred window. "Wait here. The inspector will be right with you." Brinkman closed the door.

Before Marv could complete the thought of, "Wonder how long I'm gonna be cooling my heels?" a woman, ten years his junior, walked in accompanied by Brinkman. Dressed in a nice pair of slacks, white blouse, and sharp blazer, she held out her hand and said, "I'm detective Ruth Belinsky. Officer Brinkman and I have a few questions." Marv shook her hand. She sat at the table, gestured with open palm for Marv to sit opposite her, and asked. "Can I get you some coffee?"

Marv sat and said, "No thanks, no coffee." Brinkman stood, leaning on a filing cabinet. Marv looked at his interviewer, then at Brinkman and asked, "What's going on?"

Detective Belinsky asked Marv if he lived at 1455 Turtle Cove Drive. He told her no. She asked if this was his permanent address. He said yes and explained about his transition from apartment to apartment. Officer Brinkman made a noise like a snort. At that time, Detective Belinsky turned to Brinkman and glared at him.

Dread upon the Waters

Belinsky turned to her pad and made a note. "What is your actual address?" Marv supplied the information

"Has something happened to Mom? Has there been a fire? An accident? Tell me what's going on?"

"Tell me your whereabouts on the night before last. Were you in Coleman?"

"I've been up on the St. Larry at a friend's cabin."

"Is there anyone who can confirm that?"

"My partner Joe Gaspe, we've been fishing. Why?"

"Kinda late in the year for fishing idn't it? Aren't you outdoor types hunting by now?" This came from Brinkman, making no effort to conceal his contempt. Detective Belinsky gave him another hard look.

"We fish for muskies, fall's the best time."

"How can I contact this," she looked at her notebook, "this Joe Gaspe?"

"You can't. Joe doesn't have a cell phone. He'll be gone another seven to ten days."

"Isn't that convenient." Brinkman drew another hard look from the detective. Marv glared hatred at him as well.

"Officer," Marv turned his eyes to Belinsky.

"Detective," she corrected.

"Why do I need an alibi? What do you think I've done?"

"There has been a firearm incident at your mother's apartment building."

"What incident? Mom's got no guns. Has Ricky been shot?"

"Mr. Ankara, I have some distressing news for you. There is no easy way to say this. Your mother and brother have been shot, and they have been killed."

"Shot? Who would shoot my mom?" Marv hadn't let this sink in yet, but he felt a shudder start to move up his spine. His shoulders sagged and he looked, eyes wide, at Detective Belinsky and then at Officer Brinkman. "Was this a robbery?"

Before Belinsky could respond, Brinkman said, "Execution, more like." Marv noticed, as he turned to stare at Brinkman, that the cop had a slight smirk on his face.

Joe Gaspe and the Portable Nukes

"There were a large number of bullets fired by multiple assailants. Neither your mother nor brother had a chance. They were dead at the scene."

That ripple of tension had risen to Marv's shoulders and neck. He shuddered. His eyes filled with water. He looked at the detective and said, "Mom? And Ricky? Who would kill them?'"

"There is an ongoing investigation. We will find the perpetrators of this crime." She pushed a notebook toward Marv. "Give me your contact information, please."

In the midst of his grief and shock a different uneasy feeling came over Marv. He had enemies, past and present; had his mother and brother been killed because of him? At once he was sure that was what it was. His past had come to haunt him in this way. He leaned his head into his elbows propped on the table. Marv wept.

The door to the interview room opened and a man beckoned to Detective Belinsky. She slipped out the door, inclining her head to Officer Brinkman to indicate that he should watch the suspect, prisoner, or interviewee, Marv didn't know what he was considered to be. He began for the first time thinking of his sister and how she was reacting to this. Why hadn't she phoned him on his cell phone? Was she all right? Had the cops turned her inside out?

"Can I check my cell phone for messages?" Marv inquired of Officer Brinkman.

"No."

"I need to see if my sister called. Does she know about all this? Have you talked to her?"

"Check your phone after you leave our house." Brinkman made it clear he wanted no more questions.

Marv held his head wondering what had happened to his life.

After fifteen minutes the detective returned. She sat across from Marv and asked, "What kind of a name is Ankara?"

"Whaddya mean? It's my name."

"What nationality?"

"It's German. What of it?"

Brinkman piped up, "Doesn't sound like any German name I've ever heard."

Dread upon the Waters

Marv looked at him, turned back to Belinsky, and shrugged.

"Your mother's maiden name, what was that?"

"Metzger. Also German. What's this got to do with anything?"

Belinsky looked at her notes, left the book open, took a long searching look at Marv and said, "I've just had a most interesting interview with a man from your mother's building, a man who witnessed the attack on your mother's apartment. This gentleman is an immigrant from Russia. He says that he heard a group of men speaking quietly in a Belarus dialect of Russian just before the shooting. He very proudly claimed that he was not afraid to turn in these men. Being very old, he said he was in his eighties and without any relatives, he did not fear the wrath of the Russian gangsters who shot up your mother's apartment. Do you know of any Russians who have had difficulty with your mother or brother?"

"No." Marv understood now what was happening. He hoped his expression didn't show what had just dawned on him.

Watching carefully, Detective Belinsky saw a flicker of recognition.

"What about you? Have you had a run-in with Russians?"

"Not me. There were no Russians around here when we grew up," Marv waved his hand to include Officer Brinkman, "I don't have run-ins with anyone anymore."

Marv spent several hours at the station before they were finished interviewing him. The same questions were asked over and over in slightly altered versions.

Stopping just outside the door of the cop house, Marv turned on his cell phone and checked his messages. His sister had left fifteen voice mails trying to contact him. Marv had a pretty good idea what was happening. His sister and Joe's family needed to go into hiding right way. He had no confidence that the police would apprehend these bad guys anytime soon.

Chapter 5

Akwesasne: October 3rd

Meticulous planning was the principle strength of the Mahdi and his organization. Under his direction, everything was going according to plan. The two trucks, carrying four each of the John Deere HPX 4x4 Trail Gators with towable trailers, had sailed through customs with their Mohawk drivers. US inspectors at the border had been inculcated in political correctness and did not question drivers whom they had profiled as "looking Indian." No one who had endured sensitivity training wanted undue attention from his boss. The Mahdi knew this. One truck headed south and the other moved off to the east. Planners became smug when their plans panned out.

Four Lunds with their Native American captains had taken the long slow circuit through the Richlieu River and its locks. Each lock consisted of two long concrete walls with gates at each end to retain enough water to float the boats passing through. Depending on whether the boats are up bound or down bound, the level of water rises or falls so that the boats in the lock change to the level of the next section of the waterway. This is done by pumping water in or out of the lock until it is at the level required. The lockmasters, at the locks, are lords of the adjacent waterways. They have full authority to prioritize traffic—there is a protocol for this—and instruct boats as to how and when to lock through. When their authority is unchallenged the lockmasters are very efficient. All four Lunds had stated the same destination and purpose: they were heading down to Lake Champlain

Dread upon the Waters

for some late-season perch fishing. Since the yellow perch bite was on, they would be stocking up for winter as long as the ring backs were biting. Lake Champlain perch are a delicacy and they are fat and easy to catch in October. The crates covered by tarps in the boats were identified as freezer boxes for storage of the winter catch. No lockmaster looked underneath the tarps at these coolers. At the border, they went through customs, two boats one day and two boats the next. Profiled as Mohawks-which they were, of course-no hard questions were asked.

When asked his destination each pilot said, "Going perch fishing, eh?"

"Stocking up for the long winter ahead?"

"Yes sir."

"Go ahead." Under his breath the customs agent, a catch-and-release guy, said, "Meat fisherman." His contempt was kept to himself.

Down along the shoreline of Lake Champlain, in Vermont, the boats would pick up their jihadi passengers for the rest of the journey.

The longer of the two tugs, at 174 feet, the Lillian had taken a fearful beating coming into the shipyard in Quebec, and its re-fit had been slow. Piloted there from New Orleans, the two tugs had gotten separated right away. The Madison made it around the corner into the St. Lawrence River twenty hours ahead of the Lillian, which was caught in a series of thunderstorms that blew past while it had one engine down during emergency repairs to the fuel system. It was nearly driven onto the rocky coast on the north side of the river near Ste. Iles and had a pair of plates stove in by a huge log propelled into its port bow during the final and severest of the westerly blows. The tug limped the last few kilometers into Quebec's container port, with her two bilge pumps and two emergency pumps screaming and hot enough to stroke out. Emergency repair crews were able to re-float her with air bladders while the port rescue crews got a crane slung under her and lifted her into dry-dock. Tugs like this could take an extraordinary amount of punishment and endure, but those men who lifted her didn't consider her chances of going back to work very high. The western ocean had marked the Lillian for destruction and its victims seldom escaped.

The *Madison* was expeditiously refitted and renamed. Its plates needed no significant welding and the work involved painting it with a slapdash coat and changing the name. It was now called the *Eastern Sun*. Told that he was going to New York where the boat was to be resold for a tidy profit, John Talor had his doubts about the whole project. As he waited in the wheelhouse for the float plan to be approved by the Canadian authorities and the river pilot to come aboard, he looked around at his new twenty-four-hour home. The area where the electronic aids to navigation should be looked like a pincushion because of the holes left by the removed equipment. The empty mounting holes were a series of question marks to him: radar gone. Sat-nav gone, Echo sounder gone—replaced with a fish finder that was barely suitable for a pleasure boat, Satellite fax machine removed. In normal circumstances, all these would have had secondary systems as back-ups in case of failure on the high seas. He had one radio-without backup. He could get weather reports, but these would be onshore, land-based reports, no high-seas specific forecasts were going to be available.

John had traveled enough in Canada, with its mixture of accents and nationalities, to not be worried about Sam's nationality. But his accented English and some of his syntax was decidedly odd. He had been questioning Sam-the only name given to Talor about the lack of navigational electronics, when his two assistant pilots trooped in. They were sketchy Native Americans of the Iroquois tribe, both appeared to be suffering monumental hangovers. A man identified as Sam's brother ushered them and their sea bags into the small, hot, bunkhouse, an area designed for quick refresher wolf naps, not berthing. That would be the three men's home for the voyage.

Sam handed John Talor an envelope containing one hundred $100 bills. John thought it odd to receive US dollars, since he had been hired in Canada. The trip would end at the Port of New York so he reasoned that it would be easier to spend the money in the US. "New electronics put in by new buyer, they will be." Sam had waited to say this until his brother had closed the door to the break room.

Dread upon the Waters

"Radar is pretty useful at night, in the fog, bad weather."

"You see lights, stay away other boats from you."

"The shipping lanes are crowded at the Gulf of St. Lawrence."

"Use radio only once awhile. You are paid to pilot, that's all to worry you."

"You want us to stay in the pilot house all the time. That rest room has no shower. What about food?"

"Chef will bring you very good plenty food. All day."

"I'm not comfortable about some of this stuff." As John said this, he saw that Sam's brother, who was guarding the door to the break room, pulled back his coattail. John glimpsed the butt of a sidearm there.

"You got plenty money. Just do you job, hey!" Sam's normal terse rude speech was edging into harder tones. John reached over to the intercom and said, "Engine room, are you ready to get underway?"

Sam stepped up. "I'll handle this. Crew works for me."

"I'll need to talk to the black gang as we move along."

"My job. No problem." Sam smiled a thin smile. His eyes were shards of obsidian.

"The radio crackled and the voice from the harbormaster instructed *Eastern Sun* that it was cleared to proceed into the main channel as soon as the pilot was aboard.

Sam said, "No problem." He and his brother left, The brother's eye contact with John seemed to say, "I can wait to kill you. It will be my pleasure."

The St. Lawrence River is shorter than many of the world's great rivers. Only 750 miles long, it carries a flow of water equal to the Rhine, Volga, and Nile combined. It was necessary to have an experienced pilot between Quebec City and Escoumin. John Talor's skills as a seasoned ocean pilot were going to be needed when the mouth of the river was reached and the Gulf of St. Lawrence encountered. That Gulf contained some of the most treacherous tidal water in the world.

John Talor was confident in his talent as a ship's pilot. The Portuguese were the best sailors the world had ever known and his mother's brother's had trained him and built his confidence.

Chapter 6

Lake Champlain near Valcour Bay: October 9th

In the early weeks of autumn the changing leaves on the hardwoods and the clear air of the cooler months combine to make Lake Champlain one of the most beautiful places on earth. The lake is long and narrow and sits between two mountain ranges, the Adirondacks in New York and the Green Mountains in Vermont. This lake has terrific depth and on its southern stretches is so narrow as to seem almost like a river. In early October, as the colors intensify daily toward their peak at mid-month, the leaf peepers from the eastern seaboard cities abound. Sometime late in October, the wind and rain collaborate to drop most of the leaves, and a stark, bleak, cold winter announces its imminent arrival with the winds of November.

Johann and Rad in one boat and Mo and Liv in another patrolled the lake at a bend that veered around Valcour Island. They were on two-hour shifts and planned to spend the next two days patrolling. They anticipated that their RF detectors, tuned to the correct frequency, would pick up the suspect Lunds that were expected to come down the lake heading south for the Hudson River. The boat that was not patrolling was snug in Valcour Bay. The pair of watchers who were in it were resting and enjoying the beautiful scenery.

The patrolling boat expected the RF detector to work but swept the area with binoculars for any sign of the Lunds. Johann and Mo had debated whether to expect them to transit during the day, when tour-boat traffic was steady, or at night when they could move undetected. Both scenarios held advantages and disadvantages. The obvious advantage of darkness was also a serious hazard to any pilot unfamiliar with the lake. In summer time there are many shoreline lights from cottages and cabins occupied for the season. In autumn most of the cottages and summer homes are shut up for winter. Large stretches of water have no lights at all on the shore. This is dangerous to the point of being deadly.

The bucolic scene was not entirely sublime despite the gorgeous scenery and the breathtaking mountain vistas; Mo had warned of bad weather on the way. Each of the last two nights there had been a halo around the moon. The larger the halo, the closer the bad weather, according to Mo. That halo had enlarged from one night to the next.

"Storm coming." Rad said to Johann as she pointed to the western mountains. "My dad calls that the Bull of Heaven."

There, where she looked, was a bank of gray clouds squeezing out a rain shower on the mountaintops. She thought that a strong wind from the west would be following soon.

"Then what's that?" Johann asked as he pointed east where a similar though larger and blacker cloud seemed to be rolling in from the Green Mountains. "Are we in for a Clash of the Titans?"

"Weather coming from east and west, and it looks like it's gonna meet right here." Rad let that thought hang there.

"Aunt Molly, I know where these guys are going to be! I've been lost there. Back in the day."

"Where child? Where will the young men be?" Molly Snow, Mo's oldest sister, and Amy Gaspe, Joe's oldest daughter, were in a studio where they spent most of their workshop time dreaming together. They had exercises to do that were used for practice by the dream workers at the workshop. They had just had a special session with the leader, Ruland Rush, where they homed in on their problem. During this studio time, they worked together to find and influence, in the dream world, those members of the wolf clan who, though involved in one of the four raids, were not too sure of what they were doing.

The studio was one of twelve rather large bedrooms in the nineteenth century hunting camp that housed the dream school. Ruland's wealth had enabled him to purchase and maintain one of the great Adirondack camps. Here he held dream camps and workshops for an eclectic group of seekers. Amy and Molly had been working in the advanced program for several days. Though they had spent a two hour-long session with Ruland, they worked mostly by themselves. They sat on mattresses placed at right angles to each other on the floor. Amy looked at Molly for a long while trying to decide how to tell her what was to come next in their dream work.

"My dad used to take me on trips when I was young. He'd want to spend time with me, because he wasn't around as much as he should have been. He'd get guilted into doing something with his daughter. Being the man he was, what he'd do with me was take me on a fishing trip. He didn't know how to do girly things then. After all of my sisters were born, he came to understand girls better, but with me he was convinced that he could turn me into a boy. So, one Saturday he took me on an adventure to find Muskellunge Lake in the mountains. He got lost. Twice. When we finally found the lake it was time to go home and all we did was mark a spot on the map, take a look at the water, and head home. One thing I remember was that two roads had the same name about ten miles apart. It is a name that I remember. These guys in my dream are sitting on the berm near Ore Bed Road. They are lost just like we were lost. There is a fifty-fifty chance that they are situated next to the wrong Ore Bed Road too."

"You have seen this road in your dreaming?" Molly knew the time was fast approaching where this little bird would soar ahead of her, but she continued to try to lead Amy.

"They stopped by it at night, glad to get out of the swamp but lost, and perched on a mountain side, still bedeviled by bugs and sliding downhill all night in sleep."

Dread upon the Waters

"I have seen the same group through the dreams of Billie Williams—my cousin—yours too, several times removed. He is losing his enthusiasm for this project." Molly replied.

"As you have shown me, I can dip into the minds of those people who have even a remnant of the dreaming in their lives. Last night I moved through the dreams of three Mohawks and I not only observed them, but I think I altered them. I can see the effect of one little thing changing their dreams. The confusion I visit on them is cruel to their minds but the mission they are on is one of severe hardship for our people and our country."

"Amy, we both know that you are the true inheritor of Island Woman's power. You will have power dreaming to use forever. While you live in this shadow world, you will become the most powerful woman of the Mohawks. After your life here, you will move into the dream world together with all the previous women of power, and you will be able to exert control. Right now, because I am a dream woman I can enter the dreams of some of my relatives, those who are ready to take direction. But I have no ability to influence anyone outside my clan. Unfortunately, most of my clan has lost the dreaming. You, when you are ready, and that will be soon, can dream with anyone who needs you. They will not be directly aware of your influence though. They may be upset and nervous without knowing why. You will come to the point where you can dip into the dreams of all those who need your guidance whether they are dreamers or not. You will be able to move from dream to dream in a night, altering the set pieces and the following actions as you go," Molly reassured Amy.

"But, that sounds really hard."

"It will exhaust you, my child. Sometimes you will go for days with only the dreaming, no shadow world life at all. It is a great responsibility, to be the woman of power."

Joe was straightening up the boat. He was listening to chatter on channel sixty-eight on the VHF radio. No matter how hard he tried to be neat and orderly and respect his gear, Joe was rough on equip-

Joe Gaspe and the Portable Nukes

ment. His feet hit the deck heavily when he moved, tools broke in his hand, usually when he was using the wrong tool for the job. Things fell apart in Joe's care. After any significant time on the water, Joe's boat needed attention. He didn't mind the clean-up, fix-up work. It gave him a chance to putter around by himself, listen to the radio chatter, and get his mind set for the next day's plan. He liked Sherry and, was he not married and on the job for Andre, he'd make his play for her. She was beautiful and nicely turned. Her hard-girl act didn't discourage him. It would have turned him on, but he needed time without any woman around. At home, he got his time alone in his shop. Here he got it by fixing up the boat. It was a guy thing.

Joe was on his knees trying to repair a piece of teak he had kicked loose the day before when he thought he'd had a strike from a musky. The radio crackled. He didn't hear it that well. Straightening up, he adjusted the volume and decreased the squelch a bit.

"Dr. Dento are you out there? This is Brewster calling." There was a slight pause, "Dr. Dento can you hear me?"

Joe keyed his mike, "Dento here, go ahead Brewster." Brewster was one of the charter captains from up near Ogdensburg. He'd been at the meeting with Agent Andre when Joe's mission had been introduced.

"I think I found your four friends, southwest of here. I'm at my dock now. The reason I think they're your buddies is kinda funny. You wanna hear or should I call your cell phone?"

"Marv's got the cell phone on another mission. Go ahead and tell me."

"Well... we saw these Lunds in a little slough. They were all wrong; tied up too tight to the docks, the loads covered, but not the boats, nobody around, but chanting noises coming from a camp building nearby, I thought, Friday prayers, ya know? So we went home and my mate Nolan he slips over there with some surprise packages for them and fades into the brush to watch. Sure enough, after the chanting stops a guy comes out. He's looking all around and he goes to check the loads. Not the boats mind you, but the loads."

"It didn't take long, since Nolan left him a big clue, he starts screaming and all these dudes come out and they're all jabbering and

Dread upon the Waters

shouting, pointing and pacing back and forth on the dock and the shore. One guy comes from the building with a boat hook, and he uses it to pick this package off the tarp covering the cargo on the first Lund in line. Then they sorta push this kid ahead of them and make him look under the tarps one by one. He finds what Nolan has left there and with each one there's more jabbering and yelling. The kid is forced to remove Nolan's gifts and throw them into the river so they'll float away. When it's all over—and it took awhile—Nolan is about to leave and he hears a shot, a single one. Soon enough two guys come down and dumped a bundle covered in a tarp into the water and push it out into the current. It floats away."

"What did you put on those Lunds?"

"Well, we wanted to know if these were your Arabs, so Nolan went to the pet store, got some dog chew-toys and spread them around. Nolan, he's pretty darned upset cause he thinks they murdered that kid. Anyway I figure these are the boats you're looking for."

"What was it got them so upset?"

"It was pig ears. They didn't like them at all. Those boats will be on the water tomorrow. I'm sure of it."

"Thanks, Brewster. You done good. Dento out"

"Brewster out."

Joe walked up to the cabin where Sherry was reading on the porch. He was shaking his head. What he'd heard had made him laugh but the fact that he knew that they were coming, scared him, thrilled him, excited him, and concentrated his mind.

"I know it's too dark to read. Is that what you were laughing at?" Sherry had watched him approach.

"Huh? No. It was somethin' else." He explained what he'd been told by Brewster.

Joe Gaspe and the Portable Nukes

Sherry Bronson

Chapter 7

Forty-Acre Shoal, Ontario: October 8th

There was no point in not musky fishing while they waited. Joe had an energized network of charter captains and hardcore fishermen on the lookout for those four Lunds he was expecting. He had an RF detector on his boat and CWO Rhinelander, on loan to the Canadian Coast Guard Service, was cruising the Canadian side with a detector as well. If the bugs, secreted on the Lunds, were within one mile of the RF detector the signal could usually be picked up. Then the game would begin.

Meanwhile, the forty-acre shoal area of the St. Larry is one of the best musky trolling spots in North America.

"Let's see if we can do some damage," Joe said to Sherry. He would have loved to fish this with Marv but his partner had left for home because of a family crisis. So, he would fish with the girl, a stranger who knew nothing of the outdoors and was a thoroughly citified person, until the crisis arrived. He had been told by Mo that the ocean going tugs had left first, the Lake Champlain assault had gone second and the Lunds scheduled to head down the Larry had been waiting to start.

The shoal, just inside the barrier islands where the Larry meets Lake Ontario, was a perfect picket boat beat as well as a perfect trolling run. The area, much larger than forty acres, sits astride the Canadian Middle Channel, which is a passage for traffic headed down

Dread upon the Waters

the St Lawrence River to the ocean. Joe's informants had been adamant about the Lunds using Canadian waters. Joe had people watching the American Channel as well, but he picked his patrol area because he wanted to fish these waters in Canada. Each day he moved his boat from Whiskey Nose Wes's camp on an inlet off of Mullet Creek, upstream past Clayton, through the Wolfe Island Cut and onto the trolling grounds south of Gananaque Ontario.

Teaching a strange and beautiful woman to drive a boat and to fish effectively taxed most of the patience that Joe had. He had taught Amy to drive a car and had done all right. When he'd tried to teach Kate, back when they were first married, things had not gone so well. She resisted instruction, while needing it, not wanting to appear to Joe or to herself as the lesser being in the marriage. It turned out that Sherry was an apt pupil with regard to boat handling and learned quickly how to steer. She smelled great, too.

"I get it. Just the opposite of a car." She said this to Joe while he had his arms around her from behind guiding her use of the steering wheel. They could smell each other. They also got very close when Joe showed her how to put out the trolling set of two or four rods depending on which country they were in. Two rods per angler were allowed in New York and only one each in Ontario. Joe's fantasies threatened to run away with him when he took in her scent. When hanging around with guys, he was a big talker about what he could do with women, beautiful or otherwise, who became available. The reality was different. He was physically very attracted and his ego made him believe she was too. But Joe had never been unfaithful to his wife despite being in many situations where temptation was strong. Emotionally, he had no desire to turn his life into a mess. His coincident dreaming with his daughter Amy had him wondering whether she could read his mind. He had already over-nighted twice with Sherry in Wes's cabin without incident other than her complaints about his snoring and his flatulence. Remaining faithful caused tension, but he could do it.

Joe Gaspe and the Portable Nukes

The water was calming down. The rollers coming in off the lake slackened with astounding speed when opposed by a light contrary wind. The boat was on a circuit that included a touch on the reefs off of Black Ant Island, Seven Pines Island, and Big and Little Duck Islands. The run they were on took about one hour to cover, was two thirds in Ontario waters, and had produced no fish so far.

"Tell me again why you catch these fish and don't eat them. Makes no sense to me to go to all this work just to let them go. I like to eat fish. Good for the figure." She gave him a look, knowing and bluffing at the same time.

"It's because it's hard to do. It's a problem to solve. There's plenty of easy fishing. It's because this is difficult that we are drawn to it. The more difficult it is, the more we like it. My friend Melvin, who thinks he's an intellectual, says, 'That which is cheaply obtained is cheaply esteemed.' The point of fishing for muskies isn't catching fish."

"It's about trying things, patterns, techniques, areas, times, until you succeed. Working toward a goal, a hard one, that represents something when your efforts pan out."

"But, they don't pan out all that often do they?" Sherry asked.

"No. And in terms of really big fish, very seldom. But that is the thing. This is a lifelong method of recreation. You never get too old, or too good at it. I was young once. The youngest of all the brothers, and I had to push them to include me in things. That meant I was likely to give in to my temper—which was pretty hot at the time. I'd push until something happened. My brothers would beat me up, or something would get smashed, or somebody would get hurt bad. Then it would be over and, just as antsy as I was moments before, I'd get that calm afterward. My stepmom said it was like the sensation of sitting on a bomb. But what I was really doing was closing myself off in a little world. That up and down pattern—they call it bi-polar today I guess, was exhausting. Musky fishing was what came along to cure me of the roller coaster ride. The fact that it is hard, takes a long time to succeed, that the climax is such an incredible high, but you just start over again ramping up from the bottom, that has made me able to cope with myself in a way that is non-destructive. Anyway, enough about me."

Dread upon the Waters

Sherry pulled what Joe had called a dido by sweeping the trolling lures up over a shallow reef so that the baits, one down fifteen and one down thirty feet, crashed against the rocks causing the rods to jump and bounce. She'd learned quickly how to entice the fish. A musky likes change and goes for anything out of the ordinary. They might be following a lure for a long time waiting for something to happen. When it does, they pounce.

Sherry had been surprising Joe a lot the last few days. She was deeper than he'd thought. Joe wondered how quickly she was picking up the other aspect of musky fishing.

There was a feeling that would creep over you during the hours on the water. Slowly, you'd develop an awareness of the elements; water, sky, wind, then an expectation would settle back in your brain ready and waiting. Being on the water, watching, waiting, a change would come over you as a person. Your animal nature would rise up co-equal with your human nature. Like a dog that seems sound asleep but hears everything. A man with a coiled spring of wildness within him was truly living. *Could a city girl get the feeling?* Joe wondered. When this kind of awareness was learned you listened with all six senses.

Joe felt confident with Sherry driving most of the time and him manning the trolling sets. He brought in a rod that was acting strangely to find that it had picked up a stick on one hook. He set it back out and glanced at her. She was checking the chart as she moved the boat through the pattern. Joe worried that he was going to get into trouble patrolling with this woman instead of his partner Marv. He thought he was a damned fool risking his marriage, again, by hanging around with a woman who was not his wife. He didn't think Kate would find out but was sure that Amy would know. In fact, he had felt the presence of Amy trying to intrude into his dreams the last two nights. Sherry had slept in the cabin while Joe occupied the front porch, sleeping on a camping pad. It was finally the smell of his feet that was the last straw for Sherry. She'd ragged him so badly he decided to stay out of the cabin except for using the bathroom. Kate would never believe that he was behaving himself and keeping his hands off. She would be doubly suspicious if she saw how attractive and shapely Sherry was.

Joe Gaspe and the Portable Nukes

"These lines close together here on the map," Sherry was half turned to Joe.

"Chart, not map. You gotta talk nautical here." Joe poked his little knife of criticism in, ready to give it a twist.

"The lines mean a dropoff, right?" She was serious, not yet peevish.

"Yes, they do."

"Since it's not so wavy, I'll try to hit this area over here." She pointed at the chart that showed a shoal slightly offshore from the pattern they'd been following.

"Rough, not wavy, You gotta—"

"All right, rough, Mr. Nautical Man." Her face fired up for a second.

Joe turned back to the rods, smiling. "Sure. Try it. Change is good." He yelled this since he was facing away from her.

Sherry smiled to herself. A cloud passed in front of the sun dropping the boat into shadow. She turned to port with a hard left, counted to ten and then turned back to the heading she'd been on. The lines following swung a little wider than the boat on each turn. When they swept up onto the shoal one of the drags gave a little burp, screee, screee, then it stopped for a second.

Instantly alert, Joe watched the port rod bend double and come back twice. Then the drag began letting out a continuous loud scream and the rod bent over completely.

"That's a fish! C'mon girl. Hit it. It's yours. Fish on! Fish on!" Joe jumped to the wheel, hip-checking Sherry out of the way. Sherry ran to the corner and said, "What do I do?" She slipped slightly when the boat slowed, pitched forward and caught herself on the railing.

"Pick up that rod and rip it back like you're gonna pull her head off!" Joe tried to calm himself down. He turned the boat to give Sherry an entire side for the landing of this musky.

The drag continued to scream and the rod tip slammed back telegraphing the unmistakable headshakes of a big musky.

"Keep your rod tip high and reel like crazy. You've got a musky, and it looks like a big one." Joe moved to prepare the boat for catch and release. He reeled in the starboard rod and hooked up the lure

Dread upon the Waters

placing it out of the way. He laid out the release tools, unlimbered the net, got both his cameras out of the waterproof box and placed them where they would be handy. The familiar feeling came on him: alertness, edgy-nerves taut and zinging like the fishing line. Along with the pumped feeling was a little tinge of fear, just enough to make it thrilling.

Joe reached over and clicked off the drag so the reel stopped making noise. "You're doing great, just keep on keeping on."

"My arms hurt. You take it." Joe backed away from her, hands up palms toward her.

"Your fish. You got her. Enjoy yourself." He could see that she was fired up. A strand of black hair was down across the right eye. Her cheeks were red, her eyes focused like tiny drill bits. Water sprayed off the line as she retrieved it. Then the fish took line. The rod tip slammed down one, two, three times. The reel, which she kept turning, wasn't taking line but giving some back.

"What do I do now? It won't come in anymore."

"Hold on. Stop reeling until she stops taking line. She won't run far. As soon as the line stops going out, start to reel again." Joe noted the pulse pounding in her left wrist as she held the rod. She took her right hand off the handle of the reel and shook it. Joe had a huge smile on his face. Sherry turned and looked at him.

"Smile, you're having fun," he said.

She looked daggers into him then broke into a big grin. An assertive woman who'd been on her own most of her life, she gained confidence quickly. A look of pure joy— beaming, alive, in the moment—suffused her face.

The musky was out there, seventy feet away, shaking her head but no longer taking line. Sherry started to reel in again.

"Okay. When she gets near that corner," he pointed, "I'll take the net and move in front of you. Just keep the rod tip high and step backwards. I'll do the rest." Sherry nodded her head. The strand of hair went right into her mouth where she blew it out of her way with two puffs. The sun passed out from behind a cloud and shone on the boat at that moment.

Joe Gaspe and the Portable Nukes

"Alright, let's boat this girl. Step back. Keep your tip up." Joe moved smoothly into the corner, swept his huge net through the water and had the fish on the first scoop. He was aware of how happy he was to be competent in front of Sherry. "Wow! This fish is big. She might be a fifty. Put your rod on free spool and come hold the net."

The horned dace pattern lure was across the musky's wide jaws like a bit in a horse's mouth. She was in the bag of the net, completely in the water, staring up at Joe as if she'd like to eat him.

"I'll hold the handle of the net. Take a look at her. That's at least fifty-one or -two inches. You've done it, girl." Joe couldn't disguise the enthusiasm in his voice as he stepped back and let Sherry slide past him into the corner. "Careful. If she shakes, she can throw that hook at any time."

Sherry, the city girl, looked over the side, "Oh my God, that fish is huge." Don't kill it. I want to release her."

"A couple of photos and she'll go right back. I told you we never kill muskies on purpose."

Joe switched back with Sherry so that she held the net. He had an extra long needle-nosed pliers in his hand. During the change of positions, the fish made a mighty shake, and when Joe looked again, the lure was out of her mouth and caught in the mesh of the big net. He unhooked the lure from the mesh and got those hooks out of the way.

"That measuring stick, give it to me and we'll check her out." Joe laid the floating stick in the water beside the musky. "Between fifty-one and-two, let's call her fifty-one and a half. Well, that was nice. Are you ready to hold this big girl?"

"How much does it weigh? Ya think I can hold her?"

"That's at least a twenty-five-pound fish. She's probably over thirty, too skinny to be a forty. She might hold still for a picture, then again she might go wild. A musky might take a notion to do anything."

"Let's try it."

"Lay the cameras out on the seat there, opened so they're ready to go I'll lift her, hand her to you, take one photo with each camera, and take her back, ease her into the water, and release her in good shape.

Dread upon the Waters

Put that red raincoat on and put out your arms like you're going to cradle a log. When I place her into your arms, grab her tail with your hand and cradle the head, holding on tight. You'll be facing the sun so that's great. Don't forget to smile. Are you ready?"

Sherry shrugged into Joe's rainjacket. Joe bungied the net to the boat, reached down into the cleft below the lower jaw, and lifted the fish, simultaneously grabbing the tail with his left hand. He turned into the boat, yelled, "Way over thirty," and handed it to Sherry. "Just like you're holding your own child," he said this as he spun to the cameras, leaned back, and clicked off a digital picture, set the camera down, and cranked off two film pictures as fast as he could. The film camera rewound automatically and he set that one down as well.

"Okay, I've got her." His practiced right hand slid in under the jaw and with remarkable grace for a man so big, he spun her over the side into the water. She went right back into the huge bag of the net. "You hold that handle and we'll see if she's ready to go. She'll need a minute here. Take some more shots while she's at boatside."

"How can I hold a camera when I've got the net?"

"Pull the net out from under her and set it aside. I've got her." Joe pointed her headfirst into the current and leaned over the gunwale. He relaxed a bit while he waited for some oxygen rich water to wash over her gills. Sherry leaned over the side and snapped off pictures of the fish in the water. Joe had her tail in his left hand and his right hand under her front end. The fish waited calmly.

"Joe, look at me. Smile." Sherry switched cameras again and took a few more shots.

"When I turn her like this," he rotated his left wrist so that the fish turned belly up, "If she doesn't work against that, she's not ready. Usually, when she's ready she'll flick her tail, and you won't be able to hold her. I like to let the head go when I think she's ready, so she'll swim straight down." On the second turn she did just that and swam energetically out of sight. Joe stood up, raised his right hand for a high-five with Sherry, said "Whoo hoo!" and touched her jawline with his left hand. A trace of the musky slime that covered his left hand got on her and she was conscious of the strong smell of musk that she only then realized had been in the air since the fish came out of the water beside the boat.

Joe Gaspe and the Portable Nukes

She touched her face and said, "You bastard. That stuff stinks." Joe laughed, a rolling belly laugh. The boat, which had been drifting in neutral, moved downstream in the light chop. Joe sat down, looked at Sherry and said, "That's a bigger fish than I have ever caught. Congratulations. You held her just like a baby, you don't have kids do you?"

"Thanks. Yes, I have a daughter. She's with her grandmother now. Her father's a dip weed. I don't have anything to do with him. But his mother is all right and she loves Cassie."

"You never said. I just assumed that since you are ramming around with me and Marv that…"

"Assume makes an ass of you and me."

"Yes, it does." Joe busied himself resetting the boat, putting the rods and net where they belonged, cameras back in the dry box, release tools to hand, "So do you like musky fishing now? Wanna try some more?"

"Well….yeah."

Joe moved the shifter into forward and the boat headed back toward the trolling route. "You picked a nice little hump to bang, let's hit it again. Maybe we can mark it on the GPS. There's no name for it on the chart. We'll call it Stripper Shoal or maybe Sherry's Spot. What d'ya think?" Joe was smiling, so happy with himself he was almost smug.

"What do you think, you clown?"

"If we mark it, we'll call it Sherry's Shoal. How's that? But, we're not gonna be telling anyone where it is. Except Marv of course."

"Of course."

The remainder of the day was spent in trolling that path with didoes thrown in for variety. They were rewarded for their efforts with nary a rip. There wasn't much conversation. That was harder on Joe than it was on Sherry. Marv was the quiet one of the pair while Joe sometimes rattled on pointlessly. Sherry, who had spent seven years being chatted up by lonely losers, was comfortable in her own company and had a glow about her that cannot be adequately described to someone who has not caught or witnessed a big fish like hers. The catch was thrilling but the release, safe and sound, of the big

Dread upon the Waters

girl was another matter of consequence and gave a satisfaction to one that she had never experienced. As Joe said at one point, big game hunting for dangerous wild animals with the bonus of being nice to the ladies.

When they headed in for the night, Joe said, "Even with guides who are of the people, those boats won't be traveling at night. Too many islands, unmarked shoals, and rocks; it's too easy to get lost. There are so many closed up cottages with docks that they can just tie up and wait for dawn. We'll head back for Wes's camp, eat, sleep and come back after daylight."

"How many stars do you see in the halo around the moon?" Joe asked Sherry.

"Three."

"That's how many days until we have snow."

"Snow! Don't say that."

"It's gonna be what it's gonna be."

Joe handled the Whaler on the return up Mullet Creek to the camp. Sherry's boat skills were not up to tackling narrow inlets or tricky docking maneuvers.

"If you see a lantern lit let me know." Darkness was descending at six when they rounded the last bend.

"Who'd be hanging a lantern for us?"

"That'd be Wes's nose lit up with Crown Royal." Joe let out a hearty laugh at his jest.

"You're bad." After they docked Joe built a cook fire with some charcoal and Sherry built some hamburgers, opened a can of beans and put on the coffee pot. Seated at the picnic table in the glow of the embers, they smoked and talked.

"So, how do you like outdoor recreation? Too rustic for you?"

"The only time I ever went camping, the guy just wanted to do it in the woods. He couldn't build a fire, was afraid of bugs, and almost soiled himself when we heard a rustling in the forest. We went home before the night was through."

"A real metrosexual, huh?"

Sherry rolled her eyes, a gesture Joe imagined but couldn't see in the dark. "Sure, Joe."

Joe Gaspe and the Portable Nukes

Sherry was thinking about how she liked Joe. Sure, she found him annoying at times, but that was an affectation. She liked a man who wasn't dainty about the way he went through life. He swaggered along, enjoyed his food and drink, spoke strongly, perhaps too loudly at times, knew how to handle himself and wasn't shy about pitching in and helping with the chores.

After a few minutes she said, "What I like about you and Marv, especially Marv, is that you guys can do stuff. You are quiet about it but you guys are strong, capable, independent, able to live on your own."

"As long as we've got beer." Joe interrupted chuckling to himself.

"Most guys I've known brag about stuff but it's worthless stuff. Cars and stock deals and computers and video equipment and all the gear they've got. They need constant reassurance. They're high maintenance. I don't know. You guys are different."

"Yeah, we got nothin' but fishing and hunting stuff, guns and explosives." Joe chuckled. "You've never heard about some of our escapades. We're not so special when you get to know us. Especially Marv, except for dodging Rottweilers and Doberman Pinschers-he's German you know-he's a knucklehead. Did I tell you about him when he went ice fishing?"

"Joe, shut up." She said this in an over loud voice. He stilled himself. "My first impression of you, back in the club, was as another loser. Then I heard you were the guys who raided that Sweet Cherries dump in Cincy. I thought that was pretty cool. Then I met you again here last week and you started squeezing my shoes and I didn't care for you much. But, these last four days you've been good and today when we caught the fish, you were great. So first impressions are often wrong, when they are bad first impressions."

Joe was feeling uncomfortable being praised. He said, "We better get some sleep, I'm betting on fog in the morning. If we can't get an early start, I'll show you how to shoot my nine. It's an H&K, easy to hit what you're aiming at, easy to handle, reliable. You may need to use it in the next few days." He paused. "I'll let you know after I've dreamed on it."

Dread upon the Waters

The next morning a radiation fog had rolled in over the camp. When he showed Sherry his automatic, she seemed very comfortable with the weapon. He asked, "Have you handled a gun before?"

"A little bit."

Joe went over the important safety considerations of handling a weapon, and then said, "Take aim at that beer can over there with both eyes open, then alternately close each eye. If when you close your right eye, the target does not jump to the right, that is your dominant eye. If the left eye makes it jump then that is your dominant eye. Try that. Even though I'm right handed, my left eye is the dominant one."

"Nothin' "

"You don't see any difference? Try again."

Sherry gave him a look that said, "How can you be so stupid." She said, "Nothin' "

"Okay. Well, squeeze the trigger, don't jerk it."

Sherry blew the can away with a dead center shot. For the remainder of a drizzly morning she demonstrated a perfect eye and a dead aim. She was so precise that she could hit the base of a can and flip it up 180 degrees so it almost stood on top of an adjacent can. She actually pulled this trick off once, and proved herself a much better shot than Joe. It was not even close. After several hours they were out of cans and Joe was sure that she would be handling the automatic if it were needed.

The Bermuda high that was bringing marvelous dry sunny weather to the southern United States, was powerful enough to push the incipient hurricane, boiling westward from the Azores, north. The continental high over the northern part of the eastern US and eastern Canada was not as powerful and the north flow of the hurricane curved back against that high pressure, sliding farther west as it moved northward.

Joe Gaspe and the Portable Nukes

Everyone who watched the weather- pilots, seafaring men, farmers, forecasters, any people who spent time outside- could feel the change coming. Old timers in New England and Atlantic Canada knew that the western ocean could brew up serious storms. A nor'easter in October could mean; lashing wind, horizontal rain, massive dumps of heavy wet snow, or all three. These storms could last for days as the tropical depression expended its energy against the northeast coast of the continental land mass.

The weather over the Adirondack Mountains in New York was brewing thunderstorms as the people on Lake Champlain could see. A contrary wind was sweeping in cold from the east down the Green Mountains of Vermont.

The Saint Lawrence morning fog was taking half a day to burn off even with a bright sun shining. Instead of scattering the fog, the east wind made it denser.

Far to the northeast in the Gulf of St. Lawrence the wind pummeled eastward with a fury that taxed the powerful 4200 horse-power diesels of the ocean-going tug *Eastern Sun* struggling against it. Rain fell sideways, as if a cascade were plummeting against the wheel-house. Visibility was zero. Radar was non-existent. Darkness was total, except during lightning flashes.

Amy's work with Dr. Ruland Rush was having a profound effect on her dreaming. It caused her to have so many different images, from various dreams, that she was waking in the morning exhausted and tangled in her covers as if she'd been spinning through the night. When she complained to Dr. Rush about her weariness, he gave her a practical technique and a mnemonic phrase that would enable her to settle on one dream interaction at a time. For some reason she brought her little sister Lucy's stuffed whale, Moby, along with her. She held Moby in her hand at night and repeated the phrase, "I am the dreamer for the family." This enabled her to drift off to sleep.

Dread upon the Waters

It was unseasonably hot on the mansion's upper floors, and Amy had gone to sleep with just a sheet over her. Still she was perspiring when she began to hear a roaring noise. She filed that in her unconscious mind as Molly, in the next bed, snored loudly, something she did when she slept on her back.

A roaring sound, like a passing snowplow building momentum as it approached, was coming up through the register in the room Lucy and two of her slightly older sisters shared. Lucy was wide awake, staring at the ceiling. She held a gray athletic sock, stuffed with other socks-she'd drawn a mouth and eyes on it. Amy smiled in her sleep; this was Lucy's substitute for Moby. Then a metallic clatter changed her expression, a car door slammed, and a screech of tires jumped Amy to the next scene. She pounded on her mother's door. Then pushed in and shouted in a voice deep and loud – not her own; "Leave now! This house is being torched! Save the children! Go to your sister's house in Manchester. Save your children!" This was a man's voice issuing from Amy's lips. Kate arose, unaccountably fully dressed, and shouted the girl's names as if they were all one word. The next thing Amy saw was her mom shoving the girls into the family van with Lucy straggling, throwing the sock animal down, saying, "Bad Moby," and scooting into the van door. Kate closed the door, got in the driver's side, and drove out of the driveway. She never looked back.

Amy saw the new house, the one they'd moved to because Joe worried about who might find out where they lived, burst into an orange fireball.l Only the skeleton of their home remained.

Joe and Mo were both dreaming and both restless. Flying above the action of the boats they were using, Joe above his Boston Whaler on the St. Larry moving in and out of Canada, and Mo on Lake Champlain back and forth through a dogleg left as the lake straightened out to a southerly direction.

It was all white in Joe's dream and he saw fog sometimes, snow sometimes...smoke, white and stinging his nostrils, and dust billowing in clouds. He flew as a hawk, working hard with no thermals to provide lift.

Joe Gaspe and the Portable Nukes

There was a view of four boats slowly cruising through fog, then his boat driven by a black-haired woman. When Joe looked at her he saw a raven, the trickster, in the boat. When he circled higher he heard Amy warning him of trouble if he didn't leave the company of this woman. The next circle revealed four-wheelers speeding along raising a dust cloud. Joe counted five of them. He circled again and heard through his dreams little Lucy scolding her stuffed animal, Moby. Lucy coughed and Joe saw smoke and his family automobile speeding away. The next wide circle revealed a snowstorm and, above the flakes falling thick as oatmeal, a heron being harassed by owls. Mo was in trouble. Kate and the girls were in trouble. Amy seemed to be in control but Joe was still absent from his own boat. When he circled down over the four boats again he saw through the fog, at twenty feet above the water's surface, that there were now two Lunds moving rapidly ahead. He veered back to the east and saw himself hauling another person aboard the Boston Whaler. There was the raven-haired beauty, without make-up, in fishing clothes, eyes penetrating and sparkling. Joe saw danger all around.

Moses Snow, the heron, saw the owls through the snowstorm at every turn, on every side. To a Mohawk, an owl's appearance on the scene portended disaster more serious than the raven's mischief. Mo looked again, saw the two women safe near shore with he and Johann on the second leg of the mission. He saw Amy confusing the group on the quad runners with dust clouds. He saw Joe defeating some attackers in the fog. But when he looked into the borrowed Smoker Craft, he saw only owls dive-bombing him and hooting in triumph.

More than one hundred miles apart, Joe Gaspe and Mo Snow awoke at the same instant. Each had seen a vision of conflict, dread, deeds yet to be done, and continued danger. Dread upon the water…

Mo had borrowed two boats from one of the friendly charter captains to whom Andre had spoken. He'd had extras. Mo and Liv had used the Grady–White for a day and a half. It was a beautiful and well-appointed boat but it suffered from unexplained mechanicals that made it the less reliable of the two craft. He and Johann were going to spend a few hours in the Smoker Craft, a modified sixteen-foot model that had a casting deck added up front. The plywood deck added weight and made the bow of the boat want to nosedive when

Dread upon the Waters

some turning maneuvers were attempted. Mo had determined that it was a better option to patrol with the smaller boat. His cousin, Little Snow, was going to work on the Grady at a boat launch. Little Snow was a terrific mechanic, the best in the clan, but he was arriving on this job with nothing to go on in the way of a diagnosis of the problem. Rad and Liv delivered the boat to the launch to meet him.

The Smoker Craft was steered from the back with a tiller. The bench seat had a portable cushioned seat with a backrest clamped on for the driver's comfort. Without a specific place to sit, Johann moved around. He could hunker down on some boat cushions in the front or move onto the casting deck as conditions warranted. The RF receiver was small. That and the snappers were protected, inside of a plastic dry box, from any stray spark that might develop.

Johann wore his incongruous top hat pinned to his very long blondehair. Mo concentrated on seeing into the advection fog that was developing around the bend in the lake as they patrolled their route across the narrows and back. The temperature of the air was so much cooler than the water temperature that the air condensed into fog just above the surface of the water. The dogleg in the lake and the closed-in mountain ranges had combined for a weather effect that Mo had never seen before. South of an east-west line on that dogleg in the lake, the low hanging fog was dense enough to reduce visibility to forty feet or less. Fifty feet above that fog there was bright sunshine and brisk wind. North of that dogleg line it was snowing like a banshee. The swirling wind seemed to be preparing to change directions. The demarcation line of snow/no snow was visible but not from very far away in the dense fog. Mo look at the snowline, judged how far across he'd come, and took a second to look at Johann. Yo watched the red LED on the RF power supply through the clear plastic of the box. The light's glow reflected off his face. Mo was satisfied that this boat would be all right until Cousin Little could cure the Grady of her problems.

One gets soaking wet driving around in an open boat in the fog. All aspects of one's body and gear attract tiny droplets of water from the air. That mist clings to a person until the outside of the fabric becomes saturated at which time the water starts to soak in. Johann's long hair was dripping. The ringlets eventually became so wet that they were plastered to his head.

Joe Gaspe and the Portable Nukes

Mo wore a wool watch cap that shone with a halo of water drops. The two men patrolled back and forth in this mist getting colder all the time. They watched their electronics and the snow bank to their north. It seemed logical that the enemy would be coming along soon, but they weren't sure that they would be able to see anything if they did.

James Talor knew that the North Atlantic, referred to by North American sailors as the Western Ocean, was never at rest. Learning seamanship as a young man from his Portuguese uncles, he'd seen a dead calm turn into a cyclone when a high pressure dissolved within a few hours.

The 750 miles of the St. Lawrence belie the significance of the river as one of the world's great ones. Draining the Great Lakes and almost one half of Canada, as well as a huge chunk of the northern United States, the St. Larry had its own lore and history. Because its gulf is blocked by ice each winter, the river is only open for seven months a year.

Winter was in the air as James Talor followed his brother's earlier departure down river. The second tug, longer, more powerful, and behind schedule, steamed ahead with the Aquinah as lead pilot and two Mic-Mac tribal members as alternate pilots. There was no weather radio and the fuse on the ship-to-shore radio had been pulled as soon as James was finished speaking to the harbormaster.

Before leaving, James had listened to a weather report that told of a nor'easter in the Gulf of St. Lawrence, pounding into the river's mouth. Steaming along under the bluebird skies of a high-pressure system, James wondered what was happening to his brother's tug and what the east-northeast course held for him and his vessel, *Eastern Star*.

Chapter 8

The Adirondacks: October 8th

After the first evening's lecture at the workshop, the dream partners had been instructed to try dreaming the same dream at the same time. Amy had tried to apply the learning from her workshops with Ruland Rush. Her power dreamer's mind had other ideas and it veered off in its own direction.

She clearly saw the four-wheelers sloshing and slogging through the bogs at the west end of Black Lake. The men were driving by night without lights and hiding in thickets at dawn. Everyone was covered with wet gooey slimy mud, faces spattered, hands filthy, their discomfort was beyond belief. The Saudis, unused to wet conditions, were trying to act stoic in front of the Mohawks but each one's inner dialogue was a selfish complaining rant. Having seen this, Amy's dream went through a brief period of discontinuity before jumping ahead to the four ATVs emerging single file from a forest and heading across a fallow farm field. The field was open and a slight gleam of sky made it brighter than the woods. To make up some time and reach a haul road that was supposed to be across the clearing, the lead quad runner urged the others on. They were all reaching their full twenty mph speed when Amy was awakened by the sound of a horrific metal clanging crashing grinding crash. The pain endured by the Mohawk was transferred to Amy through her left arm with which she had dislodged a table lamp and swept it halfway across the room.

Dread upon the Waters

Amy sat up and yelled, "Tractor!" and Molly was watching her from the other bed. Amy looked at the smashed lamp, then looked at Molly who said, "I guess you and I weren't sharing a dream as Mr. Rush said we should."

"Sorry," Amy wasn't clear as to what she had foreseen, but her sense of foreboding convinced her that it wasn't good.

Ruland Rush sat in the background as his executive assistant addressed the dreamers. "We will have you work in groups of two with a facilitator today. At some point in the day each pair will have half an hour or more working directly with Mr. Rush to enhance your dreaming. Since some are further along than others, your amount of time with Mr. Rush will vary. All facilitators are well-trained to bring each dreamer and their dream partner along at an appropriate pace."

Amy was eager to talk with Rush and Molly about the dream that was recurring in each session. That vision included The Old One from the wolf clan and seemed to be moving toward a goal through a sequence of vignettes, each building off the other. As she and Molly went through several exercises with the workshop facilitators, it became clear that Molly was participating in the dream but not doing so as fully as Amy. She would nod her head as parts were related to the instructor and agree that she had seen some things but be lost in other parts of the sequence. The exercises were taught from the book as written by Rush, and the workshop leader seemed to realize that Amy was into things that were very deep. As the series of exercises wore on, Amy became convinced that she would be spending some important time with the author himself.

Lunch was provided from half past noon until one. Then a walk on the grounds was scheduled to refresh and recharge all the participants. The dream ranch was on an old estate in the southern part of the Adirondack Mountains. The grounds had been one of the Great Camps owned by a minor nineteenth-century industrialist and contained several paths through woods and hills that shone with beauty both arranged and pristine on an autumn day. There was bright sunshine and no wind in the valley as Amy and Molly reached a small rustic bench. Off to the west, Molly pointed out a cloudbank sliding north over the high peaks of the central range.

"Weather over that way."

Molly's comment was meant to be an opening. Amy looked up and said nothing. Molly continued, "We'll spend some time with Ruland Rush this afternoon. It is said in the wolf clan that Rush can show us how to dream true and dream together."

Amy nodded. "He owns the land up to that hilltop over there, don't he?" She pointed in the direction they were facing. The hilltop of which she spoke was clear and sharp in the afternoon sun.

"Yes. There is a small lodge up there reserved for advanced students. Like you. I think we'll be seeing that lodge before this semester is over."

"We will see it very soon." Amy said nothing more during their break.

After the sessions resumed, the executive assistant in charge of the program came up to Molly and Amy and spoke quietly to them both. "You will not have an afternoon session with Ruland today. Don't be disappointed though. After supper tonight, I will accompany you to the hilltop lodge for a full evening of intense work. He knows the power you both have, especially you, Amy. And he is looking forward to working with you."

Amy's work with the various trainers that afternoon was frustrating to her for two reasons. First, The Old One seemed to be enshrouded in a swirling white cloud making his non-verbal messages difficult to discern. Second, each foray into the dream of the wanderers ended in a total black out, followed by a loud metallic crash that hurt Amy's shoulder and left arm more and more each time. She looked forward to help from the master on these problems.

That evening, Ruland Rush lectured Amy and Molly. "You will not find many people except dreamers who can accept the counterweight to the conscious world that comes from the dreaming.

"If you see The Old One or The Ancient One in your dreaming, know that he always has been and always will be there to guide you on the path. He exists, independent of time, in all places. He is the son of the maternal consciousness that you serve. Even though he seems impossibly old, he is a mere child in the Real World. He is hidden within each of you.

"There is no communication through technology, amazing and headlong as it may be, that is faster than the knowledge brought to us through The Old One.

"You can see this in your dreaming and others, those who you are reaching can see it too in their dreaming simultaneously, anywhere in the world and anywhere in time. His is the voice of being.

"The difficulty is in knowing that another sees the vision as you see it, at the same time. As you refine your technique you will know which others see as you have in the Real World." Rush spoke these brief statements to Amy and Molly with pauses in between each statement. He was not waiting for questions, merely waiting for his words to sink in.

The Nor'easter rolled down the St Larry, its cold air unfolding fog and drizzle as it covered the warmer water. Joe had been showing Sherry his weapons—all short-range firearms—when he had heard the squelching on the VHF radio.

"Dr. Dento, this is Musky Maniac, are you there on nine?"

"Yeah, Maniac, I'm here."

"Go to twenty-three, I've got something' for you."

Joe punched up to channel twenty-three as Sherry moved up onto the boat deck and leaned her head in to hear the transmission.

"This is Dento on twenty-three. Go ahead, Maniac."

"I spotted your Lunds in the fog this morning. These are definitely your boats. Canadian registration, but they are at a dock that I know should be empty. They got pretty far last night before the visibility shut down. They are at Sand Duck Island, and when they figure it out they'll have a straight shot down through the forty-acre shoal and into the lake."

"I'd better get out there then." Joe made a hurry-up motion with his left arm to Sherry. "Anybody but you out today, Maniac?"

Joe Gaspe and the Portable Nukes

"There'll be several of us out there but I don't know how many we'll see in the fog. At least seven boats that I know of will be on the shoal today."

"Good job Maniac. I'll keep you informed."

"You got a cell phone number I can call?"

"You'd think I would, wouldn't you? But no. My partner, Marv's, got the phone, and he's on another mission."

"OK Dento. Musky Maniac on the side on nine."

"Dento out."

Sherry had gone to the cabin and gathered up some food and drink. She shrugged into an oversize rain jacket and said, "I'm ready." Joe had been wiping the condensation off the windshield. He started the engine and advanced the throttle, in neutral, to warm it up.

Pulling into the narrow channel that would take them to Mullet Bay, Joe handed the wheel off to Sherry. Leaning in next to her ear he said, "Keep it at dead slow. Stay in the middle. I'm going to look at the chart and plan a way to intercept those boats." He tapped the chart. Sherry barely glanced at it as she stood to see over the foggy windshield and stared at the open area in the middle of the channel. She judged that she could see about one boat length, or twenty feet, ahead.

Joe stood beside Sherry. He talked to himself for effect. Trying to make her think he was very confident in the map and its information. On the sly, he glanced up often to see that she was not veering off track.

Joe set his shotgun in a rod hanger just below the gunwales. He placed his pistol barrel into an upright rod holder. Joe thought of the fog's effect on his weapons and said to himself, just loud enough for Sherry to hear, "Gotta wipe these down and oil them later—clean 'em inside and out." He placed his plastic container with the snappers in it on the storage locker in the back corner. He had placed a non-skid sheet under the box so it would not slide away at the critical moment. In an old enamel coffee cup, he lit some rotten soft maple wood to start it smoldering. It was the punk he would use to light the fuses of his snappers.

Joe Gaspe saw a crisis ahead and he was slowing down his mind in order to look into the future. He took over piloting as they moved from Mullet Bay up through Marcus's Narrows and came up just behind Sand Duck Island. Then, when they got up on the Lunds, he'd put Sherry behind the wheel. Joe deduced that the enemy would be slow starting and proceed in convoy out through the foggy stretch. He hoped to take down all four Lunds by tossing a long snapper and two or three regular snappers into each in quick succession.

"Both weapons are loaded, one in the chamber. Safeties are on." He waved at the two weapons. Sherry saw the smoke curling up from the punk. She'd seen how quickly the snappers went up when their pyro papers were nudged against the punk. She tasted fear, coppery in her mouth. She coughed. With dry mouth and shaking hands, she looked Joe in the face. He said, "We're all right now. We'll be even better later today."

"Did you put the coordinates of the island we're looking for in this?' Sherry pointed at the GPS.

"No. I haven't figured that out yet." Joe affected a sheepish look. Sherry clucked her tongue. "My fingers are too fat for those little buttons," he said.

She glanced at his ham hand on the wheel and said, "There is that."

Joe fished his RF detector, which looked like a large cell phone, out of his pocket and turned it on. It beeped and a red light came on, blinking at regular intervals.

Familiar with the feeling but unsure how it happened, Joe had a sense of confidence building in him. He had a conviction that he knew exactly where the four Lunds were, invisible ahead in the thick fog. A dead-sure mind's-eye picture showed the four boats pushing off from the dock at that rocky island, floating in the slow current, and organizing themselves for the journey out to the lake. Maybe it was his warrior's soul, maybe it was the second sight predicted for seventh sons, Joe didn't know. He spoke quietly to Sherry. "There are going to be two stragglers, boats at the back of the pack. We're going to pick them off one by one. The others will scoot ahead when they hear trouble rather than come back to investigate."

"How do you know that?" Sherry had a biting edge in her voice.

"I know."

Joe Gaspe and the Portable Nukes

"Yeah sure, you can't even program your GPS but you see into the future through the fog! Yeah, right." Sherry was getting tense while Joe calmed down, slowed time, and became assured and confident.

In that way pretty women have of being catty, often about other women, especially ones they think they're prettier than, Sherry started to ramble into a combination of a personal attack on Joe and complaints about everything and everyone.

Gaspe turned full face to her and said, "Stop! Write all that on an eight by eleven sheet and mail it to me on Monday. We got stuff to do and you are gonna hold up your end!"

Sherry looked as if she'd been whacked with a two-by-four but she said, "All right. What's my part."

Joe told her.

Sherry was trying to calm down. Her foot was tapping on the boat's deck, her ears were ringing, her neck and shoulders were knotted with tension. Joe spoke quietly to her.

"They are just ahead, hardly moving. When we see the last boat in line, I'm going to punch the throttles." The handles were advanced just over the bump that indicates movement above idle. "You grab the wheel and aim for the back corner of the last boat. Just when you think you are about to hit him, turn the wheel sharply so my back corner comes right up on him. I've got one long snapper and three regulars I'll be dropping on him. As soon as you make that turn, drop the throttles into neutral and drop to the floor of the boat. They may have guns and they may shoot."

Sherry looked at him, opened her eyes wide, and was about to speak. Joe said, "The first boat won't be ready for us. After that, who knows? Just keep the wheel steady while you're on the floor. I'll take care of 'em. Keep both motors just above idle so we can burn water if we have to get away. This fog was sent by God."

Sherry wondered about that. Joe nudged her, pointed at the RF detector, its light rapidly blinking green, and the distance-to-object display, in hundredths of a mile, rapidly diminishing. Then he nudged her again, pointed ahead, and they saw a Lund come into view. Two men sat facing forward. Joe said, "Let's roll." Ramping the outboard's up, Joe moved with remarkable grace for a bruiser, out of the driver's seat and Sherry dropped into it. Hopping to the back corner, Joe blew on the smoldering punk, it glowed orange in the mist. The water was dead calm showing the smallest ripple where the convoy of Lunds had passed.

Putting the four snappers in his right hand, using the magician's grip as Johann had shown him, Joe kneeled next to the gunwale. He didn't want to be thrown from the boat in a sudden lurch, and his body was too big a target if he stood. The Whaler closed the distance with the last Lund in line in a few seconds. The occupants of the boat turned and looked back. They had to half stand to see over their tarp-covered cargo. Each pointed and began to shout. The driver had slewed his wheel to the left when he looked back.

Joe shouted "Turn now! Punch it!"

The driver of the Lund's inadvertent movement put it right in front of Sherry. Thinking fast, she ramped her throttle with her right hand and slammed the wheel over with her left. She grunted with exertion. Joe lit the snappers in succession and tossed them into the terrorist's boat. They arced in a perfect fan as they spread along the length of the slow-moving Lund. One man tried to bring a weapon to bear on the Whaler while another looked at the burning items on the deck of his boat. Before they could act, they disappeared in the fog behind, unseen by Joe or Sherry, who opened their mouths and covered their ears. They heard a rapid series of detonations. *Crackpow-crackpow-crackpow-crackpow.* The RF detector stopped showing movement. Joe reached past Sherry and returned the throttle to dead slow ahead.

"One down." Joe dialed the next frequency on his detector. "The other boats are probably a little worried and milling around. Move ahead slow and we'll see if we can catch up with another. They're probably calling Mohammed on the cell phones to see what happened."

"Jesus, Joe. You just killed some guys."

"Yes, we did. They weren't boy scouts you know. They had bad intentions."

"Still, you killed 'em. Ya know?"

"Yeah we killed 'em and we're gonna get some more." He reached up and pushed each throttle ahead just enough to move a bit faster.

Joe Gaspe and the Portable Nukes

Dialing each of the his three remaining frequencies he saw that two boats were moving rapidly to the west, slightly south of due west. The third boat had turned north at a very slow speed. As Joe had guessed, the two teams of two Lunds and four terrorists were working on the buddy system. Their planning had redundancy built into it, and while one half of one bomb had disappeared, its buddy boat didn't know how to react. Despite his thick fingers and without thinking about it, Joe marked his GPS with a waypoint for future investigation. The first half of the second bomb was now headed toward Canada. Unknown to them, they were inching along toward the cliff-like side of a one-acre rocky island. Joe and Sherry gained on the RF signal by creeping through the fog.

Gaspe leaned in next to Sherry. She could smell his sour cigarette breath. "You done good." Joe patted her shoulder.

Sherry thought, *He's scared too. But he keeps going. That's what he's got; doggedness, bulldog stamina, and no thought of quitting.*

Joe switched again through the three frequencies on his RF detector. He couldn't see anything but a wall of white mist in every direction. He heard the waves lapping against a shore to his right; smelled nothing on the wind but his own damp clothes. The two lead boats were rapidly moving away to the west. Their course was now slightly north of due west. They would be out of his one-mile range soon. The third boat, the one teamed up with the sunken one, was closer but moving generally north. It was on an erratic zigzag course. Joe looked at the display. It read twenty-five hundredths of a mile. He tapped Sherry on the shoulder indicating he would drive for a while.

"What's up? Are we going after more?"

"They're seeking the Canadian Middle Channel to get out to the lake. They figure we can't follow over there." His wave indicated Ontario.

"We can't, can we? I mean go into Canada and do this stuff."

"We're in Canada now. Have been. Let's just follow along and see what happens. The authorities will be staying pretty close to the coffeepot this morning."

"Joe, if we are in Canada, we have no protection from arrest do we? I've got a DUI on my record. I'm not allowed in Canada."

Dread upon the Waters

"You're not allowed out of the county you live in either, are you?"

"Well, no." Sherry said.

"We'll just move along here and see what we see."

Joe Gaspe was correct. The two lead boats were trying to find the Canadian Middle Channel and locate the buoys that would lead them to the lake. They were going too fast, considering the unknown dangerous shoals and reefs in the area. But, though they were blind, they were in the right gap between islands. Luck got them into the channel.

The third boat was not so lucky. They narrowly avoided collision with the wall of an island. They crashed into some rocks before they reached the next channel west, crumpled their bow, smashing in the aluminum, but they backed off and moved farther west to try again. Sherry and Joe heard a metal screeching crash and the shouts of men and an outboard motor racing to drag a boat off the rocks by using full-reverse throttle. The enemies just kept shifting to port trying to find a way through the rocks a little farther west. The occupants of the boat were smoking harsh Turkish cigarettes. Joe was close enough to get a whiff of tobacco smoke every so often. He kept an eye on his depth finder and slowly moved west in the deeper water off the reef edge.

"Let's see what they think of this," Joe said. He lifted the shotgun from the rack and fired one slug, pumped the action, counted five, and fired a second. As the echoing roar died down, he put a finger to his lips and he and Sherry listened. They were too far away to hear the voices of the terrorists, but the distance to go on the RF detector showed increased speed from the other boat. Joe ramped his throttle, putting the Whaler on a course parallel to the enemy's Lund. The distance stabilized at one-tenth of a mile to the north. Five hundred feet separated the good guys and the bad guys.

Joe dropped the throttle into neutral when the detector indicated the boat was not moving any longer.

"Lookin' for a way through. They're not gonna find it there." Joe came up off idle turned to starboard and move ahead dead slow. He listened. The smell of that stale tobacco hit his nostrils again. He leaned to Sherry, "We're close. Take the wheel.'

Joe stepped to the stern, checked his automatic for the third time, and said to Sherry, "Slowly girl, very very slowly."

She threw Joe a look of annoyance but kept moving ahead directly north now. Suddenly they heard a loud bang, a few shouted words in what they assumed was Arabic, and the motor ahead being gunned. Then a louder crash, another ramp of the motor as it was shifted from reverse through neutral to forward. Then there was a horrible screeching, metal-ripping sound and two voices in Arabic shouting at the same time. Dead slow, Sherry moved up on the noise. Joe looked at the depth finder. It said eighty feet. The RF detector had them down to two hundredths of a mile. They were less than one hundred feet away. Looming out of the fog to their left was a rock pinnacle sticking up twenty feet out of what seemed like deep water. The depth finder still said eighty feet under Joe's Whaler. There behind the pinnacle was the Lund filling with water as the life jackets and anything that would float were drifting away.

"Hold here. Neutral." Joe aimed his firearm at the two men struggling to stay with the sinking boat. "That boat probably floats full of water. Looks like they've ripped the bottom right out. Let's see what they do."

The crated cargo rolled to one side of the Lund as the water rose in the boat. The sudden weight shift turned the boat over and dumped both men into the water. One appeared to slam his head into a protruding rock as he went over and then disappeared under the lapping waves. The other man floundered, trying to swim.

"Sidle over there, keep your eye on this." Joe tapped the screen of the depth finder. If you see it get real shallow just drop back into neutral. If we can get to this guy safely, we'll take him. If he drowns before we get there, it's his problem."

He couldn't last long. The water was cold, fifty-eight degrees at the surface and much colder a few feet down where his feet and legs were. He hadn't shucked his heavy jacket or boots, and not being a strong swimmer, he got in trouble right away. Sherry continued crab-walking the boat sideways toward him and Joe put aside his gun. He reached

Dread upon the Waters

for his fish billy, a club used to dispatch fish that were being kept for table fare. The swimmer saw them coming and tried to move north toward the rocks but he made little progress despite his hard work. Joe grabbed the back of his jacket and when he struggled and threatened to pull Joe in, Gaspe smacked him on the side of his head with the club, giving it everything he had. He knocked the man unconscious. Joe told Sherry to get on the other side of the boat to balance the weight somewhat, and he hauled the soaking man over the gunwale and into the boat.

"Mark that waypoint on the GPS," Joe said as he went to the boat's toolbox and got some zip ties out of it. He zip-tied the Arab man's hands behind his back and, linking two tie wraps, tied his knees together. Joe wrapped duct tape around the man's face so his mouth was covered and dropped the unconscious man into the stern deck.

"We won't be finding those other boats now. Might as well head for Wes's camp and see who wants this guy."

On the way to camp Joe alerted his charter captain partners that two suspect Lunds got past him, and they should see what they could see. The captains expressed doubt, since they were fogged in and blind, trolling on GPS alone. Joe used his restricted cell phone to call Agent Andre's office and explain that he had a package for pick-up by an appropriate party. An hour later the driveway was filled by a state police car followed by two white Chevy Suburbans followed by another state police cruiser. The men who exited the second Suburban identified themselves to Joe, took the scrap of paper on which he'd written the latitude and longitude of the two sunken boats, secured the prisoner, ignored Sherry, and left. As the four vehicles did three-point turns in convoy, Sherry asked, "What did they say to you?"

"No one said anything to me. No one was ever here." Joe replied.

"Cool. I get it." Sherry went back to making coffee as Joe began getting the boat ready for Marv's arrival and the move to the head of the Niagara River. Joe was nervous because he was stuck with a boat and trailer and a strange, beautiful woman when he needed to be on his horse on the way to Niagara. He had no regular cell phone and when he'd walked a long mile and a half to the payphone at the convenience store the handset had been ripped from the phone. He didn't know where Marv was—he was a day late already. Marv, the obsessive German, was never late, usually early. Joe had an ominous feeling. To top it all off Sherry—who Joe was convinced was sweet on Marv-had been getting bitchy; probably because Marv was late but Joe could never fathom why a woman behaved as she did. He tried to keep busy enough to stay out of her way. Saying to himself, *No fighting, Marv will be here directly.*

Marv was in the van wondering why he did what he did. The cops had told him not to leave town as if he was the guy who had shot up his mom and brother. He said to himself, "To hell with them." His sister had told him not to leave. She'd launched a table lamp at him as she yelled, "You and that stupid jerk, Joe!" when he hustled out the door. He'd told neither the cops nor his sister that he was involved in a mission for Agent Andre involving the Department of Homeland Security.

As he drove north, Marv obsessed, "How was he supposed to tell Joe that they were under attack at home?" Not only had Marv's family been murdered, but Joe's house had been torched and his wife and kids forced into hiding. Meanwhile, Marv and Joe would be screwing around waiting for some boats that might or might not show up. Marv was speeding a little as he tried to erase an endless thought loop from his mind. In the end he knew that doing something was the tonic he needed to clear his mind and calm his nerves. Busy with something else, he would think of a solution. Joe usually had an idea. Still, how was he to tell Joe that his house and shop were gone?

"How do you know Marv's coming back at all, much less right now?" Sherry nagged.

"I know his every move." Joe smiled like a father on Christmas morning at that ridiculous notion.

Dread upon the Waters

He looked up to see Marv's van pull down the drive. Window down, Marv leaned out and asked, "Why were the state troopers here?"

Joe would tell him on the way to their next venue.

"How can you stand this weather? You Yankees must be nuts to live in this crap." Olivia was ranting, one of those things she did.

Looking at the snow to the north of them and the dreary cold windy sea to the south of them, Rad said, "Yeah, it's bad, but didn't you recently throw in with a man who lives even farther north by marrying him?"

"Shut up." They were in the more reliable of the two borrowed boats, patrolling for an hour and tucked in behind Valcour Island waiting for an hour, while Johan and Mo hunted through the thickly falling snow for the convoy of four Lunds moving south with a deadly cargo intended for the US Military Academy at West Point. It was Friday afternoon and Lake Champlain, often busy with leaf watchers in early October was deserted because of the crummy weather. Mo had heard from a charter captain, on a perch-fishing outing, that the four boats in question had left the vicinity of the Vermont shore, heading south.

Mo knew that these terrorists were headed for the point, miles below on the Hudson, with a plan to take out the academy and the crowd at Saturday's football game against Colgate. He understood the difficulty of stopping them and to the surprise of Liv, Rad, and Johann he understood how their chaotic progress involved trucks driving through Vermont, boats traversing parts of Lake Champlain and the Hudson River, and eventually attacking the academy on off-road vehicles.

The snowstorm to the north of the east-west dogleg had become a whiteout. Huge flakes were falling more thickly than Johann, an Ohio boy, had ever seen. Mo had decided that he and Johann would attempt the search for the Lunds in the Smoker Craft while Olivia and Rad patrolled below the weather break in the good boat—the Grady

Joe Gaspe and the Portable Nukes

White. Being below the snow line the women were in a grey dismal seascape but they had visibility of half a mile or so.

Johann and Mo had the RF detector but had only twenty to thirty feet of visibility. They couldn't hear much other than the occasional beeping from the detector. Snow falls silently when not driven by wind and tends to blanket most sounds. One feels like he has cotton in his ears. Johann sat on the front casting deck looking into the white world running a snapper through each of his fingers across the backs of each of his hands to keep them loose.

Mo looked, listened, and concentrated while a small nagging question tugged at the edge of his mind. How could Johann turn those little triangular bombs through all his fingers and back without a fumble? When they had sunk the first set of boats Mo had watched as Johann held three snappers between his fingers and a long snapper between thumb and forefinger. Smoking a smoldering cigar, he would touch the long snapper's fuse to his stogie, toss it into one Lund, then quick as a cat, roll the three snappers into position, light them off with a glowing puff of the cigar, and toss them into the jihadi's boat. His training as a magician had allowed him to blow out the bottom of both boats as fast as another man might shake hands.

Two boats were gone and now they were hunting for the second pair of Lunds. Mo knew the channels in this part of the lake and patrolled the kind of zigzag course a troller would use to track a weed edge.

Olivia was looking for a boat to pull through the snow bank to the northeast, dreading the possibility of having to stop some enemy, she rode the front of the Grady White while Rad steered a blockade route across the narrows below the dogleg turn. There were no other boats out in this weather. Those pleasure boaters that had not put their craft away for winter were hunkered down waiting for a better day to come. The leaf peepers, tour boats, and private boats, were all waiting out the Nor'easter.

Then Liv heard the cracking noise of a snapper, though she saw a yellow fireball, she neither saw nor heard anything more. The radio call on Channel Twenty-Two never came. Liv turned to Rad and said, "This is not good. They should have reported, 'mission accomplished' or something."

Dread upon the Waters

Worried, the women were searching the swirling snow cloud that lay like a cotton ball on the waters to the north and east. Rad was standing at the wheel behind the small windscreen and Liv was rocking on one foot and then the other when they saw the Smoker Craft, with its bow pointing up, appear out of the snowstorm.

Together they shouted: "There they are! Thank God!"

"That's Mo waving at us. Get over there!" Olivia said

"All right I'm going! Where's Yo-Yo?"

"Why is Mosie saluting?" I don't see Johann is he hurt?" Liv asked

"That boat's riding funny. What's going on? I don't see Yo-Yo!" Rad said as she ramped up the Grady and closed in on the Smoker Craft's path.

"Why is his arm up like that? Is that blood? OhmyGod he's hurt!" yelled Olivia.

Now that it was obvious that something was wrong, Rad fell silent, worked her boat to an intercepting course, and prayed under her breath.

Mo's boat had a foot long gash in her bottom. He had been able to steer with his right hand, while keeping the boat going with the front half of it out of the water to prevent her from sinking. Johann's body was crumpled in the bottom just aft of the casting platform, which was now a crater of splintered wood looking like a crown of spikes. Rad's boat pulled up side-by-side with Mo's. He looked over at the women in the Grady and yelled above the sound of the racing motors. "Go to the dock!" He inclined his head to the west. "Yo is hurt bad—he's gone I think. We took a shot from a snapper. We're sinking. Stay beside me!" Mo turned to the front and kept up a pace fast enough to keep the front out of the water, but slow enough to keep the boat from going on plane, which would cause the leak to fill the boat faster than the bilge pump could counteract it.

With a mixture of dread and fascination, Rad saw that a plywood splinter almost four-feet long had impaled Mo through his left forearm and into and through his shoulder and out his back. He was covered with blood. He had instinctively raised his arm for protection and the explosion of a snapper had driven the giant splinter right through him. Johann was a goner. Curled in a semi-fetal position, he was not moving. Rad surveyed the damage done to the men and the vessel. Only later did she realize that she and Olivia were screaming the entire ten minutes it took to traverse the distance to the dock at the launch ramp.

Conscious, amazingly not in shock, Mo took charge of the situation. He had run the Smoker Craft right up the launch ramp to beach it. He looked at Olivia, "Call my nephew on the cell phone; tell him we need the reefer truck right away. He knows this launch ramp. Rad, you must call Andre and tell him we have been unable to halt one of the two teams set to assault West Point. Ask him what we can do." Mo paused. "Do you have any water I can drink?"

An hour later Mo's nephew had arrived with the refrigerated truck that Mo used for his bait business. He had helped Rad remove Johann from the disabled Smoker Craft. Rad and Olivia had washed Johann's body wrapping an ace bandage around his belly to keep his intestines from tumbling out of his blackened, torn, bloody, and broken midsection. They gently laid him in the truck, and covered him with a space blanket.

Absorbed in the reverential task of cleansing his lifeless body, Rad had been able to choke down her shock, horror, and rage. But, in the back of her mind, she was planning revenge. Olivia was not so calm, while waiting for the truck Mo had yelled at her twice when she had become emotionally overcome. He had stopped her from trying to pull the splinter back out of his shoulder, explaining that the bleeding would be uncontrollable without the "arrow" in the hole to stop it up. He explained that though he could get free health care in Ontario he preferred a hospital in Plattsburgh where he knew the medical director and there would be no waiting, while the bureaucracy prioritized treatment for an obvious accidental injury. Mo was also cleaned up as much as possible. The remnants of his shirt and jacket were cut away, and he was draped with another blanket from the Caddy's first-aid kit. During the wait, Mo calmly drank some of his clear tea and told the women how the trouble had come about.

"Johann had his cigar going and was doing that thing where he had a snapper between each of his fingers with a long snapper between thumb and first finger. He stood on the casting deck while I maneuvered the boat toward the signal from the RF detector. We could see nothing. Visibility out there, in the snow," he pointed with his right hand to the north around the dogleg, "was ten or twenty feet. Suddenly we came upon those two Lunds in tandem one slightly northeast of the other. As soon as they saw us, I was sidling up to them pretty smartly, the lead man pulled an Uzi out and started shooting. I ducked. Most of his shots went high but one must have clipped Jo because he dropped the snapper he had just lit and it fell to the deck. He reached to grab it and throw it. I heard him say, 'Damn, I can't reach it, Mo! Duck!' He threw the other snappers in his hand away and launched himself over the bomb and took the force of the blast. He saved my life.

When the shooting started I pulled away and they lost sight of our boat in the fog. The explosion ripped that casting platform apart and threw plywood chunks everywhere. Johann was gone and the terrorists got away."

Rad and Liv listened to the story of Yo's bravery, then Rad said, "Mo, I can't get Andre on the cell phone. Last time we talked, he told me he may be in secure locations at times, and that I must act on my own when required. Give me the rest of the snappers and the street sweeper, she meant the police issue shotgun, and I'll go after these people myself."

"One of my nephews might be able to help," Mo offered.

"No. I'm going to talk to the people at the academy as I head down there. They're soldiers. They can do war. I'm going to try the commandant then the OOD (officer of the day). Let's hope someone will act without orders going all the way up the line and back down," Rad added.

Before leaving the launch ramp in three separate vehicles, Rad and Mo's nephew towed the Smoker Craft into the main lake with the Grady and cut it adrift sure that it would sink. They put the Grady on its trailer, and Olivia and Mo headed for the hospital. Mo's nephew took off for Akwesasne in the reefer truck that carried Johann's remains, towing the Grady. Rad removed the Smoker Craft's trailer from the Caddy and left a note on it that said, "Free." Rad headed south.

When plunged into a difficult task, Rad was able to blunt her natural emotional reactions for a period of time. The longer that time was, the easier it was going to be to endure the wash of feeling that would eventually overtake her. For the first thirty miles she analyzed what was likely to be done by the terrorists.

They weren't going to boat through the Champlain Canal into the Hudson River, that would be too slow and they would be observed repeatedly. More likely they were going to get the boats out of the water, drive them around Albany, and re-launch them onto the river.

These fanatics were always interested in the big score and in their planning were eminently logical. It was their execution that was often slightly flawed. Rad smiled to herself. *Probably engineers,* she thought. *Always just a little bit off.*

The big score at West Point would fall on a football Saturday. The entire corps of cadets would be in one place as well as many distinguished alumni and guests. A nuke blown there would end the academy as it was and set back the officer corps of the US Army at least four years. Less than twenty-four hours 'til Saturday. What could Rad do? Could she even get someone to listen to her. There is a battalion of regular troops assigned to the academy with the duty of security and training. How could she reach the Officer of the Day?

Chapter 9

The Gulf of St. Lawrence: October 8th

John Talor, had spent the majority of his life out of doors or at sea. He would never have believed the level of comfort people with which some people lived. He wouldn't have been happy for long detached from the earth, sea, and sky. But he found himself in a situation on the night of October 8th where he would have been glad to be anywhere else.

The *Eastern Sun* turned out of the freshwater St. Lawrence River and into the salt sea of the Gulf of St. Lawrence. It set a course to the south-southeast. John planned to go outside Prince Edward Island, head into St. Georges Bay and travel through the Canso Strait between Cape Breton Island and Nova Scotia's main island and be in the Atlantic Ocean by Saturday.

Going around the corner of the Gaspe Peninsula, they would pass a succession of granite capes that marked North America's geological fortresses in the battle with the North Atlantic Ocean. John kept well out to sea, aware that the wind and tide would conspire to suck him toward shore. He planned to keep Cap de Rosiers ten miles to his right as he headed out of the waters of the province of Quebec. His co-pilots, David John and John Cook, were available to relieve him. One slept in the ready-room and one spent his time alternating between the lazy-bench in the pilothouse and watching the sea ahead. All three men having the name John had confused the boss, Sam, and he muttered under his breath, calling them John number one, two, or three.

Talor was watching the weather to the east. He began to chat with David. "You ever been to Gaspe, Quebec? No, eh? Beautiful spot. Has a huge cape protecting the harbor. Very unique. Dominated by a pierced rock. The hole in it was made by the sea eons ago. Little town below it called Perce. When the tide is low you can walk out there. You can stand in this hole and look at the true power of the sea that we're on right now."

David wondered why John Talor had just talked more than he had for the entire trip. He didn't ask outright, but looked at Talor with an attitude of inquiry. Talor raised his eyebrows and motioned with his head toward the east. David saw what was out there. The squall line of a half hour ago had become an immense black mountain of a cloud that loomed at them. Spray was tapping the window like buckshot.

The tapping was increasing as he watched.

"We got hell coming at us. Don't we?" David asked.

John nodded. "Soon we won't be able to see anything. We are going to be in trouble for as long as this blow lasts. Go down below and tell Sam and the guy's to get ready. I'm hoping to get us around Cap de Rosiers and into the harbor at Gaspe. Maybe we can ride it out there."

"We weren't supposed to leave the pilothouse or go down there. Boss'll be mad," David said. He glanced at Talor, judged the look in his eyes, and went out the pilothouse door, which slammed hard from the wind.

John Cook woke up in the ready room and came out scratching his belly beneath his gray undershirt. With sleepy eyes he looked around, The black-cloud mountain off to the left was curled around directly ahead. "Uh oh."

The sea and wind soon reached full storm proportions. If this wasn't a hurricane John Talor didn't know what was. The waves were bursting over the railings high enough to break over the lower pilothouse twenty-six feet above the deck. Spray slapped the upper pilothouse windows, forty-four feet above the deck. The pressure drop of the air made the men into barometers; they felt the drop in their internal organs. Turning head on into the gale, John hoped that this ship didn't want to die.

Through years of experience at sea, John had the quickness of eye, judgment, and nerve to take on this storm. He'd seen it coming. The continental high had battled the ocean storm to a standstill back to the north, but the farther southeast they had traveled, the more the ocean storm had advanced like an invading horde. He would have to face right into it, judge the tidal set against him, the hurricane winds he was facing, and the ability of his two 3200-horsepower diesels to offset these natural forces. He would be slip-sliding on his course by heading at a right angle to it. John's long and varied experience would be his only way to estimate his leeway and know where he was actually heading.

"Wish we could talk to the engine room. See how the pumps is doing." Cook said, not intending to add to John's worries but doing so anyway.

"I wonder if that crazy Indian made it to the boss's cabin? He might have washed overboard. For sure he won't be climbing back up here," John said.

"We got plenty of pumps, eh? They probably all workin' now." Cook was hopeful. John Talor considered hope to be a postponement of disappointment. As the pilot he had plenty to worry about.

When a boat is being rocked by the waves, any side-to-side movement is exaggerated by height. A roll of two feet at the waterline becomes so severe at forty-four feet above the deck that the people in the pilothouse would be unable to work even if strapped to their stations. Bucking into the tremendous surge, the boat's shape and design was its only protection against certain destruction.

It was clear to Talor that, if he could make it around Cap de Rosiers and Cap aux Ox and into the harbor at Gaspe, he'd be blown in backwards, losing way to the surge. He thought there might be reefs along there and wondered if the height of the surge would blow them over any reefs without taking out his bottom plates. She was a tough ship. Would she find a way?

◇◆◇

Dread upon the Waters

Pierced Rock at Gaspe, Quebec

Joe Gaspe and the Portable Nukes

For a long time, Amy had been aware of the tensions in her parent's marriage. They fought to a standstill about nothing and everything. Her dad never seemed to earn enough money. Her mom was unhappy with his trips away from home; she didn't always believe he was fishing. Now, in the midst of Amy's training in the dreaming, she was having vignettes interrupting her dreams involving her dad and a black- haired woman who seemed to control him as if he was a man on a string.

At the Rush mansion she was dreaming all the time: through the night, but also after each meal, and during mid-morning, and mid-afternoon. The lessons taught in evening lectures allowed her to dream independently as well as in structured workshop exercises. It was one of those independent daytime dreams about her dad that disturbed her now.

Amy saw her father at a picnic table pulling line off a fishing reel, yanking and grabbing and sweating. His face was red. His concentration was intense. He relaxed for a moment then went back at it again. Through an early morning fog, Amy saw a figure on the porch with an obvious womanly shape. The person had long black hair, worn loose and flowing. Amy heard her voice clear and true,. "Hey do you want some coffee?" Joe looked up, smiled, blew out a deep breath, and said, "Sure, great way to start a morning."

Amy was nudged awake by Molly seated next to her. She had an uneasy feeling the rest of the morning while trying to concentrate on her tasks in the workshop with Dr. Rush.

Chapter 10

Gaspe, Quebec: October 9th

The longer of the two ocean-going tugs was loaded and ready. Though rusty, the leaking plates had been welded, caulked, and covered with anti-fouling paint. The boat was dropped back into the river. A short trip through the locks and she would be steaming for an appointment with the pigs and monkeys in New York City.

The man who called himself the Mahdi was very satisfied: having limitless cash made the work of Allah more convenient. He had been able to buy the boatyard and the salvage company for no more money than the cost would have been for the two tugs. A brilliant attorney had facilitated everything. Now Mohammed Abdullah could sit in his retreat in rural Quebec and wait. The infidels were on alert, of that he was aware, but would they be able to thwart five separate attacks all across the State of New York? He doubted it. The brilliance of the strategy was in the likelihood that the first responders would be vulnerable, attempting rescue, when the second wave of strikes rained vengeance down on them. He had done well and he was sure that more great things were in his future.

The Mahdi walked down to the incinerator with the last load of papers that could be traced to him. The fire was roaring, making the air in the little first-floor shop smell sooty. When he opened the incinerator door a puff of smoke blew back before the draft consumed it. He dropped the files in. They caught fire immediately. He mentally

Dread upon the Waters

reviewed what was left on the desk upstairs; nothing of consequence there. He would lock the door, close and lock the gate, and leave this decrepit business forever. Perhaps the lawyer could sell off what was left before anyone traced the tugs back to here. If so, he would have some money left for expenses. If not, it would be the will of Allah. He pulled his Mazda through the gate, walked back and secured the padlock through the heavy chain, turned back to his vehicle, and was shot twice in the face by a .22 pistol. His assailant walked away, leaving the body where it was. The Mazda would idle until it ran out of gas. Since it was an economy car, with a full tank, that would take a long time.

Hundreds of miles ahead of the *Eastern Star*, despite being the more fit of the two ocean-going tugs, the *Eastern Sun*, was in trouble. John Talor was trying to make headway into the teeth of a storm that had turned its full fury against him. The pilot cursed his mother's Catholic God and called for his father's Aquinah spirits to show him the way through. Had he had a good set of radios and been listening, he could have pulled into Sept Iles back at the mouth of the St. Lawrence to wait out the blow that would eventually exhaust itself battering against the rock piled coast of the Laurentian Peninsula. The combination of that landfall and the strong continental high could stop the hurricane in a battle of winds that challenged any ship at sea. A boat less than two-hundred feet long, like the *Eastern Sun*, suffered in seas that were reaching toward eighty feet as the two powerful weather systems met in the Gulf of St. Lawrence.

John Talor had been trying to round the Gaspe Peninsula and past Prince Edward Island. He had hoped to skip the Northumberland Strait and slip through the Strait of Canso that separated the two large islands that formed the Province of Nova Scotia. He had to abandon that plan. John was consumed with the problem of trying to save the ship, his life, and the lives of his crew. Sam, the captain of the ship, didn't seem to care whether they made it around the corner or not. His attitude, that Allah was in control, irked John who felt the need to act

Joe Gaspe and the Portable Nukes

for himself as the instrument of God. Faced with imminent death, the spiritual Arab prepared to accept his heavenly reward while the spiritual American Indian–Portuguese crossbreed fought the heroic fight, as his nature told him he must.

John had a navigation chart that he tried to read in the blinking light of the pilothouse. It was dark because the combination of dense clouds and wind-blown spray made visibility zero. It was twilight at best and more often full dark when he looked out of the pilothouse window. All that John could see was a wall of water both when the boat was coming down the wave back and when the slashing horizontal rain hit the windshield as the boat climbed the wave crest. He had to deduce from dead reckoning where he should be. Since he had turned full into the oncoming seas, John did not figure that he'd been making much headway at all. He reckoned that he was slip-sliding to the southwest by keeping his heading directly east. If he was losing way to the westward, and he suspected that he was, despite the power of his massive diesel engines, then sometime after nightfall his back would be to the series of Capes that delineated the Gaspe Peninsula.

Cap des Rosiers, Cap aux Os, and Cap Gaspe were immense basalt battlements standing as testament to North America's defiance of the stormy Atlantic Ocean. John Talor had been here before and he knew that Cape Gaspe was the one he needed to reach. During times of good visibility he would look for the perch—the pierced rock abutment that showed the opening to the harbor at Gaspe, Quebec.

Nothing would be visible until the Nor'easter blew itself out. John had been at the wheel for twelve hours. He didn't have enough confidence in his co-pilots to relinquish his position. He had sent John Cook to check on the pumps. The pilothouse gauges showed three of the four pumps were not responding and the fourth appeared to be intermittent, at best. The boat had a list of at least ten degrees. This was hard to verify, since the boat never came back to upright status, before it was rolled again by a quartering, head-on, sea surge.

Despite his worry that Cook might have a confrontation with Sam, he needed to know what was happening below. John considered the captain to be, at heart, a primitive man who may succumb to the emotion of hate at any second, who was likely to kill any man who questioned his word, without thought or regret.

Dread upon the Waters

Cook had had to bull his way down to the engine room over the objections of the other crewmen. They, being volcanically seasick, objected to his going below but couldn't stop him.

Now he re-entered the upper pilothouse and reported to John Talor. "Three pumps conked out. One portable still working, but it is positioned so that it's sucking air on the starboard rolls."

"That's most of the time!" John shouted. "If it keeps sucking air it will burn out for sure. Can you get the black gang to move it deeper into the bilge?"

"There's nobody down there that speaks any language I know. They're Chinamen—its all singsong or shouting to me. Anyway, half of them are lying in their own puke."

"What about our leaders, the Muslims?"

"Down and out. The boss tried to stop me. Was gonna draw a pistol but when the next big roll came he fell against a bulkhead and became disoriented."

"You didn't help him along toward being disoriented did you?" Talor asked.

"Me? No." Cook affected a look of innocence.

Chief Warrant Officer Rhinelander was a guest on the Canadian Coast Guard patrol boat. He was there to observe. The usual resentment of Yanks, for being arrogant and bossy, was so obvious it was tangible. There were four people on board. The officers, one English and one French, were cordial and polite and made it clear that they despised each other. The two enlisted men, joking about their prickly officers, treated Rhinelander as an equal. Over tea and coffee they kept him informed of what was going on. The patrol boat had been going back and forth from Gananoque to Port Hope for days searching for they knew not what. This route contained a maze of islands and hundreds of private vessels. There was shore time in Kingston to provide a diversion from the boring routine of scanning the waters of Lake Ontario on one side and the forested shoreline on the other.

"Look for anything suspicious," they had been told. With nothing else to go on, everything was suspicious, and nothing was suspicious.

Chapter 11

Mullet Bay: October 9th

Marv had noticed a smile on Sherry's face, contrasting with her normal slight scowl. He assumed the worst, and thought to himself, *To the devil with Joe. Let him find out about his shop and home on his own. He's already got a woman, and now he's with the one I wanted to move on.* He went on like that in his mind, the way a man can, inventing all sorts of scenarios without evidence, not investigating any of them. Joe was working on the boat and gear with determination. Marv assumed that this meant he was avoiding conversation. Sherry was polite and friendly, but what did that smirk mean? Marv was troubled, but he moved ahead, positioning the van and trailer for towing the boat to the Niagara River.

When Joe went back into the cabin to make one last sweep and lock up, Marv sniped at Sherry, "So, you two have a good time while I was gone?"

"We fished and patrolled mostly but we did get one set of Lunds taken care of."

"Nothing else? No late night sessions?" Marv leaned forward when he made this remark.

"Oh, that's what you think? Didn't happen. We went fishing and we patrolled. Joe done his job, didn't he?"

"I don't know. You tell me."

Dread upon the Waters

"Look, I stayed in the cabin. He slept on the porch. Even through the walls of the camp I could hear him snoring. And did you ever smell his feet? Whew! They would disgust any woman. We talked about our pasts and the mission, but he never touched me."

Marv didn't want to let go of his exquisite grudge.

"Marv, stop whining. It doesn't look good on you."

Marv began fishtailing and back-pedaling. "Well, I didn't mean nothin'. I just never know about Joe. Fat and smelly he may be, but the ladies go for him —"

"And leave you behind, right?" Sherry had his number. "Well I ain't 'the ladies', got it?"

"Yep,." Marv said. "Sorry…"

Joe had hidden Wes's keys just then and walked up to the side of the van. "Let's get on the road. I wanna hear what you guys have done, then I've got some pretty bad news," Marv said.

Detective Belinsky was sure that these were outsiders, not locals, who had murdered Marv's mother and brother. She believed the Russian émigré when he said that the intruders had been speaking Russian and had just mowed down the son when he had opened the door and that the mother was inside the entryway. What the detective couldn't find was any reason for gangsters to commit this violent an attack on this woman and her slightly-off son. Sure, the boy had been in a few minor scrapes with the law, but he was a nobody, still living at home well into his thirties. Why would he attract the murderous attention of Russian criminals? Not for any reason that she'd had been able to uncover. Belinsky didn't suspect Marv Ankara, but she was angry that he had left town rather than remain and be available like his grieving sister, Tricia Why had he done this?

Leaving the sister's apartment, Belinsky thought over the content of this, her third, interview with Tricia. She didn't know where Marv had gone, nor did she find it unusual that he'd left town unannounced.

Joe Gaspe and the Portable Nukes

"I'm his sister, not his mother. He goes and comes when he wants and rarely informs me about it."

"Don't you find it unusual that he just took off and left you to grieve, arrange the funerals, and all that?'".

"I've got, er had, two brothers in a German household. To say that they are emotionally distant is like saying an elephant is a big animal. Whenever something was upsetting, they went off and did something. Worked on a big job, went hunting or fishing; something to spend their energy on so they won't have to think about their feelings. When Dad died Marv went on a fishing trip to Wisconsin; made me wait ten days to have the funeral. It's the same this time. It's what Marv does."

"Okay, I'll accept this explanation, or at least your comfort with it, but don't you wonder why this awful thing happened to your family?"

"Of course I wonder! But I know *Marv* didn't kill them."

"What about this best friend of his, Joe Gaspe?"

"What about Joe? He's a big knucklehead, but he didn't shoot my mom. He loved her. She used to feed him—since they were kids—and Joe's stomach does his decision making for him." Trish paused, "You aren't considering them suspects, are you?"

"We are investigating several leads and interviewing people of interest. Do you know of any enemies Marv had? Any from out of state?"

"Marv's had boyhood scrapes. The usual stuff: broken windows, trespassing to go fishing, pot once or twice, but he's had no sworn enemies around Muskiedaigua."

Detective Belinsky had a uniformed officer with her. They sat on Tricia's conversational grouping, their coffee untouched, no one felt comfortable.

"Your brother, he ever been out of state? New Jersey perhaps?" the uniformed officer spoke for the first time.

"I don't track his movements. Never to New Jersey that I know of, but yeah, he had a girlfriend from Cincinnati for a time."

"Did he get in trouble with someone down that way? A jealous boyfriend or something?" The cop was talking and the detective watching and listening.

Dread upon the Waters

"No it was an amicable break-up. Marv learned long ago that if you catch 'em in a bar, you'll lose 'em in a bar."

"So when was the last time he was in Ohio, that you know about?"

A change of expression passed over Trish's face for a fraction of a second. It told the detective everything.

The detective chimed in, "What? What happened in Cincinnati?"

Trish realized finally the reason for her mother and brother's murders. Silently, she cursed Joe Gaspe. Though she knew that Marv willingly followed Joe, she had found a person to blame. She looked at the cop, glanced over at the detective, and said, "I need more coffee."

Trish walked over to the kitchen stove and busied herself at the coffee pot. Each side needed a time out. Trish needed to compose her answer and the police needed to get on the same page.

The cop whispered, "The car had Jersey plates, How'd we get to Ohio?'

The detective said in a barely perceptible whisper, "This is the first lead we've gotten. Let's see where it goes."

Trish returned to the sofa resolved to come clean. "This past summer, Marv and Joe and some others rescued a local girl from captivity at a strip joint in Kentucky, just outside Cincinnati. They had some scrapes with gangsters getting her out of there. Marv never said anything too specific about the rescue, but he did mention Russians."

"Joe? That would be Joe Gaspe, your brother's friend?"

"Yeah."

"And the others? Do you know them?"

"I do not. But I know who the rescued girl is, though I don't think she lives here in Coleman anymore. Randi Deschutes. She's just a few years out of high school. She looked at Marv as a combination hero and father figure. Marv's ideas were in another direction, so they broke off contact shortly after she got back to her mother's family. Her mother and new stepfather took her with them when they moved away. To Florida maybe, I don't know."

The cops went over everything two more times with questions that were slightly altered. They eventually left with the questioning of Randi Deschutes on their to-do list.

Chapter 12

Central Adirondacks: October 9th

There were at least a dozen Mohawk dreamers at Ruland Rush's fall workshops. Most were women and all were older than Amelia Gaspe. Mr. Rush, however, paid significant attention to Amy. More so than others, who were seen in groups, Amy garnered individual consultations—always with her Aunt Molly present as a partner and chaperone, because Rush knew that Amy was the more powerful dreamer and more amenable to development. It was unclear whether he had been told this, had dreamed it, or had deduced it on his own. After the second day, Rush devoted one afternoon session each day to dreaming with Amy.

He had seen Amy warn her family of the arson attack, and he had become aware of the attempt she was making to warn off her distant cousins from completing their attack on Fort Drum.

They were in the winter parlor, a room with a paneled cherry ceiling, on the dark north side of the mansion. The room had a huge soapstone stove overlaid with painted tiles. There was a small fire chirping away, and Molly sat outside the door to keep the dreamers from being disturbed. Lying on foam pads, listening to soft drumming music on a portable CD player, Amy and Ruland Rush placed their hands on a photo of a young Mohawk man and exhaled a relaxing breath. The photo showed Mo's cousin Mikey on his four-wheeler,

Dread upon the Waters

rifle strapped across his back, smiling broadly. Someone had taken a Sharpie and written "The Deer Hunter," across the photo.

"Let's see what we can do," Rush said.

Amy's slow deep breaths transported her right into a hilly landscape. Moving on a Quad runner, she saw white clouds ahead obscuring things until she was right upon them. She saw a road sign that outlined a four-wheeler and the universal "watch for" crossing sign. She stopped at an intersection. The dust/cloud/mist kept swirling while she squinted at a road signpost with no name indicated in either direction. She turned and saw three more four-wheelers waiting for her to move on. She went straight ahead. The road was not maintained and was lightly traveled. Amy became aware that in addition to the fog, it was night. They traveled with only the lead quad-runner using its lights; the others followed her lead.

Going too fast across the field, a rare patch of flat, firm ground made them speed up. The lead quad, a Mohawk driving, jihadi behind, didn't see the rusting, hulking abandoned tractor dead ahead until it could not be missed. With a clanking metal-twisting crash the driver was flipped over into the machine that was parked where it had stopped running in the dead center of the field like a lawn ornament. His back broke with a sound like a tree branch snapping under a snow load. The jihadi was thrown across the front of the tractor, his right arm ripped from its socket as it was chopped between quad and tractor. He landed on his back beyond the tractor, bleeding out.

The Real People rushed up, looked at their tribal brother, and knew he was dead. They began to chant a death song but were silenced right away by drawn automatics of the jihadis. No lights came on in nearby buildings because no one had heard the crash on the deserted farm.

The man in charge walked up, looked down at the smashed four-wheeler and trailer and said, "Inshallah (In God's will)." He slit the throat of the bleeding Arab man. That vehicle and its two riders were just abandoned. The Mohawks noted the location hoping to return for their tribal member. In her dream, Amy was now a follower, without headlights, and they proceeded in another direction, with a new lead vehicle. All was white fog surrounded by blackness as she passed a road sign for Lead Mine Road leading back to her left. More swirling whiteness. Another road sign. Ore Bed Road. Keep following. Another sign. They

Joe Gaspe and the Portable Nukes

were stopped again. This sign indicated Oxbow Road in both directions. The leader looked at his portable GPS.and said, "This way," then turned left. The swirling white fog closed around her again. Amy looked back at her trailer. The object in her trailer, which looked like a portable generator, showed a gleaming tiny green light.

The next thing she saw was the leader pointing down a rutted dirt road that looked like a narrow driveway. He said, "Morning comes. We must wait down here until tonight." On they went.

Cell phones are funny things, sometimes they don't work at opposite ends of a building and sometimes they'll skip across several states without a problem. When CWO Rhinelander called Marv's phone from Ontario, the phone didn't realize that it was roaming in a foreign country. It was picking up the signal from a tower in the US and connected easily with the phone in the Boston Whaler on the Niagara Bar.

"Is this Gaspe? Joe Gaspe?"

"No, this is his partner. He's right here." Turning to Joe, Marv said, "Hey Big Boy you got a call on *my* phone."

Joe gave Marv an annoyed look, took the phone and said, "Yep."

"Gaspe? Rhinelander here. We met through Tom Andre, remember?"

"I remember."

"Andre told me to keep you informed about these Lunds we're both looking for. Well, they've been dodging in and out of Ontario along the north shore. We can't catch them. When they duck into Canadian waters, we head out to intercept, and they slip over into American waters. Later, when we've moved off, they are back in Canada again. They must have a GPS with a chip that shows the border."

"Well, duh."

"Anyway, they are making steady progress to the westward. The target of the power plants at Niagara appears to be a good guess. I gotta go, one of the officers is looking at me. Rhinelander out."

Dread upon the Waters

"That was a brilliant grasp of the obvious," Joe said to Marv who had raised a questioning eyebrow. "The game is on."

"What'll we do now?"

"Well, we don't have any food so we can't eat. Might as well keep on trolling." Marv swung the boat into an L turn.

Chapter 13

Plattsburgh, New York: October 10th

Olivia Shanio had seen seven marriages firsthand, four each for her mom and dad. In each one she'd seen the same mistakes and she'd sworn never to make those errors herself. Only now did she realize how hard it was to resist the temptation to change your man. He would never change, just get his back up and resist unto death At the same time, a woman had to know when her husband needed her to tell him what to do. What, despite his protests, he really wanted to do. When he had let his virility run wild; he was too stubborn to go to see the doctor, wanted to smite what he thought was an evildoer, or he was ready to put himself at undue risk… When for instance, the right action involved protecting his loved ones or achieving heroic status in their eyes.

Liv was in a quandary. Mo was going to leave the hospital. He insisted that he had to rush down to the Hudson River to assist Rad. This amounted to all three of those cases where a man had to be forced back: doctor's orders and unacceptable risk, up against an overweening heroic vision of himself. But, Mo was going whether Liv refused to help or not. Because it was early in the marriage, and because of Mo actually being a darned heroic man, Liv saw this as an exception to her self-imposed vow to not interfere like her mother had.

What the heck, she thought to herself as she draped a jacket over his shoulder. "Let's cut a trail." She said.

Dread upon the Waters

The removal of the giant splinter from Mo's left forearm, shoulder, and back had been done with only local anesthetic and under the calm direction of Mo. The inexperienced doctor had never handled a wound caused by an arrow, his experience was limited to relatively clean gunshots.

"The blood will start when you pull this stuff out of the holes. The forearm will be easy—just get the slivers and bits out, disinfect, and bandage it. The shoulder and back will have clothing imbedded—dig all that stuff out, along with the wood and splinters, douse it with antiseptic and plug both ends. I'll be all right."

Doctors don't take instruction from patients. However, this was the first time that this young physician had been spoken to by a patient as authoritative as Moses X Snow. He took the advice.

"Saw off both ends as close to the skin as you can while still leaving enough to get a Vise-Grips on the tag end. I've been wounded by arrows twice before." Neither the doctor nor the two nurses doubted Mo when he said this. The doctor did as Mo said and for the pulling part he got the help of a stout male nurse. "Pull, you guys. I'm not going to cry."

After the four holes of his wounds had been cleaned out, the nurses had painted him with two coats of purple antibiotic liquid and wrapped his chest and shoulder, pinning his bandaged arm to his chest. Mo had said to Liv, "Stay with me, my dear, while I have a wolf nap. Then we will go to help Radleigh."

"We'll what!" Olivia was going to say more but Mo's wolf nap was already underway.

"I dreamed badly again last night. Usually that only happens when I've had too much rum." Using the Mohawk appellation for all types of alcoholic beverages was a signal to the others to be circumspect about their discussions. Each morning had started off like this. No matter how little progress they had made during the night, when they were hunkered down to wait out the day, the three remaining people of the longhouse would huddle around each other. Mostly they

Joe Gaspe and the Portable Nukes

smoked and didn't speak, just sat near each other, and got as much rest as they could for the daylight hours. The three Muslims huddled at the other end of the clearing. They smoked and talked. Often several talked at once. Long after the Indians had gotten comfortable and settled down to sleep, the jihadis jabbered away discussing something.

The two groups had been traveling together for several days, traveling by quad runners at night and waiting out the daylight in rock-strewn mountains, abandoned farms, or dismal swamps. They had been unable to wash; most of what they ate was contaminated with a slick gray clinging slime that covered everything. They had become slathered in the ooze while trying to get two four-wheelers out of a sinkhole on the first night. Nothing tasted good or even seemed to fill their stomachs. An easy run to the Fort Drum Reservation, a run that should have taken five or six hours, had become an odyssey of wandering back and forth lost in fields, mines, roads, and forests, all abandoned by humans years before.

The Mohawks were losing faith. Troubled by their dreams and unable to explain their own poor choices, they were depressed, defeated and looking for an opportunity to give up the job they'd been hired to complete. First, only one of them had been troubled by his dreams. Then, as he began to relate what was bothering him, the others claimed that they too had the same troubling images.

Igor Nesterenko decided that it was time to leave Muskedaigua. He had no respect for the American police; thought them weak and ineffective, knew they were hamstrung by ridiculous rules and procedures, and considering he'd been in the US for ten years and committed many crimes, he laughed about being unknown to them.

Igor and his European-Russian friend Oleg were on the screened-in porch smoking and drinking tea. It was early. The others, Asiatic Russians, were sleeping in the cottage they had rented for a week at off-season rates. Those contemptible Asiatics had been a problem all along for Igor. The group had been warned by Jimmy Maxwell that they were to leave as little trace as possible of their passing.

Dread upon the Waters

Jimmy had instructed the group, "Move from place to place, and never stay long enough to draw attention. Speak only English when others are present, don't make a mess, get drunk, go to clubs, or do anything to cause you to get noticed." Igor knew well what happened to people who crossed the boss. They disappeared, often by Igor's hand.

Everyone had said, "Yes, boss." But now Iggie was sick of trying to keep the four Asiatics in line. They wanted to smoke in the cottage even though the list of rules left by the landlady had said to do it outside or on the porch where the two Russians now sat. They had sat in the front yard and spoken in their language instead of the back yard where they would have been unobserved.

"Like training a dog, those four. Constant corrections needed. Bah!" Igor stood up and stretched. He pulled on his Ohio State Buckeyes sweatshirt tucked his Mauser into the back of his waistband and said, "Clean up the dishes. I'll wake those ones and we'll head back to Columbus."

Oleg didn't mind taking orders from Igor but wondered aloud why he always did the dishes. Igor ignored him and moved toward the stairs to the sleeping rooms.

"I've got an idea. Let's tell the boss we got them both. We shot up one, the ugly one, and the other, the fat one, went up in the house fire. Then we can get back to the routine," Oleg said.

Igor turned and stared at the man. "Don't say more. Don't cross the boss. Don't ever lie to the boss. We'll tell him we tried. Tell him we scared these guys. But I will admit that we got neither one. He'll know what to do next. Don't worry. He won't make you disappear. Unless you lie. If you lie to Jimmy Maxwell, you will be dead within a week. He will find out and replace you. There are many replacements." He waved his arm at the stairs. "These four are replacements, easily available."

Joe Gaspe and the Portable Nukes

Agent Thomas Andre had worked within one bureaucracy or another most of his professional life. He was good at it. But the bureaucracy of the Department of Homeland Security, because it was the largest, was the most Byzantine and impenetrable he had ever encountered. He could get nowhere through channels and had begun to work the back way around to get the help he was sure that he needed.

His Mohawk contacts had told him that two ocean-going tugboats had been equipped with huge nuclear warheads—stolen former Soviet bombs. They were aimed at New York City. He had deduced that the targets were the UN General Assembly building and the Statue of Liberty. It didn't really matter what they were trying to hit, if the terrorists set off these bombs anywhere near Manhattan it would be a national disaster. The financial capital of the United States would be done—uninhabitable. Andre's one surviving informant in the Pantherville Yemeni community also confirmed New York as the target. That fellow had told him once that they would come down through Long Island Sound where it narrowed down to nothing, and another time that they would come out around Long Island and into the main harbor. Andre had to guess which scenario to believe.

He needed both the Coast Guard and the navy to help him but he knew that there was no time to go up the chain of command and get permission. Routine patrols were always taking place but he had arranged for special "training" exercises where he could get his RF detectors onto specific ships with a specific mission.

Andre knew the chances to get approval for increased surveillance of the harbor of New York would be approved. He also knew it would take too long to get approval, probably be leaked to *The New York Times*, this was the city after all, and ultimately the failure to prevent the attack would be blamed on those who actually tried to do the preventing. He had been finding another way since he began this job and he had an idea now. There were people he knew in the Coast Guard and in the Blue Water Navy. It was just a matter of getting them to do the unexpected. Perhaps the looming Nor'easter would provide his chance.

Chapter 14

Niagara River: October 10th

Marv had been waiting for the right moment to tell Joe about events in Muskedaigua, including the murders of his own mother and brother, waited to tell him about being on the lam himself. He was still waiting to tell Joe that his house had been burned down, his family displaced, his possessions gone. The right moment hadn't arrived.

They were trolling the Niagara Bar where the waters of the lower Niagara River fan out into Lake Ontario. This was salmon water and the dead-enders, those who wouldn't admit that the season was past, were still trolling at the close of the active season. The salmon, Chinooks and Cohoes, were hard to locate when the fall season matured. Hard-core trollers had been pulling them in for the two previous months and their arms were sore. The lake turned over, the thermocline disappeared, and off-shore fishing became difficult. A period of stream and tributary fishing had begun and the winter bite—consisting mainly of two trout species, steelhead and browns, was a few months off. Still, there were enough bitter enders out there that Joe was driving.

A musky troller usually goes faster than a salmon troller, sometimes much faster. Sherry had been driving when they had run up too close behind a fully rigged Salmon boat. This had resulted in shouting, rude hand gestures, and unfriendly radio messages. Joe and

Dread upon the Waters

Marv had done what they always did when confronted by aggressive drivers. They had waved and shouted to the other boat as if they were long lost friends or relatives. This usually confused the angry driver and defused the anger. Joe had slammed the Whaler into neutral over Sherry's shoulder and they had brought in their setups and, after a few minutes, had restarted their troll, heading up the river toward Devil's Hole and the rapids above the power plant discharges.

With Joe driving and Sherry watching the rods, Marv decided to tell Joe what had happened at home. He had kept everything to himself when he picked up the two at Whiskey Nose Wes's camp, loaded the boat and trailer, and driven south and west the three hours to the eastern end of Lake Ontario. Joe had asked, as they drove past the Muskedaigua exit, "How's everything at home? Why were you summoned back? Your mom's health okay, or is that wacky brother of yours in trouble again?"

Marv, who'd been behind the wheel of the van right where he wanted to be, mumbled something that Joe took to be, "I'll tell you later." And concentrated on his driving.

Sherry, who'd set her cap for Marv—a little bit—and expected him to spark her on his return, had wondered why he was being aloof. She was taking it personally, even though she knew better. When she raised an eyebrow to Joe he'd shrugged. *Maybe he thinks Joe and I have been busy in the intervening days*, she'd thought. Marv had said nothing, but Joe knew his partner. He knew something was wrong and was prepared to wait for the shoe to drop.

Now as Joe was headed for a troll up along Peggy's Eddy, Marv spoke up. "The cops are going to be after me if I go back to Coleman."

"What did you do, get a DUI?" Marv wasn't much of a drinker but that made him susceptible to poor judgment if he did drink.

"I'm being investigated for suspicion of a felony."

"What felony?"

Joe was turned around in the driver's seat. He looked at Marv who stood amidships while Sherry, who'd been watching the rods pulsing at the back of the boat turned and looked.

Marv hesitated, looked from one to the other, and blurted out, "Those cops in Coleman think I murdered my mom and brother.

Joe Gaspe and the Portable Nukes

They were shot execution style from the hallway to their apartment while we were on the Larry. They don't think much of me fishing, or you as an alibi. So I'm not supposed to leave town."

Joe's mouth was open but he knew of nothing to say. Sherry gave a little shriek and moved to Marv's side touching his left upper arm. "Oh my God," She said and stepped in front of Marv, hugging him.

Joe finally spoke. "They're dead? Murdered?"

Marv face dissolved, he'd been holding back a flood of tears. He nodded his head and held Sherry close, her black hair cascading down from her head pressed into his chest.

"There's more, Joe. Katy and the kids are okay. They got away in time. But your house is gone. Burned up. They got away. They're with her sister in Manchester. It was those Russians. They've found us and they killed my mom and burned you out."

Joe was speechless Then he held out his hand and said. "Gimme that phone, you jerk. I gotta talk to my wife."

"Before you do, there's one more thing."

"What?"

"You know that nosy neighbor of yours, where you used to live? Gus?'

"Yeah, what about him?"

"He called my sister, and he said there'd been an incident at your old house. A carload of heavy-hitters showed up and they were going to take out that brother you sold your house to. They realized at the last minute that it wasn't your family and left. They were driving one of those gold-colored Volvos. New Jersey plates."

"Those SOBs are hunting my family and you didn't tell me!" Joe stared daggers at Marv. He still had a hand out for the phone. Sherry, who'd disengaged from Marv, took over the driving, steering around a down-bound boat. The fishing rods thrummed. No one spoke.

"One more thing," Marv added. "That old Russian living on mom's floor, he told the cops he heard the shooters talking Russian, said they discussed getting the 'ugly one' and the 'fat one.' This is revenge for Ohio. Ya know?"

"Gimme the phone. I'm calling Katy, then I'm calling Andre."

Marv handed it over.

Dread upon the Waters

The quads were traveling only at night. There were no lights. Homes were either vacation cabins intermittently occupied, abandoned farms broken down and spooky, or, rarely, an isolated year-round farm where the occupants went to bed with the chickens. There were no commercial buildings with lights blazing all night. Any factories were deserted or moribund. The mines were out of business. No one ran a gas station or a convenience store anywhere near the area that they had been traveling through. Roads often went nowhere. Large tracts of the interior of northern New York State are alternately swamps and mountains. For days it had seemed to this caravan of quad runners that the only way to get out of a swamp was to go up a mountain.

They started out with eight four-wheelers ready to take a short run ideally at two separate points over a few hills to penetrate the Fort Drum Reservation, ideally at two separate points, and cause nuclear devastation to the hated 10th Mountain Division. The 10th was the despised lead unit in the destruction of the mountain fastness of Sheikh bin Laden. The raiders were down to five four-wheelers, and the scouts, the trusting natives of this country, were lost. Though the Iroquois had been kept away from alcohol, to the jihadis they seemed drunk and confused, often going one way and backtracking to try another.

"There's a river over that way, and the bridges along here are mostly gone. Nobody used them so they just fell down."

The man driving the lead ATV had a map and with a headlamp he was looking at. The map was covered in the same transparent gray slime of mud that coated everything and everyone. Mixed with a near constant drizzle, frozen overnight into an icy goo, this mud was in their eyes, ears, and mouths; it coated all their clothes and stank like a swamp. Earlier this evening, they had all had to fight to get one ATV out of a tarry sinkhole so foul that some of them had vomited. That vehicle was stuck so fast that with two ATVs towing and everyone pushing—even the jihadis, who seemed to feel they were too good for physical work—they still needed two hours to extrude the vehicle from the sucking ooze.

Joe Gaspe and the Portable Nukes

Each day while they rested in the woods the jihadis removed the canvas cover from the cargo and attempted to clean the machines underneath. Meanwhile the Iroquois tried to rest, yet whenever they could snatch a moment to themselves, they would talk about their dreams. They were spooked because all of them were having nearly the same dream each night: a dream of fog and dust, as confusing and white as their nights were black.

Looking up with his headlamp, the man with the map pointed and said, "Go see what that road sign shows."

Returning to the group after shining a flashlight on the sign, the man explained, "We're at Lead Mine Road and some other road—no name."

"No Lead Mine Road on this map here," Said the first man, his headlamp illuminating left, then right.

The man walked a short way down an intersecting road to view another sign.

The three surviving Arabs stood to the side, watching and speaking a language none of the Iroquois could understand. The third Iroquois watched them deliberately, letting them know that he had his tribe's back.

"You're not gonna believe what that sign says," Said the scout who'd gone in search of Lead Mine Road. "It shows a picture of a snowmobile and says 'watch for' above it. Watch for snowmobiles. What the hell?"

"Well, Tom, I might be able to do something for you here," the vice admiral was smiling as he picked at his Waldorf salad.

"Not for me. For the security of our country." Andre felt himself getting hot.

"Relax, just relax. I'm on your side. and I've figured out a way to solve the orders problem." The Naval Officer laid down his fork, took a sip of water, and continued. "The weather brewing in the western ocean, a whopper of a Nor'easter, will be just the excuse we need to get a frigate into the sound."

Dread upon the Waters

"It is also an opportunity for my people to do some search and rescue of our own." The Coast Guard officer said. "Weather events like this one entail an increased need to patrol proactively. There will surely be rescue missions."

The two gentlemen were in the Howard's Rock Country Club dining room that was glowing in brilliant October sunshine that belied the coming weather. "Were you fellows talking before I got here?" Andre looked from one to the other. Both nodded.

"Sure and it seems that an Aegis cruiser battle group out of Norfolk has a planned exercise. They have added a missile frigate that might just get blown off course." the Coast Guard man answered for the navy. He was smiling.

"And the weather brewing means a Coast Guard Cutter from North Carolina is heading north right now to be in position off of Rhode Island, just in case," the Navy man said. "One never knows what might happen in a big storm. Why don't you give me one of your RF detectors and I'll pass it on to one of my technical experts that spent some time in Israel, he'll be able to improve the range. He'll get it up to five miles or more. Then I'll have two made, give one to Ralph here, and we'll be able to do what needs to be done."

Andre had always known that there was a way around the glacial pace and impediments of the bureaucratic system if a fellow could find right-thinking people. He had not suspected that it would be this easy this time. Of course, to get anything done, one had to know people. Andre knew some good ones.

Chapter 15

Gaspe, Quebec: October 10th

This was the third call of the day to his superior officer in the Surete du Quebec, the Provincial Bureau of Investigation. Jacques Kilkenny might call his boss twice a year under normal circumstances. Today was the biggest day of his career. What had started out as an unusual example of an ocean rescue had become a multiple-murder investigation with new twists every few hours. The conversation, in French, was accompanied by gestures and multiple facial expressions. There was silence on the other end because the boss didn't know what to make of the events either. While Jacques welcomed the excitement, in a way, he also dreaded the impending interference that was sure to come.

A renegade ocean-going tug, *Eastern Sun*, had tied up to the public pier in Gaspe Quebec during a three-day Nor'easter and subsequently sunk. When the big blow ended and the continental high began pushing the clouds out to the east, the water level at the pier dropped from a depth of ten meters to half that. The lowering water level revealed that the ocean-going tugboat had been stove-in all along the port side and was leaning against the pier with only its uppermost works above normal water levels. There was no master or crewmember around to claim the boat. No one had arrived in town, and no float plan had been filed. The harbormaster had been in communication with no potential arrivals at the dock.

Dread upon the Waters

The weather brought by the nor'easter had been so severe that the dock had been engulfed in a sideways driving, slashing torrential rain for the previous thirty hours. No one in town had gone out. Last night the gale had reached its zenith, and somehow during that gale-force blow, *Eastern Sun,* had made it through and tied up. From where it had come, no one knew. A dog walker notified Jacques, who was the town's policeman/safety officer/justice of the peace/dog warden/harbor patrolman. Then the morbid discoveries had begun.

The Gaudette brothers, Rene and Pierre, had been called and their ocean rescue tug, *Faucon,* had been at work for hours using huge bags of compressed air to slowly lift *Eastern Sun* off the seabed. Meanwhile, they had transferred two pumps off their vessel to begin pumping water out of the derelict. Two electric cables had been run along the dock to engage *Eastern Sun's* own pumps as soon as they could be fetched from the water. Four water cannons were shooting streams twenty centimeters in diameter out of the derelict. To the observer, the pumps appeared to be refilling the harbor, since their work coincided with the tide returning the water level closer to normal. Two air compressors and four pumps set up a tremendous racket. Each new discovery brought whatever man had made the grisly find right up to Jacques, to shout into his ear.

The first find was of two men locked in a death grip, one with a machete and one with a hatchet, tangled in the companionway on the way up to the wheelhouse. They appeared to have murdered each other. As the boat continued to lift off the seabed, another man was found who had been shot in the back of the head with a bullet big enough to blow his face off. In the engine room, three Asian gentlemen, each wearing every layer of clothing he could pile on, had been executed with a small caliber weapon. They appeared to have submitted without a struggle.

Mass murder was new to Jacques Kilkenny. He had enlisted all his helpers and local government members to control the crowd of onlookers, who wanted to surge along the pier, to continue searching *Eastern Sun* and wait for the next revelation.

The discovery of the first two murder victims had meant that a car from the nearest station containing detectives, with two senior investigators, had begun driving the five hundred miles to the very edge of Quebec for the required follow-up. The discovery of another victim had meant that a small plane was being chartered to bring a team of crime scene people from Quebec City to comb the wreck. The dead Asians would bring more technicians and policeman to the scene. Since it appeared the deaths had taken place at sea and that *Eastern Sun* was a rogue boat, the Canadian Coast Guard Service had arrived on the scene. Watching the crew of *Faucon* work, they were prepared to claim, then protect, their piece of administrative turf.

Jacques stood at a lectern that his assistant Marie had found somewhere, and talked on a landline phone whose cord trailed out along the pier from the harbormaster's office. A hand-held police radio was resting on the slanted top of the podium. His laptop computer was tied into a phone line to receive e-mails as well. Just after hanging up with his boss, a man came up to Jacques and was joined by a distant cousin of his the driver for the local bakery.

"This fellow just stopped my truck down the road about ten kilometers. He took me back down a country lane and showed me a dead man slumped in the ditch. Shot in the head, executed,." his cousin shouted above the noise.

"How far away?"

"About seven kilometers, or so."

"Oh great, another murder in my jurisdiction. Can you go back there and wait for someone to come along and take possession of the scene?"

"OK, my deliveries are done."

"Thank you, cousin. Give Marie all the information that you can about the location and get the contact information for the witness. I'd give you a radio, but I don't believe the range is good enough to reach over there. It may be awhile."

"Do I get paid?"

"OK, you are deputized as of now until you are relieved."

Jacques picked up his phone again. Seven corpses now; this was becoming too complicated. Just as he was about to punch the redial button, his seventeen-year-old nephew walked up. The boy, Georges, had been one of those searching the wreck. Before Georges could

Dread upon the Waters

speak he was shouldered aside by a wiry little Newfoundlander, Red Dwarkus, who was the first mate for the Gaudette brothers. This Irishman asked in English instead of French, "You got a Geiger counter around here anywhere?"

Switching seamlessly from French to English, Kilkenny asked, "What do you want that for?"

The Newfy looked all around, turned to Kilkenny and said, "There's a suspicious piece of equipment aboard. Nothing to do with ships and the sea. It just came out of the water. Hold has been pumped out, you know. Green blinking lights, appears to be a timer chugging along. Looks to me like Russian writing on the crate."

"You read Russian?"

"No. But I was detained there for four months during the Cold War days. I have seen their writing a lot."

"Why a Geiger counter?"

"Unless I miss my guess, we've got a portable nuke under the main hatch of that tug over there. And it seems to be armed."

Jacques Kilkenny felt as if his head were about to explode.

After several moments, Kilkenny recovered his composure enough to say, "Actually there are some counters left over from that abandoned uranium mine. "Georges," he turned to his nephew and said in French, "can you go down to the storage area under the library and dig one of them up? They'll need batteries too." He turned back to Dwarkus and was about to speak when Georges grabbed his sleeve.

"Uncle Jacques, listen to me. We have a live person on the boat."

"Why didn't you say? Bring him to me."

"I can't. He is dead drunk, cannot stand or speak, but he is alive. A drunken Indian."

Jacques stared at his nephew, then at the sailor. He put down the phone. The tug floated beside the dock. Two of the pumps were no longer underwater and their rattling shut down. The noise from the two pumps on *Eastern Sun* and the big compressors still filled the air with vibration.

Kilkenny took off his cap and ran both hands over his thinning hair with his eyes closed. He motioned to Marie who had just finished sending his deputized cousin back to the body in the woods. She walked over to the podium.

Joe Gaspe and the Portable Nukes

"Watch these phones. Answer only those people you can identify by name or title. Facts only, no speculation. I've got to go look around up there." He pointed over his shoulder at the tugboat and gave her a knowing look. Her return look combined the, you-can-trust-me look with the what-do-you-think-I-am-stupid? look.

Kilkenny took the two men he'd been talking to off to one side.

"Georges, forget the Geiger counter. You get the drunken man off the boat and into the harbormaster's office. Carry him if you have to. Red, you help Georges and get another guy if you need one. Not a word to anyone about nukes, you understand?" He was switching languages as he talked to the two men and wasn't sure what each understood of the other's language. "I'm going to look through that boat."

Fifteen minutes later, Jacques knew that his problems had multiplied exponentially. Profiling as he went, he scoured the boat from top to bottom. The drunk man had been peeled out of a life-raft storage locker still firmly gripping an empty bottle of Old Bushmills. He had to be manhandled down the companionway by three men to get him off the boat. He had been in the flying bridge wheelhouse, which had remained out of the water when the bottom of the boat rested on the sea floor.

Kilkenny noticed that none these six men were white Canadians, even though he knew of almost no non-white sailors in any waters in this part of Canada. He had the bodies of three Asians—he guessed Chinese—one native Americans—judging by facial features, hairstyle, and dress, and what he would guess to be an Islamic person—he had a Koran, written in what looked Kilkenny guessed to be Arabic in a bag around his neck. The dead man who had been executed with the large-caliber weapon was unidentifiable but dress suggested another Native American.

As Jacques descended levels in the derelict, he was unsettled by the lack of all the items one would expect. No charts, no shipping papers, the GPS unit had been ripped or cut out and carried away. There were no safety items, rafts, flares, ring buoys, survival suits, life jackets. All missing. In the galley there was almost no food. What there was was all chickpeas, canned chicken, and rice. None of the usual tinned beef or pork. No hams, no canned fish. Little food with no variety.

Dread upon the Waters

Then in the first level above the cable hold there sat a blinking, green-lighted monster. It consisted of two machined aluminum housings that looked like portable generators on frames that were designed to mate with air-actuated clamping devices. One part was about one-meter long with receptacles for four posts and a central cavity. The other part was a half-meter long with posts to match the other's holes. The whole item was designed to slide together on a rail system. The two parts were held apart by wooden dunnage blocks. A sledgehammer leaned nearby, obviously intended to knock the blocks out from between the two parts.

Kilkenny thought Red was right. This boat was a floating bomb that he deduced was not meant for Gaspe Quebec. Probably not meant for any place in Canada. Jacques guessed Boston or New York or Washington. He climbed to the deck and jumped down onto the pier. He almost landed in the arms of the commander of the Coast Guard vessel.

"Constable, I am authorized by the Federal Government of Canada to take possession of this vessel and proceed with the investigation of the circumstance of its appearance in the waters of our country."

"Sure. You want it, you got it." The commander had three of his men with him. They had stern expressions and carried side arms. They were poised for action. This was all for effect and Jacques knew it. "Can we talk over here?" He gestured down the pier a few feet.

"All right." The officer walked a few steps with him.

"This is big. Everything about this boat is wrong. There are multiple crimes that have been committed. But the biggest thing is, there is a nuclear device on this boat. You can check it with your instruments, but I'd say that it is a recycled Russian bomb on its way somewhere. I am sure this is not its final destination. I will hand the boat off to you. But I'll be asking for instructions from my superiors."

The Commander stared at Kilkenny without saying a word.

Joe Gaspe and the Portable Nukes

Agent Andre had three high-security cell phones and was sometimes amazed that he could remember which ringtone belonged with which. He had a Homeland Security phone, an FBI phone, and most secure of all was a Special Projects phone. It was the special projects phone ringing with Beethoven's Fifth Symphony that he answered now.

Without explanation the caller began, "Kirwin here, we'll have both approaches covered as long as the problem of the Nor'easter presents an opportunity."

"Good enough. Keep me informed. If there is a 'kill' I want to be in on it." Andre smiled to himself.

"Roger. Kirwin out."

There is a coffee shop near where the Niagara River empties into Lake Ontario at which the charter captains discuss everything. Joe, Marv, and Sherry had dropped in for some early morning cheer when Joe saw a familiar face enter the door. He'd been wondering where everyone was and had concluded, hopefully, that they were all out fishing. He was soon to be disappointed. "The lake turned over; nobody's fishing now until the winter steelhead bite picks up. There'll be lakers all winter, too." Captain D'Onofrio was responding to Joe's question about the absence of all the charter captains.

"So there's almost no one out there now, huh?"

"No one around the bar. There're some duck hunters out and one or two musky fishermen but they are in the lower river. Nobody around the bar."

"I was hoping there would be some extra pairs of eyes out there. Oh well."

"People do the maintenance and winterizing of their boats this time of the season. Plus, there's deer hunting, both bow and muzzle loader. Guys are otherwise occupied. Why? Whatcha looking for?"

"Nothin'. I was just curious." At that Captain D'Onofrio headed for a table occupied by a lady friend of his.

Joe turned to those at his table and said, "Might as well eat." He tucked into a menu item called the Farmer's Breakfast. Sherry watched

Dread upon the Waters

him pile it on with a mixture of admiration and disgust. Joe looked up, saw her eying him and said, "Don't want to get a chill out there." He swallowed a mouthful of pancakes then laughed out loud.

Later, after launching their boat on the river, Joe, Marv, and Sherry went out again to troll back and forth across the mouth of the river where it empties into Lake Ontario. They were short-lining using big, bigger, and biggest musky baits. This was an unheard of pattern that no one who Joe knew of had tried because they didn't have any confidence that it would work.

"We've got to be ready to move on a moment's notice. So we'll just short-line here anyway." Joe said, though no one had asked. Back and forth they trolled, waiting.

Olivia Shanio was driving and using the cell phone at the same time. She was breaking the law. Repeatedly. She'd called Radleigh Loonch twice. She'd called Mo's cousin twice. She'd called Agent Thomas Andre—no luck. Now she was calling in a marker. Being from the southern half of the United States, Olivia knew many people in that gun-toting, NASCAR-loving, warrior culture. She had a younger sister whom she'd introduced to the man the sister would eventually marry. That man had an older half-brother who was the full-bird colonel of the brigade assigned to the point, West Point that is: The United States Military Academy.

Colonel Grady Charbonneau, from Covington, Louisiana, had had a brilliant career that earned him the prestigious job of being in charge of the brigade that ran the military post at West Point. Charbonneau's brigade was not involved in the academic aspects of the school; they were involved in warrior training..

Mr. Colonel Grady, as Olivia called him, owed her one. When she was a drug-rehab counselor in New Orleans, she had semi-rescued and straightened out his much younger stepbrother, George Luke. That intervention had started George on a path that eventually led to him marrying Liv's sister. It was at the wedding reception that Colonel Charbonneau told Olivia, "If you ever need anything, anything at all,

Joe Gaspe and the Portable Nukes

call me. I owe you big time." Olivia was on the phone trying to call in that favor.

Colonel Charbonneau had many ceremonial duties however, and he was attending to one of those preceding the Saturday football game. He could not hear the ringtone on his cell phone. Speeches were taking place. Bands were playing. The wind was blowing. Carbonneau would have to call her back. Olivia drove on.

Olivia was in one of Mo's reefer trucks driving like a madwoman to meet one of her husband's cousins who was holding a boat on the Hudson River ready to attempt an intercept of the last two suspect Lunds. They had eluded Mo and Johann and were going to detonate a portable nuclear device designed to take out the Academy at West Point, the entire Corps of Cadets, many visiting dignitaries, and everyone in attendance at the Army versus Colgate game on Homecoming Weekend. The successful execution of the jihadi's mission would be one fourth of the devastating assault planned on New York State for this October weekend. That was the one thing Olivia could do something about.

Radleigh Loonch stumbled as she crossed the threshold into Gino's Diner in Vail's Gate, New York. She sighed heavily as she sat at the counter. Bleary eyed, she looked at the man behind the counter of the empty restaurant.

"You look done up. Coffee?"

"Yes, please. Snow, fog, rain, sleet, dark of night—I'm tired of all that." Rad tried a weak smile. It turned out to be a grimace.

"You got that thousand-yard stare of one who's been in battle. I'm Zeke, you want breakfast?"

"Er, I don't know. Let me drink a cup first. Got any milk?" Zeke looked at the creamer on the counter then turned around and lifted a carton of lowfat out of the cooler and set it on the counter. Rad sloshed a little coffee into her saucer then doused the coffee with milk, drank a draught and poured more milk and the coffee from the saucer back into the cup. In spite of her tiredness she didn't spill a drop.

Dread upon the Waters

"Not a battle but at least a skirmish," she said.

Zeke stood in front of her with a USMC flag behind him and some 8x10 framed photos from Nam on the wall. He raised an eyebrow that seemed to say, "Tell me more."

Rad noticed the pinched feeling in her stomach. She ordered a lumberjack's breakfast and told this stranger what was going on. She spilled her mission to the diner owner and asked, "You know anyone trustworthy and brave I can get to help me? From what I read on the map, I need to stop these guys in Storm King Park. Never been there, don't have time to explore."

"The top of that mountain will be in the clouds all day. To reach the water's edge you'll have to slide down a slick granite cliffside. There's an old Chessie road, CSX now, at the bottom. Excuse me," he said, turning toward the back of the restaurant. "Jimmy, get up!"

He looked at Rad and continued, "I got a guy here, a river rat. Jimmy can help. He's a good boy. Got a little substance problem but he knows plenty of good Americans in Highland Falls ready to step up. When it comes to that section of the river, he's been hunting and fishing it all his life. The boy can survive and he ain't slack."

Rad and Zeke planned with Jimmy Raymond, a tall, slender, gristle-tough, young man with a face lined by outdoor living and hard wear, for over an hour with the only interruptions being a few early morning hunters served breakfast before heading into the woods. Once he was apprized of the situation, Jimmy knew exactly where the enemy would rendezvous and how they would approach the Academy. The plan they developed would require efforts from all three. Zeke would work the phones to the county sheriff and the Highland Falls Police Department, Both those entities would have their hands full on a day when Army played a home football game, but Zeke had a few people he knew and would try to alert. Jimmy would put Radleigh in place to intercept the attack and move down river below the Academy, near the Bear Mountain Bridge, in order to deter any escape or rescue of jihadis if they succeeded in their attack and emerged on the other side of West Point. Jimmy had some friends to help him down there. His relationship with local authorities was too problematic for him to participate with Rad in the interdiction.

Joe Gaspe and the Portable Nukes

"It's my job and also my pleasure to take these guys out. I owe them." Those were Rad's final words on the subject.

Jimmy had known the exact spot where the enemy would be able to unload the two parts of the nuke from boats to quad runners. "There's a bunch of old pilings in the water that were used when they built the tracks down there and a built up little landing area where they staged the rails and ties and stuff. They'll be able to get the Lunds in close and load the nukes onto quads and run right down the tracks to West Point. My guess is they plan to blow this thing right before the tunnel that goes under the Academy. A blast in the tunnel would destroy the school, but just outside will maximize the radiational effect. They are terrorists and radiation will cause terror, so that makes sense. Runnin' those quads down the railroad tracks will wreck the suspension on them, but I don't expect they care about that."

Jimmy showed Rad where to pull her Caddy off on a turnout in Storm King State Park. It was a local dumping spot for old appliances and such that were rolled down a ravine. Just to the south of the ravine, she scrabbled down the hill to find a position where she could intercept the vehicles that would be carrying the bomb parts.

Rad had located a good spot down near the CSX tracks that she'd reached by going down the almost vertical granite mountain of Storm King State Park. She was working her cell phone trying to get through to someone, anyone, who could help. Olivia had given her Mr. Colonel Grady's cell phone number. Rad had tried to get in touch with Agent Andre. He had his own problems dealing with the largest of the attacks headed for New York City. He was unreachable aboard a U.S Navy frigate, the USS *Troy*. Only Liv and Rad could stop the terrorists headed for the Academy.

Moses X Snow slept fitfully in the bouncing truck, a full-sized Chevy one-ton. Mo was recovering from his drugged state after discharging himself from the hospital in Plattsburgh. His shoulder wrapped and arm in a sling, he would be of limited use to Liv. Mo was on the mission because he insisted upon it.

Dread upon the Waters

Olivia hoped to catch up to the bombers while they were still in their boats and use the remaining supply of long-snappers to sink at least one of the Lunds. Liv was not confident she assumed the terrorists would have enough firepower to stop them from getting close. Liv was afraid to die, but she went on. She was not as good a driver as Rad because hadn't been as well instructed, hadn't practiced, but she was doing all right, had avoided all the Saturday morning patrols and skidded the truck into the boat launch ramp in record time. They were just a few miles north of West Point at the Yacht Club at Cornwall-on-the-Hudson. David Snow, Mo's cousin, was there waiting.

During the drive Mo spoke to calm his wife's nerves. "I'd be surprised if any of the Native People are still alive. There is nothing these followers of the Mahdi offer except the sword. We are fighting a spiritual enemy. They don't want anything but death: death for our people, death for themselves. They get to paradise by killing infidels and apostates. We can only save ourselves by converting to their religion. You'd think that what they want to do to women, gays, Jews, Christians, even many Muslims would cause everyone to be against them, but, as you know, there are many who think they can make peace with the Islamists. They can't." Mo was resting, chatting with Olivia while they awaited Rad's call that she had reached a favorable position. Liv had left messages with Mr. Colonel Grady's assistant and she waited for a return call. She was listening closely, leaning forward, squinting in the fog. Liv knew that Moses Snow was not a big talker. When he decided to speak, it was important to him and deserved attention.

"The reason we can be so effective in the fight against a spiritual enemy is that, as Mohawks, we also are a spiritual foe. Those of us who understand our culture know that we are going to be alive in the Real World forever.

"Like us the jihadis are emotional without being dramatic. They don't suffer from being reflective about life. They react to life." He turned to face his wife. "You come from a culture that thinks it has overcome that and left it behind. But mass movements still appeal to your people. Americans seem to have a need to believe in something even when that something is outlandish. Maybe you're not as advanced as you'd like to be. But Mohawks and Islamists are the same in this regard. Closer to life. More dynamic. More fatalistic. More ready to act."

"So, these young men who have already been killed...?" Liv asked for clarification.

"Some of them, maybe most. Some will never awaken in the Real World; they have never accepted their Mohawk spiritual side. They have been dead in this world and will be so in the next. They suffer under the delusion that, if they help the jihadists achieve something, they will be taken care of. When they let their guard down, thinking that the goal is reached, they will be dispatched to heaven. There is always urgency with those people."

Olivia's cell phone squeaked once. She had a text message.

The terrorists were not so foolish as to alert the Academy security. Coming in on four-wheelers from a conveniently absent neighbor's property they could approach the school along the CSX tracks before they could be stopped. The CSX freight trains came past Cornwall every hour on the hour. Getting on the tracks just after a train passed, the jihadis had fifty-five minutes to make their play.

Rad was convinced that she could stop them by herself. She had found her hidey-hole at a higher elevation just off the tracks, and she waited as the dreary daylight increased. She had her cell phone on vibrate. She had her snappers laid out before her on a flat granite ledge. She had a cigar burning-she idly puffed it occasionally to keep it going as a punk. She had a police-issue shotgun, a street sweeper, loaded and ready, and a second gun, her Sig-Sauer, holstered on her hip. She looked at her phone in the lessening fog. There was one problem-no cell phone service. She had calls in to Agent Andre, Olivia Shanio, Mr. Colonel Grady, and the officer of the day of the brigade at West Point, but no one could reach her. Beneath an overhanging ledge, she had her best chance to interdict the enemy but she was alone. She breathed deeply, steeled her nerves, and waited.

Dread upon the Waters

Radleigh Loonch was tired. She'd waited under duress for Mo and Johann to return from their mission. She'd endured the disaster of Yo's death and Mo's wounding. She'd lovingly bathed Johann's body and laid him to rest. With all that pressing on her, she'd taken off on a furious ride to the Point to warn of and try to prevent an imminent attack. She'd dialed and waited and called everyone she thought could help. She'd succumbed to delay and obfuscation from bureaucrats and operators. She'd been under severe tension for twenty hours. Now, in position—somehow she was sure she was in the right place—she had to wait to spring a trap. She had to stay alert. She had to be ready. She tried to shrug the knots out of her shoulders. She examined her gear once again with tired bleary eyes. Overcome by weariness, her head slumped onto her chest and she fell asleep.

Mo Snow was tired. He had been wounded, repaired, and stitched up. He had been drugged—intravenously—he'd hidden the oral drugs under his tongue and rejected them when the nurse left the room—he had had a long day. He'd lost blood. Despite the bumpy ride and Olivia's combination of shouted phone conversations and shouted road rage curses, as soon as he and Liv had launched the boat into the Hudson River he'd fallen asleep.

Radleigh Loonch understood about the dreaming of the Mohawks. She respected their belief in the dreaming, but she'd never been able to do it. She'd tried, instructed by Joe Gaspe, inspired by the great dreamer Moses X Snow, but she'd always come up empty. She was either unable to dream with power or she was unable to remember such dreams upon waking. She'd given up. Nodding off in the cool morning mist under her hoodie with a CBP ball cap keeping the dripping of condensed fog off of her face, she saw the riverside.

Along the gray, calm, gently lapping shore there was a snipe probing the water's edge. It looked all ways, probed with its beak, and looked up, repeating the procedure while searching a small sandy bay for food. Suddenly, the snipe saw a huge shadow overhead. The great blue heron had landed and stood, neck curled, on a nearby rock. The snipe is too small to challenge the heron and usually runs on to another section when the heron comes hunting for fish. The two birds eat different things, but still, the snipe shies from the larger bird.

This time the snipe didn't move. Rad recognized herself as the bird she'd been observing. She lifted her head and eyes to the heron and heard the familiar voice of Mo Snow.

"We cannot reach you in the shadow world. We are on our way but may be too late. You are on your own until help from above arrives. Be strong, stay out of the line of fire. Use what you've got. We are coming to help."

A trilling woke Rad from her dream. Thinking it was her cell phone, She looked down at a blank screen. There was no signal. She shook her head and said, "A snipe?" Rad shook her head again and said quietly to herself, "Mohawk e-mail from Mo. Honor the dream." Adjusting her position in order to keep the hard rocks of the spot from digging too deeply into her rear end, she thought over the most recent short dream She remembered everything for a change.

Rad heard the sound again., This was no dream, nor was it her phone. She half stood and peered over some wild rhododendrons to the track bed of the railroad just below. There, smoking cigarettes, were two men on four-wheelers with trailers. One was talking on the phone. He spoke what she recognized from her training to be Arabic. Rad ducked back behind the bushes and listened. Both men had been looking down the bank toward the river. They had neither seen nor suspected her presence. The phone conversation ended. One man spoke to the other. They started their engines and turned down the flat area toward the riverbank. Rad tried some relaxation techniques to calm her nerves. The crisis was coming. It was coming her way and it would be here soon.

Having awakened from her wolf nap, Rad was surprised to feel completely alert, given how little rest she had gotten. Wondering in her few idle moments over the last day, why she wasn't devastated emotionally by the death of Johann. Indulgently, she beat herself up

Dread upon the Waters

over her lack of feeling. This was the way she had seen her father work out emotional shocks. Get busy, do something to exhaust yourself, keep your mind on something else. Eventually, the emotional shock will come but, the longer it is delayed, the less it will take over your ability to function. But, Rad wasn't cold and austere, like her father, she was open and ready for emotion. It just didn't come to her. Sure, she'd immediately gotten on the road with a mission and a job to perform, but here she was in position, ready to act, and had a moment to reflect, while she waited for the bad guys down below her to get started. Yet, she sat in a little mental box, tormented, on edge, but not about Johann's death or revenge. Her nervousness was like that experienced before a test, limited to a desire to get on with it and start the action. She sent a text to Liv advising her that the action was about to start and that for mission silence she was turning off her phone. Her last line was, "I'm ready but I could use some cavalry."

Mo knew he'd entered Rad's dream but not if he'd gotten her attention. He saw it all now. The egret and the heron arrived at the shore. They stood on the shore as the coyotes, four in a pack, headed up the bank. Tails high, they disappeared into the brush. They were far ahead, moving with a steady loping gait. Mo and Liv would not catch them.

Mo's head came up. "Olivia we are going to be too late." Liv was looking at him. She had the phone to one ear and a finger stuck in the other trying to hear over the sounds of the boat's outboard motor.

"Wait a minute. Mr. Colonel Grady's phone is ringing. I think it has been forwarded to somebody."

Chapter 16

Eastern North America: October 12th

The re-floated tug at the pier in Cape Gaspe, Quebec had been inspected and re-inspected by numerous sets of authorities. Each succeeding set had priority over the last and had banned their inferiors from returning to the investigation. The Canadian Coast Guard had walled off the Quebec authorities who had walled off the local authorities. Everyone wanted to be in charge, but no one knew what to do.

They had a suitcase nuke—obviously much larger than a suitcase but a transportable nuke none-the-less. They had a drunken Indian in custody. He was not a Native American from Canada but a half Aquinah-half Portuguese from Martha's Vineyard, Massachusetts. That was all they had gotten from him so far. He did not seem to be the brains behind the operation. The leaders appeared to have escaped in the storm. A body found in a nearby quarry pointed toward a hijacked vehicle. An all-points bulletin was out for someone. The scarcity of roads in this part of rural Quebec should make a stranger easy to intercept but it had not happened yet. No one knew what to do, so everyone kicked the ball upstairs. It would probably be the prime minister who would make a decision, but when?

Despite the consistent efforts of its government to prevent it, Canadians still lived as a free people. They went where they wanted

Dread upon the Waters

and they spoke to whom they wanted. In addition, many were in touch with people from the United States through kinship, friendship, marriage, and business. The news of the nuke in Gaspe escaped the government's efforts to suppress the news. The backwards tug sitting on the bottom next to the city pier was big news in little Gaspe, Quebec. Even bigger news was the rumor that it carried a nuke targeted at the USA.

The rumor was in Lowell, Massachusetts within the hour. An unofficial report was circulating through the Canadian Coast Guard within two hours. At almost the same moment, CWO Rhinelander heard the first tentative report and Theresa Andre, Thomas Andre's sister-in-law heard the news. A nuke with a USA address on its ship-to file had been sidelined in Quebec. Andre's assistant at Homeland Security took the call from Rhinelander with Theresa's call in the queue waiting to be picked up. Special Agent in Charge Thomas Andre was hard to reach on the USS *Troy* but his assistant could reach him, and did so.

College football as played by teams like Army and Colgate was not the thinly disguised professional operation that it was at the major football powers. It still entailed pageantry, however, and attracted the powerful and well-heeled alumni. It was the source of innumerable wagers large and small. Colgate alums, being the products of wealthy households, more often than not, were quite different from West Point graduates and the political orientation of the two schools alumni's were polar opposites.

It was a good-natured rivalry overlaid with a subtle contempt for each other between the two alumni groups. Foremost among the beliefs of the Colgate alums, was that Army was a team that they could beat and they were usually correct in this belief. Army, a football power in the 1940s, could not point to a successful season for many years and was on several school's schedules because it represented an easy win.

Chapter 17

Gulf of St. Lawrence

No one in North America knew how close the continent was to disaster. Agent Thomas Andre knew a lot, but he was too busy to contemplate the totality of the big picture. There might have been a mastermind in the mountains of Afghanistan who knew the enormity of the impending catastrophe, but he might be buried under that mountain or he might have lost control of his movement in factional infighting. The President of the United States didn't know that one of the most important and populous states was about to be wiped off the map. The Governor of New York didn't know that his personal fiefdom was about to collapse. Andre was aware of only three sets of coiled fangs on a five-headed hydra poised to strike the second most populated state.

The on-the-ground logistics planner of the five attacks was dead. His handlers, who were also his murderers, were waiting to see what would happen. Joe Gaspe and Moses Snow knew that they each were tasked with halting or diminishing one attack. They had a dream intimation that Amy Gaspe was aware of one other strike. But, they did not know of the oversize nuke on the tugboat chugging toward New York City. They had their minds occupied with oncoming challenges of their own.

Dread upon the Waters

Amy, inheritor of the dreaming power of Island Woman, by influencing the dreams of the involved Indians, was near exhaustion from combating the overland assault on Fort Drum. Her tremendous power in the "Real World" of dreams allowed her to know at the edges of her mind that more attacks were underway. She only sensed the foreboding of the other attacks; she did not know the details of any but the one she was concentrating on. Someday, when she fully realized her power, when she and her spirit guide "The Old One" were always synchronous, she might know all that was to happen, but today she only could work out the totality of one troublesome attack.

In Long Island Sound, the younger brother of the first tugboat pilot, James Talor, was at the wheel for his second sixteen-hour shift in the last forty hours. He was not alone. The boss of the trip, Mohammed, was standing behind him, scowling, saying nothing, occasionally looking at the compass. Coming down the Sound, heading toward the west, with the sun rising behind him, James thought he saw a break in the clouds about ten miles ahead. He sighed, knowing that that cloud line was the far edge of the storm he'd been pounding through for two days. Since turning to the west he'd had the rollers behind him. Though still rough, the seas were easier going now.

On the Hudson River the two remaining Lunds had traveled through the gloom of a foggy morning. They were tied up to pilings, near the crusader's military school. They had met with the two quad runners driven by brothers who were pure of heart. They awaited the Hy-Rail truck, a vehicle with an extra set of interchangeable wheels fitted to railroad tracks, that would carry the device. The quads and the Hy-Rail, which was stolen railroad property, had been concealed at the riverfront estate of a rich investment banker a few miles north at 9 Howard Place in Cornwall-on-the-Hudson. The pilot of the lead boat,

Joe Gaspe and the Portable Nukes

Ali, marveled at how willingly Americans would abandon their best interests to further an ideological goal. They were foolish. Ali's only regret was that he would not have the pleasure of personally beheading the infidel dog whose property he had used.

To the northwest there was a stolen rental van, moving west, away from the rising sun toward Syracuse, New York. It was crammed with a TATP fertilizer bomb headed for the recruiting office of the Tenth Mountain Division. The driver, Maqmoud, consulted his Mapquest printout and glanced at his GPS. Where was he supposed to get off the Thruway, then wind his way through the city streets on a sleepy Saturday morning? The building he sought was in the university district but he wasn't sure where. He hadn't had the benefit of a practice run.

Near Gouverneur, New York the three remaining four-wheelers were sitting outside an abandoned talc mine. The dreary, gloomy, dark weather continued for a fourth day. The three terrorists woke up covered in a white powdery substance. They had been abandoned when their guides had slipped away in the night. They were determined to go on but only one ATV started and that quickly sputtered out. The air cleaners were completely clogged with talc and none of the men of pure faith knew enough mechanics to even begin repairs.

On Lake Ontario, in Canadian waters, two Lunds bobbed with their loads waiting for the meeting with the workboat. They were on the correct GPS coordinates off the mouth of the Niagara River. The combination barge/tug was to meet them and offload their cargo. It would proceed upriver to Devil's Hole for the attack that would disable the power plant discharges of both the American and

Dread upon the Waters

Canadian electrical generating stations. In the drismal gray drizzle, the people in the boats, ten feet apart, could see each other and nothing else. All the occupants were praying. They were seasick, tired, sore, and smelly but they were ready to die for the jihad.

Andre had to be somewhere during the last hours of the Nor'easter. He would be either on the frigate, USS *Troy*, or on the Coast Guard Cutter. His first assistant would take the other position. Either place entailed rough seas, high levels of tension, and limited response options caused by the severe weather.

It now appeared that Andre had guessed correctly. There was an unidentified radar image on the frigate's screen that could be the boat that they were searching for. All the legitimate boats—and there were mighty few of them in this weather—had been identified and eliminated from the kind of attention a modern naval vessel can concentrate on a target. The weather was still rough enough to ground any Sea King helicopters that could be used. The frigate was in a blocking position and two rubber boats, each containing a four-man US Navy Seal squad of commandos, were ready to execute a double envelopment when the forward progress of the ocean-going tug was stopped. Andre, Commodore Donnelly, and the ship's captain all stood in the wheelhouse while the captain quietly and expertly allowed his officer's to command his ship. They were about thirty nautical miles away from the tug that was closing inon the metropolitan area. The suspect vessel appeared to be unconcerned or unaware of the danger it was steaming toward.

Outside the Sound, in rougher water, the Coast Guard Cutter saw nothing on its screens. Far to the south, there was a sailboat in distress having turned turtle during the night. Other Coast Guard assets from Virginia were concerned with the rescue effort there. To the east, the New England waters were still foaming with powerful swells and appeared empty of vessels of interest to the patrolling cutter.

Andre waited and watched with nothing to do. The Naval officers conferred in quiet voices as they executed their orders. They knew, or thought they knew, that the target was the New York City area. They thought that, until confronted with certain failure, the terrorists would refrain from premature detonation of the bomb. It was that period of time, when the attackers became convinced that they could get no closer, that worried everyone. Would they detonate in the center of the sound? That was a scenario with less immediate loss of life but huge radiological dangers, as suburbs on both sides of Long Island Sound—heavily populated areas—would be compromised for years to come.

The Navy Seals were tasked to swoop in as soon as the tug's progress was slowed and kill or capture the adversaries before they could begin the sequence of events that would make the jihadis' mission a success. Andre was confident in the plan, but plans in war fall apart as soon as the battle starts. He had supreme confidence in the initiative and decision-making ability of average Americans, even more so in the exemplary persons of Navy Seals, but still there was always Murphy's Law.

Andre walked to the starboard side of the wheelhouse and looked into the heavy weather to the east. The sun had lightened the clouds but there was still the odd lightning flash as the pressure front of the continental high and the Atlantic low clashed. The Nor'easter had been stalled and was slowly retreating but still Andre worried.

"Hey, you guys seen an old dog wandering around here? He'd be looking lost." Paul Joshua addressed the three Native Americans who were walking in a group. The morning sky grew lighter though still dismal and gray. He held an empty retractable leash in his right hand and was dressed for a walk in rough country following a rain. He wore calf-high rubber boots, ballistic brush-buster chaps, and an open rain jacket over a flannel shirt. His cap said, USS *Buffalo* on the front and featured the gold braid of an officer on the brim. He smiled as he closed with the three men.

"Hey, where you guys been? Over in the tailings from the talc mine I'd bet." He looked them up and down, covered with white dust as they were.

Dread upon the Waters

"What kind of a dog is it, eh?"

"An old sheltie, Shetland Sheep Dog—some call it a miniature collie. He's a good old boy but he's got doggie Alzheimer's, I think. I got my rain jacket stuck on some old wire. While I was untangling it, he wandered ahead quite a ways. I called to him when he was just about gone out of sight around a bend, then he took off running away from me. He heard me but couldn't tell where my voice was coming from. Hate to lose him—best old dog I've ever had."

The local man was looking the three Natives over as he said this. They were not from the local area, they were on foot, they seemed nervous. He wondered.

"I had a girlfriend with a Sheltie, eh? Loyal as hell those dogs. Suspicious, but once they accepted you, you were ok, eh?" said William Greenblanket, one of the Iroquois.

"You boys are from Canada. Huh?"

William nodded his head. "Actually we've got a big problem. You know how to get hold of a cop? Or somebody over at the army base?" He jerked his thumb to the west where he thought the Fort Drum Reservation might be.

"Not many cops around here. This area's patrolled by the state. The county sheriff is my cousin. He's over in Theresa." Joshua looked at his watch. "Having his Sesame Bagel with Cream Cheese at Helene's diner right about now. As for the fort, lots of folks around here work over there for the division, you know. What's up?"

"We need to get word to security over there," William pointed toward the Fort again. "There's bad guys, Arab terrorists, out there and they've got stuff to attack that fort. Bad stuff."

Paul Joshua fished a cell phone out of his pocket as he looked questioningly at William and the others.

"We slipped away in the night, wanted no part of what they are going to do," William added

"Don't know if I can get any reception here. It's spotty in the hills and non-existent around the lead mine." Joshua pointed to the north. "Let me call my wife. She works for the Command Sergeant Major. He'll know what to do."

Joe Gaspe and the Portable Nukes

He got a signal, punched in a number, waited a few seconds, and said, "Margie, it's me. Can I talk to Del? Yeah I know he's busy. Okay. Okay" He waited a second his right index finger in the air. "Hey Del, how you doin'?

"Yeah, Del, I'm out near the Gouverneur mine. You know, the talc mine. I've got some guys here and one of them needs to talk to someone in authority. Yeah, yeah, I know. But we all know who's really in charge. Talk to this guy, okay? William Greenblanket's his name. Yeah, a Native American. Here you go."

It took a few run-throughs by William before the Command Sergeant Major was sure this was a legitimate call but he had people in motion before he'd even started to sort out the Indian's story. Helicopters were scrambled. Patrols were augmented in the Northeast sector, the one nearest the old talc mine, the division was tasked with additional security patrols and the boss, commandant of the division, was informed through channels. The commandant, knowing whom he could trust with initiative, approved all the moves the sergeant had made.

With his cell signal still strong, Paul Joshua called his cousin, the county sheriff, and asked that he meet them where they were.

Chapter 18

Orange County: October 12th

One of the Point's neighbors was a rich New York City money-man. Actually, that would describe many of the Academy's neighbors. The population of Orange County had flipped in twenty years from hardscrabble independent businessmen, farmers, and their families over to outsiders who had made such god-awful quantities of money that they could dabble. First, they dabbled in real estate—buying all the waterfront property except a few estates that remained in ancestral hands. Then, they bought all the properties with a view of the water, usually knocking down the old house, some going back two hundred and fifty years, and building starter mansions of twenty or more rooms to house a man, wife, and one or two children.

After consuming the prime real estate, which they considered too cheap to pass up, they dabbled in local politics and activism. These were people who had made enough money to get what they wanted and what they wanted was for things to be done their way. One of the first things on the activist's agenda was repeal of the Right-to-Farm Law. It seems that one trophy wife of an investment banker had gotten stuck behind a slow moving farm tractor and was "overcome" by diesel exhaust. Then her car was stopped by a construction delay near a pig lot where she found the smells unbearable. Soon, the political powers repealed the Right-to-Farm Law, and the prime acreage was taxed as if

Dread upon the Waters

it were ripe for development into five- and ten-acre executive estates. Concurrent with that, the sound of woodcutters in the Saturday morning forests was upsetting to some, and moves were made that turned them and their satanic mills into locally unattractive land users (LULU). In fact, noise ordinances were pushed through that targeted any noisy activities before noon. These had a chilling effect on hunting, motorcycles, ATVs, tractors, and any other thing deemed to disturb the pastoral quietude of the countryside.

It was just a matter of time before the Academy at West Point, instead of being a unique part of a proud community, was thought to be an embarrassment peopled by cretins, southern rednecks, and NASCAR types. The area's representative to the US Congress was on record as despising the military and all military types. The firmly supportive local populace had been forced, through law and economics, to move off the water into more rural counties where common Americans were still allowed to live their messy lives.

It had been easy for the jihadis, through their network of community college teachers, to find one of the Academy's near neighbors and arrange to use their land to hide two quads and the stolen Hy-Rail while they waited to meet their deadly cargo.

The property in Cornwall-on-the-Hudson had once been a restoration business where sand blasting and painting of dump trucks, propane tanks, and various pieces of municipal and military equipment had taken place. With the gentrification of the neighborhood, that business had became a LULU; eventually harassment by lawyers for the rich neighbors had forced out the sand blaster and a wealthy couple, investment bankers to the stars, had bought the property. They were in Cabo. Their gate was locked. Anything happening on their property would be classified as unauthorized use.

Two quads sat waiting on the flats just to the west of the pilings when the two boats that had eluded Johann and Mo pulled up. Four men were required to lift the packages into the flatbed trailers attached to the four-wheelers. With their cargo on board, the ATVs headed up the bank one hundred feet to the railroad tracks for lifting onto the Hy-Rail that would enable them to penetrate the Academy's perimeter.

Joe Gaspe and the Portable Nukes

Joe wasn't confident that they would find what they were looking for. The boats RF signals weren't moving and they were right next to each other. Like two boats rafted together for a social event, they didn't move apart and they barely shifted on the wind. The fog was thick, the wind was dead calm, and the waves had died to nothing as the morning wore on. Joe was sure that they'd find two empty boats and he didn't have any idea what he could do when that eventuality obtained. He cautioned Marv not to go too fast as the limited visibility would cause the object of the search to loom quickly out of the fog. He stood looking at his RF detector. Sherry, the one with the best vision, peered ahead in an active search pattern. Joe kept his right arm in front of Marv, straight out, to be raised if more speed was needed or dropped if he wanted Marv to slow the boat.

"Something's up ahead to port. I hear it cutting the water," Sherry spoke in a conversational tone. Joe looked at the RF detector and lowered his arm slowly. Marv eased back on the throttle.

"Five thousandths, slightly left." Joe dropped his right arm to his side and Marv dropped the lever back into neutral.

"There they are. A little to the left." Sherry pointed as she said this. Marv bumped the throttle back into forward and slid up to the two Lunds tied together, drifting, and empty.

Joe reached out and grabbed a gunwale. He fastened a line to a nearby cleat and prepared to climb aboard the floating derelicts.

"Careful, partner. These guys could have booby trapped them boats." Joe heard this and looked over the boat's interiors. They looked empty except for some garbage laying in the bottom. Joe hesitated, then climbed over the gunwale.

"I need to get an idea where they went, if I can."

Joe hunted around in lockers and checked the bilges of both Lunds. Sherry and Marv waited. She stood with her gentle hand resting on his shoulder. He sat waiting for Joe to be done, motors idling. Marv was restive as if ready to speak. Sherry squeezed his shoulder as if to say, "Wait a minute."

Dread upon the Waters

Joe looked up from the second Lund. "Nothin' here but scrapes. The cargo is gone. Even the tarps. There must be another boat. One we don't have any bug on. We'll go up the river 'cause we know where they are going."

"That's what I'm saying." Sherry gave Marv's shoulder a little pat and smiled at him.

"Slowly, it's still pretty foggy out here." Joe sat down after he freed the rope. He left the Lunds to drift.

The captain of the USS *Troy* was sure that the blip on the radar was the one they were looking for. He said as much to the vice admiral, addressed as Commodore while onboard. "No one would come through that storm with such certitude except someone on a mission. Any fishermen out there would have gotten the weather report and headed east so that the storm boiled up behind them. The mark here has some size to it. An ocean-going salvage tug would be about right. They are steaming in on the edge of the weather."

"They'll see us on their radar won't they?" Andre, who was within hearing distance asked..

"Couldn't miss us if they're looking," the captain answered.

"What do you have in mind?" the commodore asked.

"I'll be able to block his progress, no worries. In order for him not to get ahead of us and set off his bomb, I've got two squads from Seal Team Six poised to take down all the occupants of that tug. A second squad goes in five minutes after the first. When they decide they can't make it to the city, we've determined that it will take them ten or fifteen minutes to arm the device. The teams will stop that. I doubt it will be necessary to sink the boat." At 478-feet long, the Perry-class frigate didn't bristle with armaments like a dreadnought of old but it was more than impressive enough to halt a 178-foot ocean-going tugboat.

The captain spoke into a headset and received an affirmative response. To those present he said, "We've got a few minutes left."

Joe Gaspe and the Portable Nukes

Eastern Star

Dread upon the Waters

Seal Team Six had an eight-man squad divided into two boats ready to board *Eastern Star*. They had been disembarked from one of their Seal Delivery Vehicles (SDV). A four-man team comprised the first effort, they moved on the tug through the turbulent waves as soon as the tug slowed its forward progress. Chief Petty Officer Roy stayed in the boat with some additional equipment. CPO Sockeye, Lieutenant Snake, manning the comms, and CWO Pancho climbed ropes and came over the transom of *Eastern Star* moving up the ropes fast enough to be there before the enemy saw them. Seals use nicknames rather than formal ranks when addressing each other. This facilitates teamwork and reinforces the family atmosphere that makes them such a formidable fighting machine.

Snake was in contact with the bridge of the frigate and the other squad of Seals. He commented as each deck was cleared. Their M4s took down the lone terrorist who was on deck and Sockeye and Pancho found the last man in the area of the hold that held the hawsers, pumps, and cables trying, to arm the device. He was sweating while trying to push it along the rails connecting the two parts when he was taken down. They made no attempt to arrest him. He was eliminated.

James Talor, the pilot of the ship, sat down on the floor of the pilothouse and interlocked his hands behind his head. When the Navy Seal entered the pilothouse he said one thing, "Cold and dark."

To Talor Lieutenant Snake said, "Stay there. Don't move. Someone will come for you." He wheeled about and went down the companionway.

"Where the hell is the guy I'm supposed to talk to? I need to reach this Homeland Security person." The Canadian caller was tense and testy but didn't want to say anything to an underling.

"I'm patching you through right now." The operator rolled his eyes and punched up a special code for Thomas Andre's secure phone. Andre was on the bridge aboard the USS *Troy*. He had two radios and three cell phones laid out around him. He hadn't heard from Rad or

Joe Gaspe and the Portable Nukes

anyone at West Point. It was eleven AM and the football game at the Point was scheduled for noon. He had no news from Joe Gaspe at the other end of the state. He tried the cell phone number given to him and got the "not available" message. He had just heard from CWO Rhinelander about the Canadian Coast Guard losing track of two Lunds in Lake Ontario. The third of his cell phones announced a call with its ringtone. He picked it up.

Andre listened for a few moments, then looked at his watch: five after eleven. He looked a little dyspeptic when he said, "Okay, I understand," and put down the phone. Another phone rang. He picked it up when a voice came over the intercom. "Team Six recovering two squads at eleven oh seven. Enemy vessel is cold and dark. All secure."

Into his phone Andre asked, "Excuse me what was that?" Andre closed his eyes and massaged his temples while listening to the Canadian voice in his handset. He asked no questions, said "Okay, thank you," and disconnected. He laid that phone on the console and said to himself, "Couldn't have waited any longer could you?"

The sailor manning the helm asked, "Were you speaking to me, sir?"

Andre looked up and said, "No young man, I was talking to a deaf ear."

The sailor shrugged and continued with his assigned duty.

On the bridge a few minutes later Andre explained to the captain and the commodore that the other salvage tug had been found at the tip of the Gaspe Peninsula in Quebec armed and loaded with what looked like a moderately sized Russian nuclear weapon. The Canadians had had this information for two and one half days but had been sitting on it.

"This phase of the game is apparently over then." Andre said. The commodore raised an eyebrow toward the captain.

A boarding party from the Coast Guard, in a small patrol boat, was timed to arrive on station just as the Seals faded into the fog. The navy handed the tug over to the Guardsman. With control of the tug assured, the Seals disappeared, the USS *Troy* continued on its training mission and Special Agent Thomas Andre would sail into the Port of New London on the captured tug. He hoped New York's media would never know how close this portable nuke had gotten.

Chapter 19

Orange County: October 12th

Something had woken Rad from her dream. It might have been the dream itself. She heard Moses tell her that the army had been notified. She was not to be on her own. The day had worn on and the morning was stretching toward noon. She heard the four-wheelers laboring up the path toward the tracks. When she looked, they were down below on a flat area loading both halves of the device into the truck. The quads detached their trailers and took up position as guard vehicles in front and back.

These were her bogies. Rad was sure of that. She had her doubts, but they were about the outcome, not about what she had to do. She repeated her mantra of self-confidence, "Overcome doubts with action, do what you know is right." She'd learned it years ago when her parents had sent her on a character-building vacation and received in return a daughter who was always able to assert herself effectively.

Rad's training made clear that the two "halves" of the portable nukes would have to be activated to be armed and assembled in order to detonate. This process would take from ten to fifteen minutes after they were placed in close proximity to the Academy. Therefore, taking out one half of the device would effectively disable it.

Rad checked the loads in her weapons. She was confident in her preparation, but like her mantra, the preparation was a prayer of sorts.

Dread upon the Waters

The power of a ritualistic observance would improve her concentration on the important things to be done. She remembered her father's voice, although she was glad he had no idea of what she was about to do. Agent Andre, aware of her mission, would have to run interference in the future, if there was a future. She was about to cross the line into illegality and break numerous rules of engagement of both the CBP and the FBI, her two agencies.

Radleigh Loonch didn't believe she would make it through this confrontation. She had firearms but she assumed that the shooters leading and following the nuke would take her down with their weapons. She had been unable to contact anyone nearby for reinforcements. She would be outgunned. "Well," she thought, with mixed relief and regret, "at least I won't leave a grieving husband or babies."

She blew on the end of the cigar to keep it glowing and prepared for the moment when the two ATVs and the road-rail vehicle would come right past her. The first vehicle began bumping and jerking up the tracks. The driver was armed with an AK-47. When the truck came smoothly along and before he picked up speed, she had to throw her two long snappers, both aimed into the pick-up bed of the Ford. Then, if she could, she would drop down, grab two regular snappers, and launch a second pair of bombs at the trailing guard ATV. At that point, she planned to scuttle to the left as quickly as she could, keeping her right hand free to aim her Sig-Sauer. Rad had no idea how the concussion would effect her or the rider on the leading ATV. She had screwed two sets of earplugs into her ear canals and told herself. "Remember to keep your mouth open wide."

The Command Sergeant-Major had the most important job in the army. Everyone respected him. Everyone listened to him. He could get anything done in or out of regs. His boss expected him to be right about everything. Sgt. David Bolden was a supremely confident man, but he was way out over his skis on the maneuver he was presently involved in. He was damp under the armpits, in communication with everyone except his boss, the colonel, and had three ops going at once. He had sent a patrol to the Academy's dock to do recon for a possible riverside attack. He had sent an enhanced platoon,

Joe Gaspe and the Portable Nukes

complete with heavy weapons, to lead a recon to the Conrail tracks below the Academy grounds. He had scrambled two helos, both Black Hawks. One helicopter was an MH-60L gunship and the other a modified troop carrier bringing eleven fully equipped infantrymen. Bolden was on his own as far as leadership. He was unable to get any messages past a punctilious staff officer who blocked direct communication with the colonel.

Because congressional VIPs were at the Point for the football game, Colonel Grady Charbonneau was occupied in attending a canned tailgate party, catered by mess orderlies, and lacking any spontaneity at all. His snarky staff officer, Major Hoople, had been planning this affair for too long to allow anything purely military to intrude. The partiers, stiff and formal, unused to the culture of tailgate revelry, were deep in conversation. Colonel Charbonneau was trying to accomplish the impossible, by convincing a ranking member of the House Armed Services Committee—ironically the local district's representative and a stalwart opponent of anything good for the Point—to increase funding for electronic monitoring of both the United States Military Academy and New York's famous Fort Drum.

The congressman's every need was being catered to thanks to the major. Caviar at a tailgate, who would have thought of that? Charbonneau tried hard to not to listen too closely to what he considered to be left-leaning statist drivel dripping with contempt as it spilled from the representative's lips. The VIP tailgate party wasn't outside in the gloomy morning mist, but in an officer's lounge beside the stands of the stadium. Over the pre-game sounds, the Colgate marching band muffled by concrete, Charbonneau thought that he heard helos crossing overhead. He glanced at his watch—too early for the pre-game flyover—what was up? He looked for an enlisted man that he could use to make an end run around Major Hoople and find Sergeant Bolden.

Bolden was on the top of the cliff looking down, barking into his radio with his faithful corporal beside him. Both were turned out in full web gear on the word of a civilian woman who claimed to be the colonel's sister-in-law. Doubts assailed Bolden but he surged ahead. "Let's start down," he said to Corporal Dennis. Dennis assigned a

Dread upon the Waters

private to the point and one to cover their back. The four-man command team started down the steep trail toward the tracks.

"Nothing at the docks. No boats. No tracks. No sign of people," the man at the river told Bolden.

"There anything up or downstream from you?"

"Can't see anyone upstream or downstream. Nothing out of place. Not on our property."

"Hold on, I have another report coming in," Bolden said.

It was the recon squad. "Sarge, we are being signaled by a boat on the water. They want to approach. I am going to deploy in three squads and allow them to come close enough to talk."

"Roger that."

It was Olivia's boat signaling. She stood as she angled the borrowed Smoker Craft toward shore. She wanted everything to be transparent. The troops were ready for her with guns pointed generally in her direction though not at her person. She idled the motor forward then slipped it into neutral until she got about fifteen feet from the soldiers. She drifted on the current.

Waving her right arm toward the north along the riverbank, she shouted, "You've got terrorists in the woods right next door. They unloaded from two boats there. They are bringing a bomb up the tracks on ATVs, Quad runners!"

The platoon leader said, "Identify yourself!" to Olivia and spoke in an aside to his radio operator, "Report what she said, but identify it as unconfirmed."

Up the river and a half-mile north, Rad puffed on her cigar to get the tip glowing. When she stood up, the sun popped out of a hole in the clouds and shone right on her. She bowed her head so the CBP ball cap shaded her eyes. Looking down she saw that the Hy-Rail truck was right where she wanted it on the tracks.

A pressure wave from a helicopter started to come over and down the cliff when Rad lit the first long snapper and flicked it toward the tracks. She lit the second long snapper, tossed it underhand ten feet north of the first one, and ducked down to grab two more firecrackers. She straightened up just as the first snapper cracked off, blinding her with flash and debris. She was throwing blind when she dropped the next two snappers right onto the eruption of the first two. They cracked off after Rad went down behind a rock. She scuttled on her hands and feet to the north, dirtying her automatic as she used the hand holding it to scrabble away.

Everyone on the cliff was aware that this was no drill. The platoon at the shore and Olivia, standing, and Mo, seated, in the Smoker Craft looked north as the explosions, two large cracks followed by two smaller bangs, took place. "That is Radleigh," said Moses X Snow.

The noise of the next few minutes drowned out all that was said. The crew of the lead helo saw the flashes as instantaneous yellow flame balls on the cliffside below and to the left of them. They would have to turn around to train their guns on the line of dirt clouds.

Sergeant Bolden heard the snappers go off and said into his mike, "All squads report in! What do you see?"

He listened as the confusion mounted. To his group who were just descending the cliff he said, "Go, go, go!" waving them down toward the action.

To the helo platoon leader he asked, "Can you see anything that needs taking out?"

To the platoon at the shore he asked, "That anywhere near you?"

"Negative." From the helo.

"Negative," from the platoon at the dock. "We can hear 'em, can't see 'em."

Bolden heard from the recon platoon leader over his radio net. "We are deploying in three squads: cliff top, shore side, and reserve. The action is right ahead of us. Just north of dead center below."

Bolden had heard the snappers go off through his headphones. Then he heard a burst of AK-47 fire, a sound that was recognizable to him.

The man in the lead ATV, seeing his mission being destroyed, stopped his quad and turned his weapon onto the area on the hillside where he thought Rad's bombs had come from. His firing went high, ripping through the trees and brush up the cliff from Rad's previous position. The second of Rad's two regular snappers had hit a remnant bird's nest in a scraggled maple tree, bounced off a branch, and landed almost at Rad's feet, just on the other side of a twenty-ton granite outcrop that she was hiding behind. It was the last to detonate and the concussion slammed Rad back against the cliff face. She smacked her head on the rocks behind her and was knocked out cold.

The attack on West Point was over. The Hy-Rail truck took a direct hit from a long snapper. The passenger, not wearing his seatbelt, was killed instantly when his head was propelled into the windshield. The tires were blown out and an eight-inch diameter tree was felled across the bed. The driver tried to bail out and was eviscerated by the second long snapper when it bounced off the top of one half of the nuke and exploded in his back. The green ready lights continued to blink on each piece of the cargo. The ATV following the bomb was hit by the force of the third snapper and was immediately blown backward. What was left of the guard was wedged under a downed maple twenty feet below the tracks. His beard disintegrated and his clothing blasted right off the front of his body.

After loosing a burst with this AK-47, the lead guard turned around and started to run. Then he turned his AK-47 on the helicopter gunship. He loosed a two-second burst at the helo before he was shredded by hundreds of rounds from the 7.62 mm Mini-Guns. The four men had come to die for the jihad and they had done so.

The terrorist who had been left at the boat landing was walking back up the tracks idly hoping that he would be far enough away to survive the nuclear blast. The sound of the battle initiated by Rad made him quicken his pace. He would survive and escape into a nether world that was neither in the jihad nor out of it.

The two platoons converged on the scene, recognized what they had averted, and began to sort out the forensic evidence. Command Sergeant Major Bolden took control of the scene when he arrived. Colonel Charbonneau heard the sound of the helicopter's 7.62 mm Mini-Gun. No one else recognized that sound during the pre-game ceremonial flyover. The other noises, down the cliff and muffled by rocks and woods, went unheard at the football game.

Rad was found alive, concussed and sprayed with mud, but still wearing her CBP ball cap and carrying ID that named her as an agent of the Department of Homeland Security. She was hospitalized on the post, but was too foggy to be debriefed.

Olivia and Mo, after being relegated to listening to the incident, were debriefed to good effect. Despite their mad dash, Liv thought that they had been too late to help Rad. No one told her about Rad being found alive and the interrogators ignored her requests for information. She was kept separated from Mo—a precaution so that they couldn't arrange their stories. It was only later that Liv learned that her call to Mr. Colonel Grady, received by Sergeant Bolden, had been the trigger to bring reinforcements to help Rad.

Midway through the first quarter, Colonel Charbonneau left his guests at the football game and came over to sort out the situation. He was flabbergasted to see his sister-in-law from New Orleans being interrogated, her roommate, whom he had met, in the infirmary, and to hear that they had stopped a nuclear attack. While controlling the investigation and cleanup, he sent word up the line about the attempted attack. In return he received reports of additional encounters around the State of New York. He was satisfied with the outcome and proud of his men, but also grim at the prospect of what might have been.

"They had to go this way. Let's proceed. Slow and steady wins the race." Joe took a rag made from an old tee shirt and wiped the barrel of his shotgun. He handed the automatic to Sherry.

"Marv, you get behind the wheel. Sherry you make yourself small in the front end but keep looking ahead. This fog may clear when we get between the banks." He tossed an olive drab poncho to Sherry. "Put this on over your rain jacket. It'll get heavy when it's wet but you don't want to be too well seen."

Because Marv knew they were on a serious mission, he didn't resent Joe ordering him around as he usually would. Joe moved around the boat arranging needed items and betraying his nervousness. When on edge, Joe gave speeches or told stories. He didn't have any stories for this occasion. He just rattled on.

"I don't think they can get past the plant discharges in Devil's Hole. Unless they have an airboat they'll get stopped at the whirlpool. There's nothing to attack at the whirlpool. So they have to be after the cooling water discharges from the Canadian or American side. A nuke on either side will disable both anyway. They're right across from each other. I wonder if a call to Rhinelander will do any good? These guys have been in Canada and they may still be there."

Joe was standing and the low hanging fog hugged the water. Marv, sitting behind the wheel was substantially blind. To him the river looked like the inside of a cotton ball. Sherry, molded into the bow, looked right along the water's surface. She could see a little bit farther down on the rippled face of the river. She hoped to notice any disturbance to that surface before they were on top of it. Joe's head poked through the fog. He could see up the cliffs on both sides. They were in the center of the river. Joe saw the crazy cantilevered nightmare bridge that was an art exhibit at Art Park on the American side.

"Move over near the Canadian side. Close enough so you can see that you are going parallel." Marv sidled to the west. He could hear the water lapping at the shore before he saw the steep rising bank.

Joe thought about calling the Coast Guard but was not sure if he would get anything but arrested by them if they showed up. Besides that, the boat was definitely in Canada, out of the Coasties area of control.

The Whirlpool Bridge loomed ahead and far above them. The water swirled in large round boils as the cooling water, released from the two generating plants and coming through pipes far below the surface, rose to the top in round up-wells that buffeted small boats side to side and made control difficult. No boater likes the feeling of having the front of his craft pushed left or right without his steering, exerted on the stern, being able to correct it.

If this had been happening during salmon fishing season, they would be passing fishing boats drifting downstream all crowded together to harvest those anadromous fish struggling upstream toward the falls. They were not in salmon season, but in that slack time

Joe Gaspe and the Portable Nukes

between warm-water and cold-water fishing. That meant there were no boats in the river that day. Joe kept looking and talking, Marv chugged ahead slowly, and Sherry watched and listened trying to stay on task and calm her nerves. Normally annoyed by Joe's blather, they were both comforted by the stream of consciousness as it flowed.

Joe pulled two of his extra-heavy musky poles from a rod locker and hooked up huge trolling plugs to them. The lures, known as Plows after one especially successful model, were thirteen or more inches long and carried three huge ten-ought treble hooks. Joe looked at Marv and said, "Just in case."

"Whattya going to use them for? Grappling hooks?"

"Who knows?" Joe shrugged. Marv shook his head and rolled his eyes in that gesture between friends that meant, "You're my pal but you are nuts."

Marv's phone rang just as Joe was about to pick it up. "Yep?"

"Is this Gaspe?"

Joe acknowledged.

"Rhinelander here, we've lost these bastards in the fog. You see anything?"

"They abandoned the Lunds—the cargo is on another boat. I think that they headed up the lower river. We haven't seen them yet but we're on the trail. Can you alert the authorities on both sides, US and Canada? They're headed for the warm water discharges at Devil's Hole. I'm sure of it." Joe glanced at his watch. "It's eleven fifteen. This is going down today. Can you contact the US Coasties?"

"I am an officer of the US Coast Guard."

"OK, how about the Canucks; can you alert them?"

"I am currently on a Canadian Coast Guard vessel. We'll see what they want to do."

"We're hot on their trail. Get 'em to meet us at Devil's Hole if you can. Dr. Dento out."

"Rhinelander out."

Their proximity to the cliffs of Canada caused birds to squawk as the Whaler cruised by. Joe had stopped talking. He was either out of words or getting his nervousness had redoubled. "There's the US discharge over there." He pointed to the east. "The Canadian one is up a bit more."

Dread upon the Waters

Marv slowed without being told to. He went a little too far towards idle and began losing way. He bumped the throttle ahead a little bit.

"Handsomely, now. Steady as you go." Joe had been reading sea stories and sometimes talked nautical because he was unable to help himself.

Sherry snorted, thinking neither of these guys was handsome. She rested her head on the bow just over the cutwater and felt the rhythmic thrum of the Whaler slicing against the current. She listened and watched. She was able to see along the river's surface below the fog that made everything above it disappear. A noise anomaly brought her attention to the starboard side ahead.

In a hoarse whisper she said, "Joe! Shut up!" She pointed to the right ahead. "They're right up there."

Marv, slowly moving along on one of the two four-stroke outboards, was making almost no sound with the boat. Confident that the enemy would be standing or sitting trying to see, Joe signaled to proceed. He clicked the safety off on his shotgun. "Sidle up to them slowly and silently," he whispered in Marv's ear. Sherry, eye to the surface, pointed to the right and pumped her arm twice indicating that she heard two different voices. She switched her automatic to her right hand and pointed with it. Marv was getting very near the shore, dominated here by huge concrete discharge flues just above the rocks. He checked his depth finder. It was thirty-seven feet deep, only fifteen or so feet from shore. Sherry held her hands apart for Joe and Marv to see. With her gun in one hand and the other empty, she moved them toward each other to show that the distance was closing.

The Arabs on the boat were talking, smoking cigarettes, and though armed, were inattentive. They had their boat, a work vessel of thirty feet with a crane arm over the low center cutaway deck, tied to two tough volunteer trees incongruously growing out of the rocks on shore below the discharge works of the Ontario Hydro power plant. The wire rope of a crane was over the side and two compressors rattled with their air hoses threaded into the water. One man sat in a chair operating the crane, two others stood guard armed and unready, one in the bow and one in the stern. Another man chatted with the stern guard. He appeared to be unarmed. They considered their job complete. The diver's below would be ready in ten minutes. Then the armed device would take five minutes to detonate.

When things happened only Joe with his Mohawk mind's ability to slow down time, would remember everything. Sherry and Marv would only have their own part to think about. No one on the other side would tell any tales.

The Whaler appeared out of the fog as an apparition with everyone ready to do his or her part. The bow, with Sherry crouched low just peering over the gunwale, slipped past the stern of the workboat. She looked up and dropped the enemy security man in the bow with two shots to the brisket, close enough together to cover with a playing card. He loosed an errant three-round burst from his AK-47 before crumpling to the deck.

Marv brought the Whaler up beside the crane and slowed his speed to match the downstream flow of the current. This required a deft hand on the throttle. He kept them there until he was wounded. A bullet from the AK-47 hit the boat railing next to him and the aluminum shards thrown off stung his right forearm like a nest of hornets. He lost throttle control and that caused the Whaler to fall off down current and the bow to pull away from the enemies.

Sherry turned her weapon to the wire rope on the crane, shredding it halfway with two shots, then taking new aim and severing the remainder with a double tap. Marv looked at the blood spurting out of his right forearm, grabbed it with his left hand and said, "Wow! Great shooting! That's my girl!"

In the stern, Joe had come abreast of the two enemy combatants when Marv quietly cut the water with his bow. "Hey, Mohammed!" he yelled and loosed a shotgun blast that killed the security man and blew off the left side of the other man's face. He fell backward, down, but not dead.

Joe dropped the street sweeper onto the seat beside him and grabbed a rigged musky rod. As his boat sluiced away at the bow, he placed a short accurate cast scraping along the workboat's waterline. He meant to catch the two air lines going to the divers below. The Plow caught the stern air line nicely and at first pulled it toward the

Dread upon the Waters

Whaler, ripping holes in the line that leaked air. Then, as the Whaler turned away, the hooks tore the airline completely so that it gushed air and whipped across the water's surface like a runaway snake. The forward airline was left intact because the action of the Whaler, losing way in the current, pulled Joe's lure out into the river before it scraped that far along the boat's side. He reeled in his lure and reached for the other rod but the boat was too far away. Marv putting pressure on his wounded right forearm to stop the bleeding, had no way to control the boat.

Joe paled looking at his partner, Marv yelled, "I'm all right!"

Sherry, moving toward Marv, said, "The cargo has gone down to Davy Jones' Locker."

Joe gently moved Marv out of the driver's seat and glanced at the enemy vessel. The crane operator sat at the controls and stared. The officer down on the deck rolled around trying to rise. The two guards were dead. The cargo was no longer under control of the crane. It was on the bottom. One diver was gone. No air being fed to him. The other diver? Who knew what was going to happen to him? It was time to get away.

Marv's cell phone, sitting in a plastic bag on the console, rang. Joe picked it up with his left hand while he steered the boat back upstream to make another pass at the bad guys. "Yep," Joe answered.

"Rhinelander here. I've got the Coast Guards from both sides on the way up. These patrols are more than routine. Where are you?"

"We're at the discharge on the Canadian side. They can mop up—this operation is over. We are going to vamoose."

Joe headed the Whaler east into the fog, planning to drift down the American side as quietly as he could. He wanted no opportunity to explain himself to the representatives of his northern neighbor. He hoped he could slip past the US Coast Guard as well. By just using enough throttle to keep the Whaler in the current, they slipped downstream. Joe watched as Sherry concentrated on wrapping Marv's shot-up arm with everything in the first-aid kit. She had removed his jacket to do her work.

"Toss that overboard." He said. "Put all the firearms below under the rain gear in the slop chest." He saw the flashing blue lights of the

Joe Gaspe and the Portable Nukes

US authorities screaming upstream to the west. He was sure they couldn't see him since all he saw of them were the blue flashes. Joe deduced that they would eventually close off the river when they figured out what had happened on the Canadian side. He hoped to have his Whaler on a trailer back to Muskedaigua by then. His hope proved correct.

Chapter 20

New York State: October 19th

North Central New York was not unscathed by the attacks of October 12. But it could have been worse. Two members of the Tenth Mountain Division's administrative staff, both young unmarried women, were killed when a semi-successful truck bomb blew the front corner off the disused gymnasium that was their recruiting center and collapsed the roof. The sergeant, "running the clock" in a security check, died in a roof collapse, while the lieutenant, preparing to open the doors, was obliterated in the initial blast.

In Theresa, New York, the local sheriff, alerted to the discovery of the confused Iroquois young men, was on point near the abandoned talc mine when the three Arabs came walking up to him, sat down twenty feet from his cruiser and put their hands on their heads. Right behind them, herding them along was a patrol from the military police at Fort Drum in two Humvees. The Arabs thought it better to surrender to the civil authorities rather than face the army's wrath.

Dread upon the Waters

The season was far advanced for diving when UDT (Underwater Demolition Team) 10 was brought in to try effecting recovery of the items that had been sunk in the St. Lawrence River. The United States had possession of some of the devices aimed at it and the Government of Canada had possession of one of the big ones, but evidence, to establish the provenance of these devices, was always useful.

Joe Gaspe had supplied the GPS coordinates of the boats that had been sunk off the shore of an island hard by the watery border between the two countries. There was some worry that winter and currents would send the device to an unknown location. So the specialists of the US Navy were brought in. The frigid water temperatures required dry suits and very short durations for the underwater dives taking place. Two-man frogman teams descended to a shelf of rock thirty feet down and searched for the devices. There was a sheer drop to eighty feet right off the shelf into US waters. If the package had slid off into those depths it could not be pursued until the water was warmer, if ever. It had already been decided that the two devices lost in the sinking of Lunds in Lake Champlain would never be recovered. Those depths were too great unless an underwater dive vehicle was used. That would not happen during "the season" when the lake was busy with recreational users. It was hoped that at least one of the two parts of the nuke on the St. Lawrence would be accessible since the boat had foundered almost on shore.

The dive boat was secured with anchors and shoreline leads. One of the two teams of divers was searching along the rock ledge when comms were established with the support personnel on the boat.

"Deep Diver to Big Snatcher, I've got something here. Looks right!"

"This is Big Snatcher. Roger that Deep Diver. Can you verify? Will send down a recovery line, if you verify."

Through a series of hand signals the two divers agreed that the object was what they were searching for. Each diver was attached to the boat with a strong line to prevent him from drifting downstream too quickly to do the work. They would need a heavy cable to raise the item and would need to keep clear so their tethers were not entan-

Joe Gaspe and the Portable Nukes

gled in the cable. A float line was being attached by one diver when the other diver exclaimed, "Wow, would you look at that!"

"Did not copy that, Deep Diver is there a problem?" Big Snatcher, the sailor on the dive boat, asked.

"No. No problem. There is a really big fish watching Deep Diver two. That's all."

"Lines coming down for attachment."

"Roger. I've got one. There's the other. Securing lines. Will tell you when we're clear."

"Big Snatcher. We are read… Oh my God. Unbelievable!"

"Deep Diver repeat that. Do you need assistance?"

"No sir. We're good. There is just the biggest monster fish watching us down here. He's right there. Must be eight-feet long. You can go ahead and start the pull. We are clear."

Half of one portable nuke was thus recovered. The second half had rolled into the depths and would remain there.

Joe sat between Rad and Marv. He was tucked into his plate of appetizers and eyeing the basket of chicken wings. Though one would think a trencherman like Joe couldn't eat with such consuming gusto and also be observant, he would be wrong. Joe noticed that Marv, with Sherry beside him, was completely absorbed in his true love. Sherry was flashing her dagger eyes alternately at Rad and Olivia. Earlier, Joe had told her that these two "college girls" were uninterested in Marv but Sherry said, "I'm pretty sure they're idiots."

"Olivia is married to Mo, a man you don't know well, and Rad just lost a close boyfriend in our recent action. Leave them alone. Just try to get along." He looked at her face for confirmation.

"Those cows better not cross me or come after Marv." Sherry stared at Joe for a minute. Then she said, "OK I'll ignore the lame bimbos."

To himself, Joe remarked, "Women!?!" and shook his head.

Mumbling through a stuffed jalapeno he waved at the plate of wings, "Mm mm, eat up, have some wings."

Dread upon the Waters

Olivia watched the door to the next room where Mo and others were in discussion with Special Agent Thomas Andre. She said nothing. Rad took one lonely chicken wing and set it on a plate with several sticks of celery and a tiny dollop of blue cheese dressing. Marv, flaunted the bandages on his wounded forearm where he's taken the ricochets from the AK-47, looked at Sherry, and did not move toward the food. His sipped his soft drink. Sherry said to Joe, "This stuff ain't no good for ya, ya know?"

Joe noticed how people sometimes tried to exaggerate their diction in certain situations. Here was Sherry, who he knew was desperate to educate herself, using her educational deficiencies vis a vis Rad and Olivia to talk like an ignorant jealous knucklehead around his friends. He shrugged again and piled half a dozen wings on his plate, took a prodigious draft of beer from his glass, and stored that idea in with all the other mysteries of dealing with women that he kept filed away.

They were in the glassed-in banquet room of the Tuscarora Falls Inn, facing through to the adjoining room. The falls, low in water in the late fall, burbled a soothing song outside a window that was open a crack. In that other room Andre was talking to Mo and Uncle Mike and Chief Johnson, all Iroquois. Incongruous as it seemed, Joe's daughter, Amy, was with that group as well, seated beside Mo's sister, Molly.

In the manner of the Mohawks, each speaker was given all the time he needed to make his points. Interruptions, considered rude until the speaker had yielded, did not happen. Chief Johnson had spoken at length. Uncle Mike had added context and prescience to the position that the chief had posed. After a time Agent Andre spoke—he had prepared remarks—praising the contribution of the Mohawks for their efforts in the recent events. Each of his salient points was punctuated with a gift, an interesting antique pipe for Uncle Mike, a box of expensive cigars for Chief Johnson, a leather bound book for Mo and fine examples of bead work to the ladies, moccasins to Amy, and a decorated pouch to Molly. He had words of sorrow and regret for those people of the longhouse who did not survive the difficulties. Andre was confident, knowing that his team had killed no Mohawks and only a few of the errant brothers had been captured and interro-

Joe Gaspe and the Portable Nukes

gated. At great length, Andre came to the point where he asked the Chiefs and Sachems in concert with the Women of Power to work to improve the teaching on the reservations. He leant a historical perspective to his remarks, reviving the Iroquois' honest broker role in the security concerns of Canada and the United States. Uncle Mike seconded his prescription for the tribal elders to be more diligent in overseeing community education.

When Andre was done speaking and Uncle Mike had stood up and given a second short address, it was Moses X Snow, a man with no official position but known as a wise orator respected within and without his community, who summarized the meeting. The Mohawks were brought their dinners as well as generous quantities of coffee and tea. They tucked into their food while Mo and Andre stepped into the falls viewing room.

The tension was palpable. Andre glanced around, sat opposite Joe, and motioned for the waitress to enter. Mo sat beside his wife Olivia. His left arm was wrapped against his chest under the loose shirt-jac he wore. He said nothing.

When the waitress had left with the orders Andre began to speak, "I will be talking generally until she returns:" He nodded toward the door. "When we have our food, some specifics will come into play. Eventually, the results of all of our efforts will be told to the extent that security concerns allow. One more person will be joining us." He motioned toward a man posted outside the door from the porch room into the main bar. That man opened the door and CWO Rhinelander entered. He sat beside Sherry. Andre took a sip of water and said, "We have succeeded in ending the most serious threat to our country that has ever existed. All of you are to be commended for your part in this and those of you who are not employees—here he looked from Sherry to Marv to Olivia—will be receiving a check and can consider yourself part of this network organization for the future. Assignments will be given to you when your particular skills are required. That will be intermittent at best. Those of you who are employees will be getting a bonus and will remain engaged. Here his glance passed from Rhinelander to Joe to Rad and settled on Mo. "My assistant will be giving you envelopes shortly."

Dread upon the Waters

"There will be no official recognition of your part in this successful defense of our borders. Over the last number of years we have blunted the sword of Al Qeada in a great many ways. There has been almost no publicity in these cases. No one with an ounce of sense believes that the major news outlets in the US would hold close to the vest information favorable to America's image of itself. At the same time, publicity detailing the foiling of attacks would make available to the enemy intelligence that we would prefer they do not have. The Coast Guard," here he glanced at CWO Rhinelander, "has had multiple successes, all accomplished quietly. The navy, army, and marines have thwarted the enemy worldwide and at home. Many countries have helped to defeat them in detail and keep them on the run in general. These countries have an interest in secrecy due to their particular domestic considerations. If it were known in France that they have worked with the US Air Force in the African continent to destroy enemy formations, their continued cooperation would be impossible. The Bush Administration never publicized their completed operations—again for intelligence reasons—they were content to let historians make the judgments of their worth. The present administration has continued to downplay their achievements for the reason that their domestic supporters would eat them alive if they knew. So no one will know what you have done."

Joe rushed in with a comment, "Stupid Taliban," he said, apparently unable to remember the Mohawk way of listening politely. Radleigh elbowed him in the ribs.

"While the *New York Times* will not be told of what happened here, you team members deserve to know," Andre continued. "I will move from west to east in my roundup of the attack. There were five prongs to the plan. In the west the portable nuclear device was aimed at the power grid. While each of these attacks aimed at specific strategic targets, the cumulative effect was to be to make New York uninhabitable and to cause considerable loss of life.

"In the west they aimed at disabling the power grid at Niagara by taking out the warm water discharges on both sides of the border. Our enemies are students of history. They have noted that in past power disruptions to the US grid Ontario Hydro power had filled in the gap

Joe Gaspe and the Portable Nukes

and contributed to a quick recovery. So they planned to prevent that. This attack was foiled by Joe's team both on the St. Lawrence River and at nearby Niagara. The level of cooperation from the Canadian authorities was enhanced by the work of CWO Rhinelander. The Canadians are now in possession of the two devices sent that way. They are disarming and examining these but their provenance, where they originated, is already known. These devices were spirited out of the former Soviet Union and sold to Middle Eastern brokers for a substantial profit. The device that was sunk in the St. Lawrence was recovered thanks to GPS information. The device at Niagara was recovered along with two prisoners who will be interrogated in cooperation with the Canadian authorities. Since all this took place in Ontario waters, no US persons were involved other than CWO Rhinelander as an observer." Andre paused and looked at Joe. Joe nodded.

At that moment, the waitress and an assistant were allowed to enter with the dinner orders for the group. Andre waited until everyone had been served and the door closed behind the servers.

"There was a massive truck bomb detonated at the Syracuse, New York recruiting center of the Army's Tenth Mountain division. Two young women, a lieutenant and a sergeant, the only occupants of the building on a Saturday morning, were killed. While there was some damage to surrounding buildings and many books belonging to the university were destroyed in a nearby library annex, no other casualties occurred. This was our only defeat and as far as the world knows, the only attack."

"An attempt to take out Fort Drum, home of the 10th, with portable nukes was foiled when the Mohawks, misguided cooperators with the enemy, deserted the operation and abandoned the terrorists in rough country to the north and east of that military reservation. Though I don't know how, there was a wavering of resolve on the part of the Indian guides. There were three terrorists captured in this incident. They are being debriefed at a secure location." Agent Andre looked at Joe for a moment. Joe spoke the word "Amy," silently. Andre read his lips and nodded.

"There was an attempt to reuse the old invasion route down through Lake Champlain and down the Hudson. Remember these

Dread upon the Waters

people are students of history. The plan was to attack the United States Military Academy at West Point. That attack was foiled by an heroic effort by members of the group seated here. We lost one man, unofficially, here in a combat operation on the lake. The Mohawk guides for this operation and the one on the St. Lawrence have disappeared. We have assumed the worst. The final attempt on the Point was foiled by decisive and valorous work on your part." Here he glanced alternately at Mo, Olivia ,and let his gaze rest on Rad.

"One nuke was recovered at the Point while the other was lost in the deepest part of one of the deepest lakes in North America. It will never be recovered. There were no prisoners taken there. Unfortunately, the property of a neighbor of the Academy was used for this attack and there may be a publicity problem here. This neighbor happens to be an attorney, so we will see."

Joe said, "Stupid Lawyers." Mo looked at him. Rad elbowed him in the ribs. He parried the attempt and smiled.

"The largest of these attacks, two devices each with a fifty megaton yield, was targeted at New York City. It is clear that the motivation was to destroy the State of New York. They wanted death and destruction as always. They wanted revenge on the 10th Mountain Division that had been instrumental in taking out the Taliban in Afghanistan. They wanted to eliminate the army's future officer corps at West Point. They wanted to disrupt the economy of New York and, by extension, the world. They wanted to disrupt recovery by taking out the power grid. And last, but by no means least, they wanted to kill Jewish Americans. They are still wedded to the belief that they can scare us into surrender.

"So the Nor'easter helped us in several ways. It made many of our responses invisible to incidental prying eyes. It harmed the enemy's timing, and it disabled one of the two ocean-rescue tugboats. That boat was blown ashore at a seaport in Quebec; Gaspe, Quebec by the way,"

Andre looked at Joe, who smiled and said, "My kind of town." He laughed.

"Through fortunate weather, cooperation from members of the US Navy and the Coast Guard, as well as second thoughts from some of the Native Americans," here Andre nodded toward Mo Snow,

Joe Gaspe and the Portable Nukes

"neither of these nukes were able to be used to any effect. You all deserve credit for a job well done."

Andre paused. Not constrained from interruptions like the Mohawks, Marv asked, "Did you recover enough material to determine how these nukes got into the US?"

Sherry nodded and said, "Yeah," as if that question were her idea.

"Some of these devices are in the possession of the Canadian authorities. But some are also under our care. Though we will be waiting for a report from our neighbors to the north," Andre sent a stern glance Joe's way after he loosed a snort from his nose and lips. "We have enough information about the ones we recovered to know that they are re-engineered items stolen from the Russian inventory."

Andre concluded his remarks by saying, "Several of you have suffered injuries as a result of your work. Your government will see that you receive the best of care. What can be done to mitigate your difficulties will be done. You have my word on that."

Rad raised her hand and asked, "What happens if word gets out about loss of life or vigilantism with regard to these events?"

"I will do my utmost to see that word does not leak. I expect the same from each of you."

"Are you gonna get in trouble for what we've done?" Joe asked.

"I don't believe so." Andre concluded with another thank you to the group for a job well done.

It was time to eat.

Handy Order Form

Postal orders:
All Esox Publications
P.O. Box 493
East Aurora, New York 14052
Fax orders: 716-655-2621   Phone Orders: 716-655-2621
Email orders: info@allesoxpublications.com
Website: AllEsoxPublications.com

Please send more information on Publications: Yes_____   No_____

Name: _____

Address: _____

City:_____State/Prov:_____ ZIP/Postal Code_____

Please send the following materials. I understand that I may return any of them for a full refund, for any reason, no questions asked.

Quantity	Title	Price	Total
_____	*Dread upon the Waters*	$37.50 US	_____
_____	*Girls Before Swine*	$37.50 US	_____
_____	*Fireships & Brimstone*	$37.50 US	_____
_____	*The Accidental Musky*	$ 6.95 US	_____
_____	*The Quest for Girthra*	$16.95 US	_____
_____	*Becoming a Musky Hunter*	$14.95 US	_____
_____	Understanding River Muskellunge (DVD):	$15.95 US	_____

Sales Tax: NYS residents add 8.25%................ _____
Shipping: U.S $4 (Can $5) for first item
$1 (Can $1.50) each add'l item....................... _____
Total... _____

Payment: Check____ Credit Card_____ Visa___ Mastercard____

Card Number _____

Name (print)_____Exp. Date_____

Signature_____